J

FANS OF THE IMPOSSIBLE LIFE

Kate Scelsa

BALZER + BRAY

An Imprint of HarperCollins Publishers

FOR AMANDA
AND MOM AND DAD

Balzer + Bray is an imprint of HarperCollins Publishers.

Library of Congress Cataloging-in-Publication Data
Scelsa, Kate.
    Fans of the impossible life / Kate Scelsa. — First edition.
        pages   cm
    Summary: At Saint Francis Prep school in Mountain View, New Jersey, Mira,
Jeremy, and Sebby come together as they struggle with romance, bullying, foster home
and family problems, and mental health issues.
    ISBN 978-0-06-233176-2
    [I. Best   friends—Fiction.   2.   Friendship—Fiction.   3.   Gays—Fiction.
4. Bullying—Fiction. 5. Mental illness—Fiction. 6. Foster home care—Fiction.
7. Family problems—Fiction.]   I. Title.
PZ.1.S335 Fan   2015   2015005754
[Fic]—dc23   CIP
                                                                              AC

Typography by Jenna Stempel
17 18 19 20 21   PC/LSCH   10 9 8 7 6 5 4 3 2 1
                                            ❖
First paperback edition, 2017

"Just the place to bury a crock of gold," said Sebastian. "I should like to bury something precious in every place where I've been happy and then, when I was old and ugly and miserable, I could come back and dig it up and remember."
—Brideshead Revisited
Evelyn Waugh

You have been here before.

The highway winding north through dark New England forests. White dunes towering above the sides of the road, looking like the moon.

You can come back. Even after you hurt each other too deeply to comprehend. Even after the impossible becomes just that. Too far out of reach even to dream.

Love remembers the places where it touched down, left an invisible trail on your bodies. Follow it back. You can follow it back to them.

PART 1

JEREMY

The first day of my sophomore year of high school I somehow lost the ability to tie a tie. It was one of the same ties that I had worn every day since eighth grade, when the male population of St. Francis Prep got switched over from clip-ons, but on this morning it felt like an unfamiliar object in my hands.

"Jeremy?" my dad called up from downstairs. The clock on my nightstand said 7:49. I was going to be late.

Dad came up the stairs and stuck his head in the open door of my room.

"You want a coffee thermos to go?" he asked. "Dave's got a fresh pot downstairs."

"No, thanks."

"You sure?"

"Yeah."

"You okay?"

"I can't get this," I said.

He looked at the disheveled knot hanging below my collar. "Want some help?"

I nodded. He came over to me, undid the knot that I had made, and retied it. I watched his face while he concentrated. His lips moved a little, as if he were trying to remember something.

"Thanks," I said.

"No problem," he said. He finished and stepped back, examining his work. "Very dapper."

"It's the same uniform I've always worn."

"It's a dapper uniform."

He lingered for a moment, and I turned away from him with the excuse of putting something in my backpack. I didn't want to talk. I didn't want him to say anything about this morning.

I was saved by the cat slinking in the door and weaving her huge, fluffy white body between our legs.

"Dolly Parton the Cat is here to send you off," Dad said. He always insisted on calling her "Dolly Parton the Cat," as if someone might mistake her for the real Dolly Parton.

"Thank you, Dolly Parton the Cat," he said. "Won't you sing Jeremy a song for his first day of tenth grade?"

Dad went down the hall singing, "And eyeeeeeyeeeeee . . . will always love meeeew . . ."

I sat down on my bed with my backpack at my feet. Dolly Parton the Cat jumped up next to me and pushed her head under my hand, demanding that I scratch her ears.

"Time to go back," I said.

* * *

Fifteen minutes later Dad stopped his car at the bottom of the small hill that led up to the main building of St. Francis. St. Francis, caretaker of creatures great and small, probably didn't have a midlevel prep school in mind when he stood with his arms outstretched to the hungry birds of the forest. But here in Mountain View, New Jersey, this was his legacy.

"You want me to go in with you?" Dad asked, watching the crowd congregating on the front lawn before the first bell, the girls in their uniforms of blue polo shirts with blue and green kilts, the boys all in khakis, blue button-downs, and blue and green ties like me.

"No," I said. "I'll be okay."

"You'll go right to Peter's office?"

"Yes." I pulled my backpack up from where I had wedged it between my feet.

"Okay," Dad said. "See you tonight. I'll be home from work by six."

I got out of the car, shut the door, and turned back to look at him. He gave me a thumbs-up and drove off. I stood at the bottom of the hill for a moment, then took a deep breath and made my way up to the building, through the front doors, and down the familiar hallway to Peter's office.

He was sitting at his desk doing something on his computer when I came in. He looked up and smiled when he saw me.

"Welcome back, Jeremy," he said.

MIRA

First days of school were not designed to be easy, and this one was no exception. Mira had thought that it might help to have Sebby here with her on this morning, but as soon as he met her on the bench at the bottom of the small hill that led up to the main building of St. Francis, she knew that it had been a mistake to invite him. He was a reminder of her other life, her real life, and that had no place here.

It was an unseasonably warm day for September, and the wool of her school uniform kilt was lying hot and itchy on her legs. The tights that she was wearing underneath to keep her thighs from rubbing together when she started to sweat were not helping the situation. This was weather that seemed to be stuck in someone's vision of an idealized childhood summer. Blue sky, sparkling sun, eighty-two degrees. A day for ice cream and Slip'N Slides, for falling asleep in the grass with a Popsicle melting in your hand.

"Shouldn't this place have a big iron gate or something, to keep out the riffraff?" Sebby said. He was lying with his head in her lap, playing with the pleats of her kilt.

"I think we're the riffraff," she said.

"Exactly."

If she could have picked her own outfit for this day, it might have made things easier. Possibly the silk muumuu with puffed sleeves, red with a white bamboo pattern, paired with a neon yellow belt and green slip-on sneakers. Pink lipstick, silver painted nails. Then she would have at least felt protected in the armor of one of her aesthetic visions: "shuffleboard grandma goes glam." Or possibly the brown A-line button-down chiffon that tied in a bow at the neck with a lacy cardigan, "librarian chic," to commemorate her return to academia. But the uniform was meant to erase all individuality, guarding against anything that could be deemed "inappropriate attire for those representing the institution of St. Francis," as explained by the student handbook. So she had done what she could. Silver nails, but no lipstick. Out of context she found that bright pink lipstick lost its sense of irony. She tied her hair into a messy bun on the top of her head with a ribbon that hung down the back of her neck, bright green against her brown skin. Her curls stuck out of the ribbon at odd angles, on the verge of escape, betraying her inner desire to run away from this place as fast as she could.

At her old school she could wear whatever she wanted. But that was public school. Mountain View, or MouVi, as the kids called it (or at least the kids who liked it enough to enjoy giving it a cute nickname), was the regional public school where Mira had spent the past ten years. But MouVi was not prepared to handle Mira's "special needs." They had made that very clear. And after nine months of absence, St. F was the compromise.

"Look at these assholes," Sebby said, surveying the students making their way up the hill.

"Just consider them easy marks," Mira said. "More fun for you."

"An easy mark is never fun," he said, sitting up. "No challenge to it. How am I ever going to improve myself?"

"You could try going to school. I hear it's all the rage."

"I go to school. How dare you."

"Then how come you're here with me right now?"

"I like to keep them guessing when it comes to my actual attendance. Anyway, you know school's not really my thing."

"Yeah, well I don't think it's my thing either."

"But you have such potential."

She rolled her eyes.

"You'll never get anywhere in life with that bad attitude," he said.

"Oh, god, I don't know if I can do this."

He grabbed her hand and looked into her eyes. "You can do . . ." he said, with a dramatic pause, "whatever you set your mind to." Then he started laughing maniacally.

"Okay, thank you."

"Wait, I'm not done. You can achieve . . . all of your dreams."

"No, you're done."

She stood up, pulling her worn thrift-store army bag onto her shoulder. It was the same one that she had used at her old school, the patches and buttons that used to cover it now removed.

No slogans, logos, or images allowed on any attire or accessories, declared the St. Francis handbook. *Erase all evidence of your individual personality, please. Turn yourself over to the land of the soulless drones, if you wouldn't mind.*

"How about I reach for getting through this day without having a nervous breakdown?" she said.

"It's a start, I suppose." He stood up and kissed her on the cheek. "Don't pretend that you're not destined for greatness, my love."

Mira was impressed with herself that she managed to stay away from the nurse's office for the entire morning. She got through her classes by sitting quietly in back-row desks. It was easy enough to go unnoticed amid the excitement of first-day reunions of returning students comparing new hairstyles, new shoes, new mannerisms picked up over the summer.

But lunch was a different story. It inherently demanded interaction. The cafeteria was made up of twenty large, round tables set up to divide the student population into a self-mandated hierarchy based on a complicated algorithm of shared history, shared interests, and shared status. And so Mira found herself holding her damp lunch tray piled with food that definitely did not fit the rigorous requirements of her mother's elaborate dietary-restriction plan, looking out over the sun-filled second-floor cafeteria and attempting to stave off a slowly rising panic. The antisuicide windows were cracked open to the warm air, younger students gazing down longingly at the juniors and seniors who enjoyed "outdoor privileges" during their free periods. Like prison, you earned it through years of good behavior.

An unlikely rescuer appeared at Mira's side in the form of her neighbor, Molly Stern.

"Miranda! Oh my god!" Molly gave her a kind of half hug in an attempt to not topple the lunch trays they were both holding.

"Hi. Hey, Molly," Mira said.

"My mom said she thought she heard that you were coming to St. F this year, but she wasn't sure and I didn't want to get my hopes up if it wasn't, like, totally for sure happening."

"Well, I'm here," Mira said. "It's happening."

Molly lived down the street from Mira in a house that was enormous even by the standards of their McMansion-loving neighborhood. They had played together as kids, sometime afternoons of lemonade stands and sidewalk chalk. Even then Molly had had an air of desperation about her. She had three older brothers who were infamous for launching street-hockey balls into people's windows. Something in Molly's face had always revealed a suspicion that fate had unfairly tricked her into life without a sister, and she would never quite forgive it.

They'd lost track of each other when Molly started at

St. Francis and Mira followed her older sister to Mountain View Elementary. Mira caught glimpses of Molly on their street every once in a while over the years, but this was the first good look at her she was getting since puberty had hit. Her nose was still too big, her face had not grown to fit it, but to compensate she had cultivated a huge mane of hair to try to balance things out. A few diamonds on a pendant hung from her neck in a style that was popular with a lot of the St. Francis girls.

"You have *got* to come sit with us," Molly insisted, grabbing Mira's arm and leading her to a table whose occupants were deeply engrossed in the passing around of an issue of *Cosmo*.

"Ladies," Molly said when they arrived at the table, sitting down in two conveniently empty chairs, "this is Miranda. We've known each other since forever."

"It's actually just Mira now."

"What?"

"I just go by Mira. No one calls me Miranda anymore."

"But on our street we always did," Molly said. "Molly and Miranda's Lemonade Stand. Remember? Oh my god, we were so cute. We live on the same street," Molly informed the table.

"Well, it's just Mira now," Mira said again.

"Oh, well, I love nicknames. I wish I could have one, but my name is already so short. Just Molly! That's all anyone's ever called me."

Sarah, the blond and perfectly coiffed unofficial leader of this particular lunch table, snickered and whispered a mocking "Just Molly!" to her number two, Anna, an Indian girl with a tight ponytail and a permanent smirk.

The girl sitting on Mira's other side stuck out a formal hand to shake.

"I'm Rose," she said.

She had a dyed black pixie cut and severe glasses with large black rectangular frames.

"Hey." Mira shook her hand.

"How's your first day going?" Rose asked.

"It's okay," Mira said. "I just had English with Mr. Sprenger."

"Everyone calls him Peter," Rose said.

"Oh my god, you are so lucky that you have Peter," Molly said. "He is the absolute hottest."

"He's also a good teacher," Rose said.

"Yeah, I guess," Molly said. "I'm, like, 'What did you say, Peter? I was too busy staring at your face.'" She looked around the table for confirmation. "Right?"

But Sarah had other topics on her mind.

"So you're a freshman?" Sarah asked Mira.

"Sort of," Mira said. "I didn't finish last year at Mountain View, so I need to retake a bunch of stuff. They let me into sophomore English and history, but I'm stuck with freshman classes for everything else."

"She's so not a freshman, though," Molly said. "She's older than me. You should be, like, a junior."

"I'm sixteen," Mira said, worried from the emphatic nature of Molly's tone that they might think she was in her thirties.

"Wow," Sarah said. "Mountain View, huh? Did you get a

scholarship to come here?"

Molly jumped in before Mira could respond. "I can't believe it's been so long since I've seen you," she said. "We used to do all kinds of crazy stuff on our street when we were little. Didn't we?"

Molly had a terrible habit of ending almost everything she said with a question, as if she couldn't be sure about things until she had taken a poll of everyone in the room to find out what they thought.

"Lots of lemonade stands," Mira said.

"So what happened?" Sarah asked.

"To the lemonade stands? I don't know. Winter?"

"No, at Mountain View," Sarah said. "Molly said you were having a lot of problems."

Molly started tearing nervously at a bag of chips.

"Honestly, Sarah, I didn't say that."

"Oh, I'm sorry. I thought I heard you say those exact words right before you went over to ask her to sit with us." Sarah looked at Anna in mock confusion. "I guess I misunderstood."

Anna snickered.

"I was sick," Mira said.

"Like, in the hospital?" Sarah said.

This was more than Molly could take.

"Sarah, you are being really rude. It's Miranda's first day."

"So I'm not allowed to ask her questions? I'm just making conversation."

Mira stood up.

"I gotta go get something else to eat," she said, picking up her tray. "This grilled cheese is like plastic."

"Oh," Molly said, sounding disappointed. The initiation into the group had evidently not gone quite as planned.

"Well, hope you're feeling better, Mira," Sarah said in a sugar-sweet voice that could be heard two tables over. "And not still feeling sick." She said the word *sick* like it was some kind of hilarious euphemism.

"Thanks," Mira said.

She made her way to the trash can and dumped the rest of her lunch in it, piled the damp tray on top, and walked through the cafeteria doors.

Downstairs she headed down the hall to the nurse's office. She turned over her permanent doctor's note to the nurse, gave in to the sagging comfort of the standard-issue cot, and tried not to cry.

JEREMY

No one talked to me on that first day back except for Peter. Not that I gave them an opportunity. Head down, I counted the minutes to the end of each period, knowing I just needed to be able to say that I made it through the day.

When I got home after school, the front door was unlocked and I let myself in.

"Dave?" I pushed my shoes off my feet and set them in their place on the carefully curated shoe shelf by the front door.

"I'm in the kitchen," Dave called back.

I dropped my backpack at the bottom of the stairs and followed the smell of bread baking into the kitchen. Dave was laying out cookies on a baking sheet.

"Hi," I said. I sat down on a stool across from him. "You're home early."

He shrugged. "Work was slow," he said.

"You're not here to check on me?"

"I'm here," he said, uncovering a fresh loaf of bread from the bread box on the counter, "to make you a snack." He cut off a large slab of soft bread and spread fresh peach preserves on top. Preserve making was a new hobby of his. Half of the basement was currently filled with colorful jars that he couldn't give away fast enough. Dad said he should start a stand on the side of the road if he was going to keep this up.

Dave handed me the bread on a plate.

"Thanks," I said.

"Cookies will be ready in ten minutes," he said.

"Cookies and bread?"

"Don't tell your dad. He already thinks I'm trying to fatten us all up."

"And you're not?"

Dave smiled. "Eat your snack."

I took a bite. It was still warm.

"You're not going to make me talk about my day?" I asked, mouth still full.

He picked up the baking sheet and bent down to put the cookies in the oven.

"Do you want to talk about your day?" he asked, closing the oven door and setting the timer.

"No," I said.

"Okay, then."

He cut himself a slice of bread, spread on preserves, and we sat and ate in silence.

MIRA

It was only after the school nurse gently suggested that Mira might "like to try going back to class" that she reluctantly abandoned her post on the cot and managed to finish up her first day. Four more periods before she was able to get on the bus, claim a seat by the window, and stare out at this route that she would be following from now on, twice a day, five days a week. She counted the blocks home as they passed by the window. Nothing had ever seemed so far away.

The bus let her off at the bottom of her driveway, its double doors shushing shut behind her.

Their house was the one holdover on the street from an age before people in the neighborhood started building faux mansions that went up to the edge of their property lines, elaborate chandeliers displayed prominently in soaring front-hall windows. Mira's family's house looked like a refugee from 1920s Savannah, with a decorative wicker rocking chair on a wraparound porch. Her mother thought this gave it charm. Mira thought it looked lonely. Like it had outlived its friends.

She took a deep breath in an attempt to cleanse herself of this day and tried to think of something positive to report to her mother. Her mother was into positivity. It had never been Mira's strong point. She would not mention the nurse's office. Let her mom believe that she had made it through the day upright.

Mira made her way up the front steps. There was no avoiding it. She lived here. She would have to go in sometime.

"Mira? Is that you?" her mom called when the front door banged shut behind her.

"Yeah."

Mira made her way back to the computer alcove by the kitchen, where her mom could usually be found these days. Fourteen months ago the law firm she had worked at for the past decade decided to let her go rather than make her partner. Unfortunately this was the same firm Mira's father worked at. And he was a partner. After she was let go, Mira's mother sued the firm for gender discrimination, and since then the topic of work, a thing her parents had always shared, as if the firm had been a third party in their marriage, was avoided at all costs.

Today her mom had on sweatpants and a T-shirt declaring that she had completed some 5K run, as if to prove that she had once been a person who spent all her time doing 5K runs and not growing pale in pajamas in front of a computer screen. Her frizzy hair was pulled back into a high ponytail that created a cascading pouf on the back of her head. She called this her "Jew fro."

There was a framed picture of Mira's parents on the mantel in the living room, taken during their days together at Columbia law school, both of them making goofy faces, her very white mom's hair teased out to match the retro-looking Afro her dad had sported back then. Mira loved that picture of them.

"Let me see you," her mother said.

Mira pulled a chair up to the computer alcove and presented herself for inspection.

"So?" her mom said. "Tell me everything."

"It was fine."

"Just fine?"

Mira sighed. She didn't have the energy to live through this day and talk about it too.

"I'm tired," she said.

"Tired tired? Or just tired?"

"Tired tired." It was their code. It seemed better than other words they could use, loaded with the baggage of diagnosis. As if all she needed was a really good nap to finally feel better.

"Scale of one to ten," her mother said.

"Eleven," she said.

Her mom was looking at her as if she was trying to remember which encouraging piece of positive-speak she hadn't used in a while.

"What?" Mira said.

"Eleven means we need to go see Kelly."

"No, Mom, please. I'm following the diet. She's just going to make me choke down those awful horse vitamins."

Kelly was the holistic nutritionist her mother had started taking Mira to when she had asked to go off her medication last spring. The pills had been making her feel jumpy and constrained, like her head was trying to hold her brain in place and somehow failing. Kelly had been the compromise.

"It's Kelly or Dr. Hellman. Your pick." Horse vitamins or jumpy drugs.

"Just give me a chance to get used to this place, okay? Did you think it would be filled with some kind of special air or something that would immediately make me all better?"

"I just want to know that you're giving it a chance."

"I am giving it a chance. I went to all my classes except gym."

"Mira . . ."

"Mom . . ." She tried matching her mother's tone in an attempt to turn this into a playful conversation instead of yet another panicked planning session about "what we should try next."

Her mother sighed. "I just want to make sure we're doing everything we can."

"First days are hard. Just give me some time."

"Okay. I get it. But we have a standing appointment with Kelly next week and we are not missing it, okay?"

"Yes. Sure."

"And you need to stick with the elimination diet until then. Or else we're just wasting her time and ours."

"Of course, Mom."

"What did you eat today?"

"I don't know. Nothing, I wasn't hungry."

Her mother shook her head and turned toward the computer. "No, absolutely not acceptable. Your blood sugar, Mira. It's like we did all of that glycemic index work for nothing. I'm making you lunch tomorrow." She was clicking through pages of recipes on her favorite all-allergy-free-cooking website. "Look. Vegan, gluten-free quiche."

"What exactly makes it quiche?"

"Well, the shape, I guess. It's quiche shaped."

"Sounds great."

"Your sarcasm is not appreciated."

"Sounds gross."

"Thank you. Honesty."

"You don't want honesty. I was honest with you that I'm tired and you totally overreacted."

"All right. Let's start over, okay?"

"Okay."

"So, did you make any new friends today?"

"You don't just 'make friends' on the first day of school."

"But did anyone seem nice? Did you see Molly Stern?"

"Oh yeah. I saw Molly Stern, all right."

"And?"

"I mean, she's Molly Stern, what do you want me to say? She's like if a chipmunk became a human girl."

"Are you sure you're not just being a snob?"

"A snob? When am I ever a snob?"

"Molly may not be that cool, or whatever," her mom said. Mira automatically rolled her eyes. "But she's a nice girl and she might be able to help you get adjusted."

"So I should use her to get 'adjusted' and then drop her when I find 'cool' friends?"

"You know that's not what I mean."

"That's what you said."

"If you are half this difficult with the people you meet, it's remarkable to me that you have any friends at all."

"I don't. Remember?" Mira stood up. "Sebby didn't come by, did he?"

"No," her mom said. "But no visitors until you finish your homework."

Mira grunted.

"I assume you have homework?"

"Tons."

"Mira . . ."

"What?"

"You're going to give this place a chance, right?"

"Yes. I am. I promise."

"Okay."

"Okay."

Mira hoisted her school bag with exaggerated effort.

"I'll take a thirty-minute nap, then do my homework, then make lots of new friends, okay?"

"Set your alarm," her mom called after her as she made her

way up the stairs to her room. "Your father said he'll be home for dinner. He wants to hear all about your day."

Mira woke up an hour after her alarm went off, dreading the impending dinnertime recap of her day for her dad, and called Sebby. Contacting him wasn't always easy, since his cheap cell phone had usually run out of minutes, which just meant that he hadn't gotten around to pocketing another prepaid phone card. The best way to reach him was unfortunately to call his house.

The phone was picked up on the first ring.

"O'Connor residence. Stephanie speaking."

Mira breathed a sigh of relief that it wasn't Sebby's foster mom, a woman who thought it was sinfully rude to hand over the phone to anyone before inquiring for at least ten minutes about the health and well-being of every member of the caller's family.

"Hey, Stephanie. It's Mira. Is he home?"

"I don't know, Mira, what's it worth to you? Ow!"

The unmistakable sounds of older-sibling aggression were accompanied by a declaration of "Give me the phone, maggot child!" then pouting shouts of "I'm telling!" and finally Sebby's voice on the other end.

"Sorry, babes, this place is crawling with maggot children."

"That is gross, Sebby."

"It's the truth. They leave little trails of slime behind them. Hold on."

There was the sound of children screaming and a baby crying in the background. Then it was quiet.

"I am literally in the closet," he said.

"What's going on over there?"

"Big Momma is the last person in the world to still have a phone with a cord. It only reaches to the pantry." Big Momma was what Sebby called his foster mom, which he thought was hilarious since Tilly O'Connor was so thin she had to buy her belts in the children's section.

"No, I mean what's going on with the screaming?"

"New shipment. Twins."

"You're kidding."

"Nope. It's insanity over here."

Tilly was a full-time foster parent, taking in those in need through a referral service at her church. At least twenty children had gone through her care since her husband had died in a construction accident nine years ago. Her current household had three other kids, two boys and Stephanie, all younger than Sebby.

"Wow. Twins. Jackpot for Tilly."

"And listen to this. She's moving Stephanie into my room with me because she needs space for the two cribs."

"Oh no."

"Yup. Me and little Steph are getting real close over here."

"Is Tilly allowed to do that?"

"The state says it's fine as long as we have our own beds. Believe me, I checked to see if I could make an anonymous report."

"Maybe she thinks you'll be a good influence."

"Maybe I should tell her that I'm a godless homo and get myself kicked out of here."

"Don't joke, Sebby."

"No, do not joke about being a godless homo when stuck in the religious lady's pantry. It's just too ironic to be amusing."

"And here I was calling to complain about my day."

"Yeah? How was it?"

"Awful."

"Anything in particular?"

"You know, mild panic attack in the nurse's office."

"Oh, that's all."

"That's all."

The screaming returned, with a loud cry of "He's in here! He's hiding in the closet so he doesn't get in trouble!"

Sebby sighed. "See? Not even funny."

"It's a little funny," Mira said.

"I better go. I need to make an appointment to have some earplugs permanently implanted."

"Talk to you tomorrow."

"Bye, babes."

"Bye, Sebs."

Mira hung up the phone and lay back on her bed. She looked up at the wall above her. A set of stretched nylon wings hung from a hook, like a trophy from a successful fairy-hunting mission.

She made a wish on the wings that everything would be okay. For both of them.

JEREMY

Two weeks into the school year Peter decided that he wasn't going to let me get away with never talking to anyone.

I had been spending my lunch periods in his office, balancing the contents of whatever food Dave had packed for me on my sketchbook while I pored over an art book from the library. It was the best part of my day. The only interruption was the occasional student looking for Peter's attention with the excuse of talking about a paper or an extra-credit project.

Peter was the most adored teacher at St. Francis, at least ten years younger than any of the others and the only one who had his students call him by his first name. A long face and dusty-brown hair topped a body that moved with a kind of loping confidence through the halls, upright enough to inspire authority but casual. Accessible.

If I was sitting alone in Peter's office when another student came in, they would eye me jealously, wondering why I thought

I could be so familiar with his space. Then they would remember, and a look of discomfort or pity would move across their face like a cloud, and I would turn back to my sketchbook and let them leave.

On this day I headed to his office as soon as the bell rang for lunch. His door was open as usual, and I dropped my things on the floor and made myself comfortable, pulling a cookie that Dave had packed up for me that morning out of my pocket and eating it, crumbs spilling onto the book of Impressionist paintings that the library had just gotten in.

"Jeremy, my man." Peter came in behind me, tossing his lunch bag on the desk. "How goes it?"

"Fine," I said, attempting to gather up the cookie crumbs.

"Mind if I join you?" he said, sitting down on the other side of the desk.

"It's your office," I said.

"I'm glad you're here. I wanted to show you something." He grabbed a piece of paper off the shelf behind him and held it up in front of my face.

"New club registration," I read.

"They're looking to fill out the after-school club roster, and I thought that you might be interested in starting an art club."

"Me?"

He laid the piece of paper down on top of my open book.

"Maybe something for the students who want more time in the studio than they get in class."

It was true that the actual studio art class was mostly

useless. An artistically frustrated former painter had been drafted into teaching the same perspective drawing lessons and color-wheel combinations over and over. I would try to finish up any assignments as quickly as I could so I could get back to the sketching that I had been doing all day anyway.

"You think the school would let us have extra studio time?"

"If it was for a club, I'm sure they would."

I picked up the paper and examined it. Half of it was lines for signatures and email addresses to list other students who might be interested in joining.

"And you want me to start it?"

"Just get any ten student signatures and you've got yourself a club. I'll be your adviser."

I could feel my hands start to sweat as I stared at those lines. Ten people. I hadn't talked to ten people in the past week.

"It would be great for your college application too," Peter said. "Starting a club shows a lot of initiative." He dumped out the contents of his lunch bag and started unwrapping a tuna-fish sandwich.

"But I don't have a lot of initiative," I said.

"Listen, I know you would love to get more time in the studio, and if it means taking on a small leadership role to get it, then that's the price of admission."

"You're just trying to get me to talk to people, aren't you?"

He smiled and took a bite of his sandwich, sat back in his chair, and looked at me while he chewed.

"I'm being set up," I said.

"Just get ten signatures and we'll go from there," he said. "I promise it won't hurt."

"Easy for you to say," I said, shoving the paper into the back of my sketchbook.

"It wasn't easy for me to say, I have a mouth full of tuna fish."

I did have friends before everything that happened. Or at least I had people I talked to. There was Simon, the sci-fi obsessive and chess player from middle school, who moved away after eighth grade. And Ahmed, newly made captain of the math team, who now hung out exclusively with the other math team members. But that was all before last spring. And now I couldn't even think of ten people who would sign a stupid piece of paper for me.

I sat in Peter's English class that day staring at the sign-up sheet, compulsively pulling it halfway out from the spot in my sketchbook where I had stashed it, then pushing it back.

Peter's class was mostly sophomores like me, kids who had been indoctrinated into the cult of Peter the previous year and were now back for more. Almost everyone spoke up in class, wanting desperately to say something smart to impress him. The most aggravating of the Peter kiss-ups was a girl named Talia, who always got to class early to make sure she got the seat directly to his right at the large round table that Peter preferred for his classroom. She was tiny with a commanding voice and white-blond hair that she wore in a conservative braid down her back.

On this day Talia was lecturing us about the fact that you couldn't read Kurt Vonnegut's *Slaughterhouse-Five*, the book we had been assigned over the summer, without reading William Faulkner's *The Sound and the Fury*. Peter, who seemed perpetually amused by his students, was the only one paying attention to her.

"You can't really understand Vonnegut without knowing the reference," she was saying.

Talia and I were both St. Francis lifers. We tended to be an awkward species. Lifers started St. F in kindergarten at the lower school building, moving across town as we progressed to the middle school and finally high school. After ten years together in an institution this small, we all knew far too much about each other. A claustrophobia had set in somewhere around third grade that was proving to be difficult to shake.

So when someone new came into this world of preordained power structures, someone who looked like they might understand a certain kind of emptiness, you might notice her. Or I might. I noticed her.

"Mira." She said her name on the first day of class when we went around the table to introduce ourselves. Her curly hair was tied up in a ribbon, her silver-painted fingernails tapped absently on the table.

I was so desperate not to look into familiar faces that I often found myself focusing on her. The back of her head in my history class in the morning. Her sitting across from me in Peter's class in the afternoon, her curls making progress in their mission to escape order as the day went on. She was the only other person who was as quiet as I was. While I sat there drawing, she often not-so-subtly worked on homework for her other classes. An open algebra textbook in front of her was only half concealed by her English notebook.

I had seen her after school too, always running down the hill to meet a lanky boy in street clothes who waited for her on the bench every day. The afternoon sunlight would shine on his blond hair, giving him a backlit halo.

Now I was sketching in between sneaking glances at the sign-up sheet, each time I pushed it back into my sketchbook hoping that it would disappear forever. An image of myself sitting alone in the art studio flashed through my mind. Would they let me have a club for only one person?

Talia was still insisting that "it's a direct literary inspiration," when I looked up from my sketchbook and saw Mira looking at me, or at least at the space that I happened to be occupying. She didn't seem to really be looking at anything. But then I was looking at her looking at me. It took a minute before her eyes registered our accidental crossing of planes of vision. I felt myself freeze in embarrassment. But then she smiled, tilted her head toward Talia, who was somehow still talking, and rolled her eyes. I laughed, more out of shock that she had noticed me than anything else, that someone would make a joke for my benefit. The girl next to me glared at my drawing and

Mira's blatantly open algebra textbook. Mira smiled and went back to her homework.

The final period of that day was interminable, because I had decided that I was going to ask Mira to sign the Art Club sheet.

My last class was in the first-floor biology lab, and it provided an excellent view of the parking lot where some of the seniors, who had the privilege of arranging their schedules, had managed to get themselves a study hall for their final period. Teachers in final-period study halls were notoriously willing to let students leave early, since it meant they could leave early too. A moment of truth, that none of us wanted to be stuck in that building anymore.

It was fifty minutes of fruit-fly lecturing before I could bolt out of the classroom, grab my jacket and backpack from my locker, and push my way through the throng of kids bottlenecking at the front door, out into the welcoming afternoon air.

I stood there with the form in my hand, watching the groups of kids pouring out of the building behind me. I didn't see her anywhere. The bench at the bottom of the hill was empty.

I looked down at that piece of paper. Why did I think she would sign it? Because she was new? She didn't know any better? Did I think that she hadn't gotten the message yet that I was invisible?

I took my backpack off my back, crouched down to unzip it, and shoved the form inside. When I looked up again, she was suddenly there, walking past me, her uniform kilt passing close to my face.

"Mira!" I said, still crouched over my backpack.

She turned to look at me. She had her hair in that unmistakable messy bun, secured with a purple ribbon today, and matching purple lipstick.

"Yeah?" she said.

"Um, it is Mira, right?" I said, standing up.

"Yup."

"I'm Jeremy, from your English class."

"Yeah. I know. What's up?"

"Oh, uh, I'm . . . getting signatures to start a new club. It's an art club. Just for anyone who wants to have some extra time in the art studio after school. I need ten signatures and I was wondering if you might, uh, if you want to . . . sign up?"

I pulled the form back out of my bag and held it up like a shield in front of me.

"I don't take art," she said.

"That's okay. You don't have to actually be in the club. I just need signatures from any ten students."

Mira took the piece of paper from me.

"Do you have a pen?"

I produced one from my shirt pocket. Was this really working? All I had to do was ask?

"You need my email too?"

I looked at the form as if I hadn't been studying it nonstop for the past three hours. "Yeah. I guess so. Then I can just email anyone who signs it and let them know if it's happening."

She took the pen and paper and tried to balance it on her other hand to write.

"Oh, here." I pulled a book out of my backpack and held it out for her to lean on.

She signed the page, wrote her email, and then took the book from me, handing back the paper.

"What is this?" she asked, opening the cover. It was a book of work by my favorite artist, Nick Cave, a birthday present from my dad and Dave.

"Oh, he's an artist. He makes these crazy costumes."

She was flipping through images of people covered head to toe in colorful fringe and furs and elaborate embroidery.

"That one's my favorite," I said, pointing to a photograph of a stick creature peering out from the cave of its own body, an empty basket where its face should have been.

She examined the picture for a minute, then closed the book and handed it back to me.

"So are we going to make stuff like that in this club?" she asked.

"Just whatever we want, I guess." I leaned over to put the book and signup sheet back in my bag.

"Cool. Thanks for asking me."

I looked up at her, sure that this must be sarcastic, but she was smiling, as if we were sharing a joke that I just hadn't figured out yet.

Suddenly the boy from the bench was behind her, grabbing

her around the waist and picking her up.

"Do I have to carry you to the mall, woman?" he yelled. "What could possibly be taking so long?"

"Put me down, evil she-beast!" she cried, attempting to kick him. He let her go, laughing. "This nice young man is asking me to join his secret society." Mira pointed at me. "These things can't be rushed."

"Oh, in that case." The boy turned to me and held out a hand. "Sebastian Tate. Sebby. If you're starting a secret society, you're definitely going to want me to be your secretary."

"He's got the outfit for it," Mira said.

"Oh, I . . . it's a school club," I said. I felt as if a tornado had descended on me. The air around me seemed to be spinning.

Sebby turned to Mira. "What's his name?"

"Jeremy." She was still smiling in that way that was trying to assure me that this was not at my expense.

Sebby turned back to me. He grabbed my hand. "Jeremy, I am coming to your club, okay? This is for your own good. When is it?"

"It doesn't exist yet," I said. I could feel my hand getting hot.

"You'll tell Mira the minute that you know."

I nodded, mildly terrified.

"What do we do in this club?" he asked.

"Art," I said. "It's an art club."

"Fantastic. I love art."

"Sebby, come on," Mira said. "Release the poor boy. We've got places to be."

He smiled at me, raised my hand to his lips and kissed it, then let it go.

"Released," he said, and walked away from me.

Mira was already halfway down the hill.

"See you later, Jeremy," she called back.

I looked around to see if anyone had witnessed any of this, but as usual I had been invisible. I touched my hand where he had kissed it, so casually flirtatious, so easy for him. Where did these people come from? I felt emboldened by the inter-action, as if having their attention even for that moment had bestowed a kind of approval upon me. At least it meant that I wasn't invisible.

I walked up to the next nine people I saw and got them to sign the form.

MIRA

They had already managed to get themselves kicked out of both Victoria's Secret and Hot Topic when Mira's phone beeped with an incoming email. She and Sebby were sitting on a bench eating giant "New York style" pretzels from Mama's New York Style Pretzel Shop. Sebby was making faces at the Hot Topic salesman who had banished them from the store after catching him trying on the glittery fake eyelashes. Sebby just pocketed them on his way out. And grabbed some blue nail polish for good measure.

Mira took her phone out of her bag.

It was an email from Jeremy, the boy from her English class.

Thanks for signing the Art Club petition. We'll meet
Wednesdays right after school in the studio if you
want to be a part of it.

"I guess our new friend got his signatures," she said, handing the phone to Sebby.

"Great," Sebby said, reading it. "I'm free on Wednesdays."

"You're free every day."

"You don't know my life."

"I do, actually."

The Hot Topic salesman was eyeing them from behind his counter display of goth jewelry and Manic Panic. He was too old to be working there for any reason other than that nowhere else would have him, with his long, greasy ponytail and fading Ramones T-shirt. And being harassed by two teenagers did not seem to be helping his sense of self-worth on this particular day. Mira recognized the look in his eyes from her many afternoons spent at the mall with Sebby. He was debating whether or not to call security.

"Let's get out of here," she said. "This guy has it in for us."

"Never admit defeat!" Sebby said. But he hopped off the bench and blew a kiss at the Hot Topic guy, and they set off on a stroll through the halls of commerce, passing by the chain clothing stores, from preppy to slutty and back to preppy again.

Mira stopped to look in a window promising THE HOTTEST LOOKS OF FALL! and featuring tiny mannequins in skin-tight jeans and cropped cardigans.

"These clothes are like death," she said, "and anyone who wears them is dead inside."

"That kid was cute," Sebby said, not interested in one of her regular rants against mass-produced clothing.

"Art boy? Jeremy?"

"Yeah. Art boy was cute, right?"

"You flirted shamelessly," she said.

"That wasn't flirting. That's how I say hello."

"You were shameless."

They kept walking, away from the offensive clothing toward the less controversial chocolate-and-candy section of the mall.

"So which one of us should take him to prom?" Sebby asked.

"You can have him," Mira said.

"Yes, but do I want him? Did he even mention me in that email?"

"Yeah, he said, *P.S. your friend is a huge flirt.*"

"He didn't!"

"No he didn't, but I think you completely terrified him. I've never even heard him speak before, and I have class with him every day."

"Maybe he needs some friends."

"Well, I'm not looking for any more friends. I have my bestie, Molly Stern."

"God, I don't even know Molly Stern and I already love her."

"Take her. Please."

They made their way past the big fountain that hadn't worked in two years. A sign declaring THE FOUNTAIN WILL BE BACK THIS SPRING hung crookedly off the top spigot.

"I just think you should keep an open mind about this Jeremy," Sebby said. "He obviously has a crush on you."

"On me?"

"Yes. He asked you to be in his club."

"He just needed ten people to sign that paper."

"He emailed you right away."

"You told him to!"

"I'm intentionally changing the subject because you are getting overexcited. So, what are you going to make in Art Club? Oil painting? Bronze bust?"

"Oh lord, do I actually have to go now?"

"Why not? You have something against the arts?"

"I have something against spending any more time in that building than I have to. Seven hours a day is enough. I can barely keep my eyes open for that long."

"Perhaps you will find energy through an expression of creativity."

"Yeah, I doubt it."

He stopped in front of the bulk candy store.

"Okay, number one: I need Sour Patch Kids. Number two: You're definitely going to Art Club, because I'm going with you. I told Jeremy that I would and he's obviously counting on me."

She followed him inside the store as he grabbed a bag and helped himself to samples from the large plastic bins.

"And what exactly are you going to do in Art Club?" Mira asked.

Sebby found the Sour Patch Kids and took a handful.

"I am super artistic, okay? I'll paint a mural. Children holding hands. World peace. Very tasteful."

"Uh-huh. You got enough candy there?"

"Almost." He opened another bin, grabbed a giant jawbreaker, and stuck it in his pocket, making a large bulge in his pants.

"Yes, I am happy to see you," he said.

"Lovely."

"Okay, let's go."

They walked out of the store, the teenager at the counter barely looking up as they left without paying.

Sebby held the bag of candy out for her to take some.

"I swear my mother has developed the ability to smell sugar on me," she said.

"Life is short," he said. He picked out a neon-green Sour Patch Kid and held it in front of her face. "Do you accept this little sugar man and his mission to bring you peace and fulfillment with the risk of a major sugar crash to follow?"

"I do," she said. "I accept the terms of the tiny sugar man, and the wrath of my impossible mother."

She ate it out of his hand, intentionally biting his finger.

"With pleasure comes pain," he said, filling his mouth with candy.

SEBBY

You took different paths when you were at the mall without Mira. You had other things to accomplish when you were alone.

It was easier to pocket things in a way, because you could move more quickly. But then a teenager alone always aroused more suspicion. Easier to catch what your hands were doing on security cameras without an extra body to mask you.

On this day you managed to grab a few sets of earbuds, a pack of rechargeable batteries, and a necklace from Claire's that you thought Mira would like. You had seen it earlier and remembered it, used a group of gum-chewing twelve-year-olds carefully examining the plastic earrings to block you, and got in and out quickly. Now you stuck your hands in your pockets, feeling the satisfying jangle of the chain as you walked away from the store. The guy who lived on the corner of your block would give you a few bucks for the other stuff. And now you were feeling that adrenaline happy of seeing and taking. Desire and consummation uninterrupted by something as crass as money changing hands.

There was no point in risking lifting anything else on this day, so it was time to go look for some company. You could usually find Sam in the record store all the way at the south end of the mall. The store was a relic, plastered with twenty years of band posters and ads for concerts long ago jammed to. They had actual LPs alongside the CDs, both a hard sell to anyone other than diehard collectors.

Sam unfortunately fit the mold of the main record-store clientele. Clothes that didn't quite fit right. Hair that had been brushed a little too vigorously. And too old to be hanging around a record store at one o'clock in the afternoon instead of at a job, which probably meant that he lived with his parents. But then you shouldn't have been there either.

He was in the jazz section on this day. Sam loved jazz. Also indie rock. And folk. "Anything but metal."

"Hey," you said, peering over from the perpetually uninhabited gospel section.

He looked up cautiously, as if convinced that you couldn't possibly be addressing him. There must be someone behind him, or maybe you were quietly calling to a person on the other side of the room. It seemed that he had been hurt by making assumptions about such things before.

"Oh, hey. Hey, Sebby," he said, finally accepting that you were actually talking to him.

"Anything good?" You nodded at the LPs tucked under his arm.

He shrugged. His eyes never quite met yours. They were always just a little to the left or right of you. Or else they were watching your lips when you talked, as if he had to look at your words to understand them.

"Want to get something to eat?" you asked. It was your job to get him out of the store. The first time he wasn't so shy, but from then on it had been up to you.

"Okay," he said. "I'll just pay for these."

You waited for him outside the door.

"Food court?" he said.

"Sure," you said.

He bought you a burger and himself a Coke, and you sat at a plastic table and ate while he talked about how he might get to fill in for his friend's three a.m. radio show on the local college station the next week. He had been working on the playlist all month, but then he worried that maybe he was overplanning it, and that it would be a better show if he just went with inspiration in the moment. You nodded politely, although you wished Sam wouldn't talk about his life because it just made you sad. More for yourself than for him.

You finished your burger. He hadn't touched his soda.

"You want to get out of here?" you asked.

This meant going to the handicapped bathroom on the top floor of the Sears, the floor where they sold mattresses, and you couldn't help but appreciate the irony that you were so close to so many actual beds, but not quite there. One thirty in the afternoon on a Monday, not even the salespeople could be bothered with coming up here. There was a homeless guy who liked to take naps on one of the beds sometimes. You caught him out of the corner of your eye as you and Sam made your way down the aisles. He looked comfortable.

The bathroom was mostly inoffensive. No one ever cleaned it, but no one seemed to use it either. Maybe just the homeless guy. If he did, he kept it very neat.

No matter how many times you had been in there with Sam, it was always awkward to start. You thought that this was why people liked to be drunk for this. Mutual unremembered fumbling would have been so much better than this very clear-eyed vision of Sam carefully lowering himself to the floor as you leaned up against the wall next to the hand dryer. His knees creaked a little and you were forced to reexamine your calculation of how old you thought he was. Twenty-five? Thirty? But then Sam was the kind of person who'd probably had creaky knees since he was ten.

But once he got your zipper open, you no longer cared about the awkwardness, the total inelegance of the situation. You no longer cared about poor Sam or Sam's poor knees or yourself or anything.

One nice thing about Sam was that he didn't seem to mind you making noise. Sounding like you were actually enjoying yourself of course revealed your own attitude about this encounter. That you couldn't find shame in all of this mess like a normal person. But Sam never seemed ashamed. He was just a guy who couldn't get a date, spent too much time in the record store, didn't get enough sunlight. It was possible that his time with you in the handicapped bathroom on the top floor of the Sears was the one thing in his life that Sam wasn't ashamed of.

So you made noise. What did you care? You wanted to get caught. You wanted them to know how nice it could be there in the handicapped bathroom. Inspire the world with your own ability to embrace pleasure in unlikely places. You accidentally hit the side of the hand dryer with your fist, setting it off. You smiled as the hot air blew out next to you. Your life was absurd. You tried not to think about it.

And then you couldn't think anymore and that was the loveliest place of all. Where your head went away and there was only a cloud on top of your shoulders. A moment of suspension right before you crashed back down to earth. There. There it was.

Afterward, he kind of held you, his head resting against your leg. You wanted to touch him but you didn't want to disturb the moment he seemed to be having, and anyway you would rather just stretch your arms out, hugging the wall behind you, feeling the air from the dryer, which had gone off again.

When he finally got up, Sam went to the sink and washed his hands and face. You felt close to him watching him do this. Like the two of you were married, at home. Maybe you just finished brushing your teeth. Now you would get into bed together. He would spoon you and say he set the alarm for early because he had a meeting in the morning. You thought about asking him to pretend with you. You could lie down on one of the mattresses. Ask the homeless guy to turn out the light.

The first few times you offered to reciprocate, but he shook his head and changed the subject to the release date for the new Arcade Fire album. So then you didn't ask anymore.

You said good-bye to Sam at the bottom of the escalator. Some days he offered to buy you something else, besides the food, if there was anything you needed. But on this day you made a quick getaway before he could mention it. You were anxious to get back to your block and see how much you could get for the earbuds, impatient to get the necklace to Mira. The sweet calm of the moment in the bathroom had faded and your brain was already on to the next thing. Kind, slow-moving Sam has served his purpose for the day, and you had places to be.

Sam stood where you left him at the bottom of the escalator. You looked back once and he hadn't moved. He was staring into his plastic bag as if it might contain some answers. He was a nice guy, and you always had a soft spot for nice. Next time you would think of something in advance for him to buy you. It seemed to make him happy.

You wondered if he would head back to the record store now. Maybe he didn't even like records that much. Maybe he just waited there for boys to meet him, and you were part of an elaborate network of dropouts and delinquents who turned to Sam to break up the monotony of an empty afternoon.

JEREMY

The day of our first Art Club meeting, Peter assured me that he would meet me in the studio as soon as he finished his after-school department meeting, but he insisted that I prepare the room myself and greet my new club members. I was still not convinced that anyone was actually going to show up. I had gotten a few "thx" responses to the email, but I couldn't imagine a world in which I was about to spend the next hour doing anything other than sitting alone in the art studio. Of course then at least I wouldn't have to talk to anyone.

I was sitting in the corner with my sketchbook when three freshmen came in. They seemed to have emerged from some sort of St. F emo subculture, two girls with black nail polish and a boy with his tie loosened and shirt half unbuttoned to reveal a vintage Morrissey T-shirt hiding underneath.

"Is this the club?" the boy asked.

"Yeah, yes," I said, realizing that there was no getting

out of it at this point.

"Cool," the boy said. He chose one of the drafting tables, and the two girls sat down on either side of him.

I knew what Peter was trying to do, force me into human contact like some kind of immersion therapy for loners, and I was half annoyed and half flattered. That was how Peter got things done. It was impossible to be too mad at him for meddling, because you were so busy feeling grateful that he cared enough to meddle in the first place. But I was still silently cursing him when Mira and Sebby walked in the room.

I felt my heart start to race at the sight of the two of them together. I wasn't sure how to prepare myself for the return of the tornado of energy that Sebby brought with him. I had not forgotten his playful good-bye from the week before, the feeling of his lips on my hand as he planted a kiss and then dropped it. The casual ease with which he seemed to navigate the world.

"Hi, Jeremy," Sebby said, smiling.

"I'm so sorry," Mira said. "He insisted on coming."

"Oh, that's okay. It's good, uh, that you're here," I said, having trouble looking directly at him. He was like a light that was too bright. Like the sun.

Sebby smirked at Mira. "See? I told you. He wants me here."

"My friend has a huge ego, Jeremy. Please do not encourage him."

Peter came in the room behind them, and Mira pulled Sebby over to a drafting table in the back.

"How goes it?" Peter said, coming over to me.

"Okay, I think," I said.

"Looks like some people want to be in your club."

"I guess."

"Should we get things started?"

I nodded.

"Great."

He turned to the two occupied tables.

"Hi, folks," he said. "I'll just introduce myself. I'm Peter. I think I know most of you already." He greeted each of the emo kids. "Liz, Greg, Courtney. Nice to see you here."

Courtney blushed through her long bangs.

"And?" He turned to the back table. "Mira. And I don't think I know your friend."

Sebby, thrilled to be given an opening, stood solemnly.

"Sebastian," he said, gave a regal nod, and retook his seat.

"Nice to meet you, Sebastian," Peter said. He looked at Mira with a squint that stopped just short of being a wink. She attempted a polite smile in the interest of not being busted for bringing her nonmatriculated friend.

"I'm going to serve as the faculty adviser for this club," Peter said. "Mostly I'll just be available to you for any questions you have. For now I will turn the floor over to Jeremy."

He sat down on one of the desks with characteristic breeziness and looked expectantly at me. I was saved by some new arrivals, Rose with Talia trailing along closely behind her, mid-sentence.

"Oh, are we late?" Talia asked, situating herself as close as she could to Peter while trying to look casual about it, laying a notebook and pen set out carefully on the table in front of her. Rose took the opportunity to escape and make her way to the back of the room.

I watched as Mira introduced Rose to Sebby, wishing that I could be sitting there with them instead of stuck at the front, ready to completely embarrass myself at any moment.

"Jeremy?" Peter said. "Ready to address your club?"

I took a deep breath, took a last look at the notes I had in front of me, bullet points rehearsed to the point of absurdity, and began.

MIRA

Mira had finally agreed to bring Sebby to Art Club after endur-
ing a torturous required meeting with one of the school guidance
counselors in which she was informed that she should have started
working on her college application essay when she was in kindergarten. Because of her "unusual circumstances in coming to St.
Francis," they were evidently "worried about her progress" and
"ability to successfully work her way into the social and academic
world of the school."

In trying to cut short a worried comment about the number
of hours she was spending in the nurse's office, she brought up
the fact that she was helping to start a new club that was meeting for the first time that week. This seemed to show enough
interest in waking life that she was let go without further insult.
And now here they were.

At least Rose had showed up too. Mira had gotten to know
Rose, the girl with the cropped hair and severe glasses, a little

over lunch since the first day of school. She had a kind of twitchy rebellious streak in her, revealed in moments when a regular laugh would morph into a wicked cackle. Mira wasn't always sure what was so funny, but something about Rose made her want to know.

Rose joined Mira and Sebby at the drafting table in the back, and Mira made the proper introductions.

"Rose, this is Sebby," she said. "Sebby, Rose."

"Oh yeah, Sebastian, right?" Rose said. "I've heard about you."

"Only terrible things, I hope."

"The worst."

They were waiting for Jeremy to actually get the Art Club meeting started. He was mostly keeping his back to the room, flashing a terrified look at their table whenever he was bold enough to turn around.

"Thanks, everyone, for coming," he said finally, sounding like a person speaking above a whisper for the first time in his life. "It's, um, really great that you're all here." He glanced quickly at Mira, Sebby, and Rose's table, then turned back to his papers.

Sebby raised an eyebrow at Mira.

"So today we need to work on our mission statement." He nearly yelped out the words. "I . . . I know it's kind of boring. But if we're going to be an official club and get some money from the school for supplies, we need to have one."

"I love this," Sebby whispered. "You guys pay a fortune to

go here and then have to beg them to give you twenty bucks for construction paper."

Rose gave him a look that said "no kidding."

"Mission statements are a great way to focus the energy of a group," Peter offered to the room.

Talia was actually taking notes, scribbling furiously in her notebook as soon as Peter opened his mouth.

"Isn't this club just for us to have extra time in the studio after school?" the girl named Courtney sitting at the front table asked.

"Yes, but . . . we have the opportunity, if we want, to do other stuff as a group," Jeremy said. "Like, have an exhibit of our work. Or go on field trips. If everyone wants that."

"Is he sweating?" Sebby whispered.

"Oh man, keep it together, Jeremy," Rose whispered.

Talia raised her hand.

"Yes?" Jeremy said.

"I vote for an exhibit," she said. "At the end of the year." She looked around the room to confirm that everyone agreed with her.

"Well, we're not really ready to vote on anything yet," Jeremy said.

"It's the best choice in terms of college applications," Talia said. "We'll each make a portfolio with documentation of the exhibit. Field trips are a waste of time as far as colleges are concerned."

"Who is this girl?" Sebby whispered to Mira.

"You do not want to know."

Peter came to the rescue. "Some great ideas there, Talia. Thanks for getting the conversation started. Jeremy, why don't you pass out paper to everybody, and you can all write down your ideas about what you would like to get out of the club."

Jeremy, grateful to be given instructions, passed a stack of blank paper around the room and then retreated back to the corner.

Sebby turned to Rose. "Okay, what's this kid's story?"

"Who? Jeremy?"

"Mira and I have been fighting over him and we need this settled now."

Mira rolled her eyes. "We're not fighting over him. You're just a huge flirt."

"I think you have a better chance of winning that fight," Rose said, pointing her pencil at Sebby. "That's just my educated guess."

Sebby smiled at Mira, victorious. "I win!"

"Yes, you win. Mission statement, people," Mira said, tapping her pencil on the blank page in front of her.

"I was at St. F Middle School with him," Rose said. "He's actually had kind of a hard time since we moved up here. There was this crazy thing that happened with his locker last spring. Someone wrote something really evil on it about a month before the end of the year. It was a pretty big deal."

"What did they write?" Mira asked.

Rose drew something in the corner of her paper and showed it to them. It said *Jeremy ♡s 2 suk dix.*

"Are you serious?" Mira said.

"In spray paint," Rose said. "Really big."

"Why would someone do that?"

"I guess if you're an asshole in the mood for a hate crime, you don't really need a reason."

"They don't teach you people to spell here?" Sebby said, examining the paper.

"Evidently not," Rose said, scribbling out what she had written. "But they do teach us how to make a huge deal out of things like that. Not that it wasn't a big deal, but we had to spend the rest of the year doing special 'sensitivity workshops' for, like, hours a day."

"But that's better than just ignoring it, isn't it?" Mira said.

"Sure. But the whole thing became a big joke. The rest of the year you would see 'J Sux Dix' written everywhere. It was a huge mess."

"What happened to Jeremy?" Mira asked.

"He didn't come back. I hadn't seen him until school started again this year. He's always kind of been a loner, but since he got back he barely even speaks."

"See, this school needs me," Sebby said to Mira. "I'll start all kinds of secret societies pledged to destroying assholes."

"You do have your own school, you know," Mira said.

He picked up a pencil and wrote on the blank page in front of him: *My school sux dix.*

Rose laughed.

* * *

After the meeting, Mira and Sebby took the bus to his house. She wanted to avoid whatever her mother was cooking for dinner, and Tilly wouldn't care if they ordered a pizza.

As soon as they walked in the front door they heard the screaming. At least three children seemed to be waging some kind of war in the kitchen.

"Okay, maybe not," Sebby said.

"We'll just go to your room," Mira said.

Tilly stuck her head out of the kitchen. She had one baby in her arms and another one strapped to her chest. Crayons were flying through the air behind her.

"Oh, good. Sebastian, I need you to run some errands for me, okay?"

"I have homework."

"Well, when you finish your homework, then."

Sebby pulled Mira in the direction of his room.

"I'll be doing my homework all night," he called back.

"Sebastian, I need your help. This is nonnegotiable," she was saying as he closed his bedroom door behind them.

His room had changed since the last time Mira had been over. Until five weeks ago he had shared it with his foster brother Jonathan, who had packed up his stuff on his eighteenth birthday and left without saying good-bye. Now Jonathan's side of the room was stuffed full of everything pink and glittery that little Stephanie had managed to get her hands on in her nine years of life. Tiaras, feather boas, posters of pink ponies, and a fairy princess dress were some of the main attractions.

"How is it that you are not even close to being the gayest thing in this room?" Mira said.

"I know. It's impressive, right?"

He sat down on his never-made bed under the watch of the few posters he kept on the wall. The Velvet Underground's Warhol banana was Sebby's way of being both retro and inappropriately phallic at the same time. One thing Mira could say for Tilly, she let them keep their rooms however they wanted. In the last place Sebby had lived, he and the couple had parted ways when the father realized that Sebby wasn't so keen on the baseball-themed bedroom that had been carefully decorated for a child who had never been born.

"Why is Tilly under the impression that you have homework to do?" Mira asked, falling back onto his bed.

He rolled his eyes. "She just assumes I'm back at school, I guess."

"You guess?"

"I make sure I'm out of the house between eight and three."

"Don't you think someone is going to notice that you're not going?"

"I go sometimes."

Mira raised an eyebrow.

"Fine, I'm going to go. Everything's fine, okay? Don't worry about it."

"I wish you could really go to St. F with me," she said.

"Yeah, in what universe is that even a possibility?"

"They have scholarships."

"For kids with amazing grades. Not loser dropouts."

She shook her finger at him. "No self-shaming talk, Sebby," she said. "What would Dr. Samuels say?"

"Dr. Samuels liked you better than me. Dr. Samuels thought I should shame myself more."

"Ha ha."

"Do you believe that story Rose told us about Jeremy?"

"Oh god, that poor kid," Mira said. "No wonder he's so quiet."

"And I love that all their overdone liberal bullshit totally backfired," he said. "Of course it did. People are assholes. End of story."

"The world according to Sebastian Tate."

"It's a philosophy that has gotten me far in life."

At that moment the door slammed open and Stephanie stood in the doorway, glaring at them.

"Can you learn how to knock, maggot child?" Sebby yelled at her.

She was standing with her hands on her hips, wearing a pink Barbie T-shirt stretched tight over her round stomach.

"Were you looking at my stuff?" she asked, seeming to already know the answer.

"Oh, yeah." Sebby turned to her side of the room and stared at her wall of pink paraphernalia. "We've spent the last hour entranced by the sparkle coming off your tiara collection."

Stephanie looked at her possessions with alarm.

"We weren't messing with your stuff, Stephanie," Mira said.

She had always felt a little bad for Stephanie. Sebby had to be the most annoying big brother in the world. And Stephanie had lived in this house her whole life, years before he had shown up. She had once been one of those adorable babies Tilly had fawned over with such devotion. Mira hoped that Tilly had managed to hide her disappointment in the fact that Stephanie had grown up into a walking, talking person of her own. And Sebby's arrival three years ago must have seemed even more unfair to Stephanie than accumulating younger siblings. He was much more difficult to boss around.

"We were just talking," Mira said.

Stephanie marched over to her bookshelf, grabbed a locked diary with a unicorn on it, and clutched it to her chest.

"You shouldn't be talking with the door closed," she said.

"Well, we weren't just talking," Sebby said, "we were also doing it, so we figured we should shut the door."

Stephanie's face shriveled up in a look of exaggerated disgust.

"That's not true," she said, not quite sure.

"Oh, yeah it is." Sebby jumped on top of Mira and started tickling her.

"Get off of me, you idiot!" she squealed.

She kicked him across the bed and he laughed, pretending to zip up his fly.

"See?" Stephanie looked horrified but vindicated. "She wouldn't do that with you."

"You don't even know what sex is, troll girl," Sebby said.

"I do too." Stephanie clutched her diary tighter.

"Well, the next time Mira and I hook up, we'll leave the door open so you can watch, okay?"

Stephanie seemed to be weighing whether or not she was going to try to come up with a retort to this or storm out on her little pink Keds. Her face was scrunched up into a scowl that made her look like an old man with pigtails. She finally decided on storming out, slamming the door behind her as she went.

"See?" Sebby said. "Privacy."

"You really are traumatizing that poor girl."

"Well she put Jell-O in my bed two nights ago, so I like to think of it as just engaging her sense of competition."

He lay down on the bed, put his head in Mira's lap.

"So, what do we think about little Jeremy?" he said.

She played with his hair, sticking it straight up and then pushing it down onto his face.

"The Shyest Boy in School," she said. "You better stop flirting if you don't mean it."

"Who says I don't mean it?"

Mira let out a fake shocked gasp. "Are you saying you *like* a boy?"

"He's cute."

"Yes. He's very cute. Like a little Chihuahua that shakes whenever someone gets too close to it."

"Maybe he needs some friends," Sebby said. "We can help him get accustomed to human interaction."

"Oh, is that what the kids are calling it these days?" She

made air quotes with her fingers. "Human interaction."

"If the boy finds me irresistible, then there's nothing I can do about it."

"You really want us to make friends?" Mira asked.

"It's for your own good. You have zero friends."

"Hello? You?"

"Yeah," he said, "but I'm going to be busy making out with Jeremy, so . . ."

She grabbed a pillow and pretended to smother him with it.

"Do it," he said, his voice muffled from under the pillow. "Put me out of my misery."

She threw the pillow across the bed.

"No way," she said. "You're not leaving me here alone. Who will listen to me complain about my stupid life?"

"Your life is not stupid."

There was a crash in the living room, followed by a scream and Stephanie shouting, "Not me! Not me!" over and over.

Sebby sighed. "My life, however, is idiotic."

Mira stood up.

"Let's tell Tilly we're doing homework at my house and we'll go eat pizza in the park."

"Fine," he said. "God, I don't know why I ever come here."

"I am sorry to say that you live here."

"Thank you for your sympathy."

"My pleasure."

JEREMY

The St. F homecoming dance was the second Friday in October. It was the first big event of the school year, matched only in importance by the spring semiformal. I told myself that I was going for the same reason I always went to these things, to keep my dad from accusing me of not trying hard enough to make friends. Basketball games, school plays, pep rallies. I had spent most of any middle school and freshman-year events standing in a corner for an hour trying to look as inconspicuous as possible before calling him to come pick me up.

"Was it really that bad?" he would ask when I got in the car.

"Yes," I would say. "It was."

But even as I stood in my bedroom staring at my dresser and wondering if I should try to make an effort and not just show up in my school uniform, I knew that for the first time in my life, I wanted to go. Because I was hoping that they would be there.

This felt a little dangerous, this interest in other people. It meant that there was something that I needed, or at least wanted. It seemed to demand some kind of action on my part, and I had no idea what was supposed to come next.

We had met for Art Club three times now, and Mira and Sebby had been there each time, making jokes with Rose at the back table. But there was a distance I wasn't able to cross between them and me, and I was finding myself desperate to know what might happen if I could.

So I would go to the dance, and hope that they would be there, and hope that I wouldn't make a complete ass of myself. I was also a little worried that a nighttime event could bring out any simmering bad behavior that might be lying in wait among my peers. The dance would be chaperoned, but the formal structure of our daily lives would not be there to protect me. If someone wanted to give me a hard time, this night would provide them with a great opportunity.

My bedroom door was open and I could hear my dad and Dave in the kitchen, Dad's version of talking quietly still audible a floor away.

"I'm just glad he wants to go," he was saying. "I really wasn't expecting this."

A mumble of a response from Dave, whose voice rarely went above a whisper even when he spoke normally.

"But even before everything he was so resistant to these things," Dad said.

Another mumble. I shut my door.

I didn't really have any clothes besides my uniform, a nice suit for funerals that I had nearly grown out of, and my summer cutoffs and T-shirts, now relegated to the bottom drawer of my dresser.

Dolly Parton the Cat was watching me from the bed.

"This is a bad idea, isn't it?" I said.

She put her head down on her paw.

"Dolly Parton, if you think I should stay home, do nothing."

She looked at me and let out a small mew.

MIRA

Mira was in her room, standing in front of her closet, trying to make some decisions. She had never gone to a school dance before, even at MouVi, and Sebby had only convinced her to go to this one because he thought it would be funny.

"I think you and I have different definitions of what *funny* means," she said to him.

Her closet was overflowing with her once-victorious thrift-store finds that now went neglected five days out of the week.

"I'm sorry," she whispered to them.

She called Sebby and put him on speakerphone.

"I'm stuck on the outfit," she said.

"What have we got?"

"I mean, anything's an option. They're all crying out to be worn."

"Well, it's homecoming. Is there a theme?"

"Yes, the theme is stupidity. I can't believe you're making me go to this."

"Something about school spirit? Cheerleaders?"

She rooted through her closet, dresses falling off their hangers as she went.

"How about the rayon magenta stripe?" she said. "Sort of fifties cheerleader deconstructed by the eighties?"

"That and a pom pom in your hair."

"I don't know if I'm looking for that much attention."

"Live boldly, woman!"

"Yeah, yeah." She hung up on him.

Yes, the magenta stripe would do. The pattern of small vertical stripes was interrupted along the chest with a diagonal pattern of thicker stripes. A high rounded neckline and long sleeves with elastic around the wrists, elastic waist, and an A-line skirt. It had been a great find. Seven dollars at Arc's Family Thrift last spring. Black Converses, gray tights, and a black headband to finish off the look.

She sat at her vanity in front of the mirror that was mostly covered with scarves and necklaces. A hand mirror that she used for seeing the back of her head was propped up on the table. She was pinning her hair up around the headband when her phone rang. The caller ID said "Sister Woman."

She picked up the phone. "Hey, Julie. What's up?"

"Sister Woman" was a joke from when her older sister had gone through a phase of being obsessed with the history of Mormonism when she was ten years old after watching a PBS special about polygamy (Julie had been the kind of ten-year-old who enjoyed spending her time watching PBS specials). She had misunderstood the central concept, thinking that it was a society based on a bond between biological sisters, and had sentimentally started calling six-year-old Mira "Sister Woman."

Now Mira could hear the crackling of wind on the other end of the phone. It was possible that it was generated just by the fact of her sister being unable to stop moving. Julie couldn't tolerate even the air around her staying still.

"Do you know where Dad is?" Julie said without introduction. "He's not answering his phone."

"Probably at the office," Mira said. "He's not usually home before nine."

"Are you serious? You have to talk to him about that, Mira. He can't be neglecting family time."

Before she went to college Julie had always been the organizer of "family time," essential to the health of any successful family, according to her. Like many things with Julie, "family time" did not happen because it was something that you wanted to do. It happened because it was dictated by some outward force of propriety.

Now that Julie was at college (not just college, of course, *Harvard*) there was no one left to tell them how to behave. For the past year Mira and her parents had each been occupying their own separate worlds inside the same house, only beginning to realize just how dependent they had been on instructions. There were still family dinners that included her father when

71

he got home in time, but those moments felt like echoes of a shared history. Their life now mostly consisted of Mira in her room, her mother in her computer nook or doing the crossword puzzle at the kitchen table, and her father trying to relax in front of the TV when he finally did get home, roommates in a slowly deflating house.

"I think work's just been really busy for him," Mira said.

Julie let out a long sigh of disappointment.

"I'm sure if you email him a nightly family itinerary he'll follow it," Mira said.

"I know you're joking, but you seriously need to be monitoring this situation."

"What do you want me to do about it?"

"You guys have to be spending time together as a family, Mira."

"Well, we're not a family without you, Julie," Mira said sarcastically, only realizing after the words came out that it hit a little too close to home.

"All it takes is a little effort." Julie's voice had the usual touch of condescension in it that her extra four years always afforded her.

"I'm just trying to keep Mom and Dad happy by going to school," Mira said. "That's about all I have the energy for at the moment."

"I thought you were at St. Francis now."

"Yeah. I am."

"So isn't it easier?"

"What do you mean?"

There was either a particularly strong gust of wind or another sigh on Julie's end.

"Are you walking through a wind tunnel?" Mira asked.

"Just headed to the library. I thought you left Mountain View because you were having trouble."

Mira put down the bobby pins and let her hair fall.

"St. F isn't easier, it's just different."

"Well, Mom says you're doing really well with this new diet and everything. That's great that you're trying to lose some weight."

"It's not about losing weight," Mira said. "It's a food-allergy diet."

"Oh, she just said diet."

"Food-allergy diet."

"Well, that might help you lose weight, right?"

"That's not the point of it."

"It couldn't hurt, though."

Mira didn't say anything. She rested her forehead in the hand that wasn't holding the phone.

"Hello?" Julie said.

"Yeah, I'm still here," Mira said.

"What, are you mad that I said that? It's true, Mira. I'm sorry to be blunt, but you've gained a lot of weight in the past few years, and that's probably why you haven't been feeling well."

"That's not the problem," Mira said.

"Well, what does your doctor say?"

"It's none of your business, Julie."

"If it's none of my business, then why are you telling me about it?"

"I'm not. I'm not telling you anything, because you don't listen."

Now it was Julie's turn to not respond. Another gust of wind blew through her end of the phone.

"Look," Julie said finally, "I'm about to walk into the library and I'm just trying to get ahold of Dad for a quick question about my law and ethics lecture."

"Why don't you ask Mom? She's home."

"Right," Julie said. "So I'll just call Mom on the house phone then."

"Great."

"Okay, take care, kiddo!" The forced cheer in Julie's voice was unmistakable.

Mira hung up the phone and let it fall onto the table, accidentally knocking the propped hand mirror over, so that it lay there like the surface of a small and unflattering pool of water. The reflection of a double chin stared up at her.

Mira's body had not been her friend for a while now. In the hospital they had tried to teach her that she could help her body by helping her mind. But almost a year later she still harbored a belief that it was against her. It wasn't just about being bigger, it was the exhaustion that seemed to come out of nowhere. The way she felt literally weighted down to her bed in those moments. So she had decided that because she couldn't love her body, she would try to love what she put on it. The clothes, the makeup, the scarves, everything in this room was an attempt to keep self-loathing at bay, to not give up when something that fit yesterday no longer fit today.

She looked down at the mirror again. That was her sister all right, a reflection set at an unfair angle, shoving her flaws right in her face. Julie the Perfect. Julie the Achiever. The Thin. The Athletic. Mira had always been bigger than Julie, even when they were little. And obviously to her sister this was just another sign of weakness.

She propped the mirror up again so it sat vertically on the table, now reflecting all of her face back to her. She picked up a bobby pin and half-heartedly stuck it in her hair. "Ugly," she thought, looking at her reflection, as if something inside her was naming itself against her will. She took a deep breath. It was just a conversation with Julie. It was nothing. She was meeting Sebby in half an hour at the dance. Everything would be okay.

She picked up a purple-tinted lipstick that matched one of the stripes in her dress. She could feel the familiar heaviness in her shoulders, the sensation that something was pushing down on her. She wanted to lie down in bed and cry until the feeling stopped. She wanted to curl up in a ball and go to sleep.

No. She would put on lipstick. She would leave the house. Sebby would be waiting for her.

"Everything is fine," she told herself.

* * *

Her mom dropped her off at school at eight. Sebby showed up on his bike ten minutes later, looking impeccably messy as usual in a worn gray hoodie he had found during another trip to Arc's. He examined her outfit.

"I stand by my recommendation for a hair pompom," he said.

They headed up the hill to the entrance near the gym. Around them people were moving in packs that had congregated beforehand to secure their group status in the face of such an important social ritual. Through the crowd streaming into the building, Molly Stern bounded up to them wearing a skintight beige dress. She looked basically naked.

"Mira, we missed you at the diner," she said, grabbing Mira's arm just a little too hard. Her main concern seemed to be steadying herself. She had invited Mira to go to the diner with the girls after school—"And then, you know . . ." "You know" seeming to be code for drinking wine coolers in the parking lot, and Mira respectfully declined. She couldn't imagine a less enjoyable way to spend an evening than downing pink liquids with the same group of girls she was barely able to tolerate at lunch every day.

"Yeah, sorry about that," Mira said. "Sebby and I had some things to do."

Sebby raised his eyebrows at her lie.

"Sebby, this is Molly Stern," Mira said.

"Oh, Molly Stern." He took her hand, relieving Mira from

supporting Molly's entire body weight. "I have heard so much about you."

"Really?"

Mira followed behind as she heard Sebby tell her, "You know Mira just talks about you all the time."

Queen of the Table Sarah and Number Two Anna were hanging back from Molly.

"She is such a lightweight," Sarah said, rolling her eyes.

Music blasted out from the open doors of the gym. In front of them Molly was making a noble effort at crossing the threshold without losing her balance.

"Omigod," Sebby said in his best Valley Girl voice as Molly teetered away from them. "We're going to have so much fun with your best friend Molly at this dance."

Mira pushed him inside the gym. The echoing temple to forced games of volleyball had been transformed into what looked like someone's slightly skewed idea of a high school dance. St. F was so small that traditional rites of passage often ended up seeming like miniaturized versions of the real thing. A machine next to the DJ booth was shooting out rays of colorful lights onto the small group getting the dancing started early, while the others clung to the edges of the room, testing the air. It felt like a setting for instant nostalgia, a place where big moments of lost innocence should take place.

"Wow," Mira said, looking around, "super fun."

"When do they bring out the pig's blood and dump it on the

head of the awkward girl with telekinetic powers?" Sebby asked.

"Not until ten, I think."

"Well, what are we supposed to do until then? This was not well planned."

The kids dancing in front of the DJ booth looked strange out of dress code. Carefully put together T-shirt and jeans ensembles had been crafted to prove that they were just like other people. No ties tonight. No stifling wool kilts. This was the students of St. Francis desperately wanting to prove to each other that they were normal.

Talia came in the door behind Sebby and Mira, her long braid hanging down the back of a shapeless floral patterned dress.

"Hi, Talia," Sebby said, delighted for an opportunity to engage with the most infamous member of Art Club. "Done any good sketches lately?"

"Excuse me?" Talia was distracted, glancing past him to the rest of the room.

"Oh, are you looking for someone?" Sebby asked.

Mira tugged on his arm, begging him to end this interaction.

"Yes," Talia said. "What are you saying about sketches?"

"Just, because of Art Club," Sebby said. "Do you sketch in charcoal? I prefer pastels myself."

"Is that supposed to be a joke?" Talia said.

"No, I'm serious, I would love to know more about your process."

She looked at him, sizing him up.

"Did it ever occur to you that it's inappropriate to spend all of your time at a school that you don't actually attend?" she said.

Sebby feigned a look of shock.

"Why, Talia," he said, "I thought you would be happy to see me!"

Talia turned to Mira.

"Have you seen Peter?" she asked.

"No," Mira said. "Why would Peter be here?"

"He's a chaperone for the dance," Talia said in a tone that suggested that Mira was a complete idiot.

"No," Mira said, now pulling on Sebby's arm with the silent plea to stop laughing. "I haven't seen him. Why? Is everything okay?"

"Yes," Talia said. "Everything's fine." After an uncomfortable pause she added, "Bye," and walked off toward the back door of the gym.

Sebby doubled over in laughter.

"Oh my god. Talia!" He jokingly reached out to her. "Come back!"

"Do not tempt her."

"I thought we were friends."

"That girl doesn't have friends. She has humans she is forced to tolerate because her ship crash-landed on this planet."

"Talia, phone home."

"Exactly."

They had made their way onto the dance floor. Sebby faced Mira, took her hand, put his other hand on her waist.

"Best. Dance. Ever," he said.

"As usual, your standards are way too low," she said.

JEREMY

I walked into the gym behind a group of squealing freshman girls and immediately regretted not making more of an effort to look like everyone else. Why didn't I buy some new jeans and a fake faded band T-shirt at the mall? The irony of getting to be out of uniform of course was that everyone still looked exactly the same as everyone else.

I spotted Mira and Sebby as soon as I walked in. They were impossible to miss, Mira in a magenta dress that twirled around her as she danced, Sebby in his fraying thrift-store khakis. They were doing some kind of tango in the middle of the gym, oblivious to everyone around them.

I stood on the side of the room watching them, realizing that I had no game plan for this evening. My normal "stand in the corner, call Dad after an hour" strategy was not going to work if I wanted to actually participate in some way. But standing in the middle of the room staring at people wasn't an option either. I looked around desperately for a place to go and settled on the refreshment table. I could just drink punch all night.

Rose was sitting behind the table piling cookies into a tower.

"Hey, Jeremy," she said.

"Hey," I said. "What are you doing?"

She placed a final cookie on top.

"Leaning tower of cookies," she said. She attempted to make the tower lean. It fell over pathetically. "I'm just working off some detentions. Mrs. Pierce is such a hard-ass about getting to class on time and she has the last classroom on the second floor, so I'm always late." She picked up a broken cookie and held it out to me. "Want one? They're free."

"Okay," I said.

"I'm surprised to see you here," she said. "You're not usually much of a dance guy."

"Yeah. Not really."

"You're not much of an anything guy these days. Except Art Club. I guess you're Art Club guy now, huh?"

"I guess."

"I'm into it. We've got the Art Club bond, Jeremy."

She held out a fist. I stared at it.

"Bump it, Jeremy. Fist bump."

"Oh, sorry."

I shoved the rest of the cookie into my mouth and bumped my fist against hers. Rose laughed.

Suddenly I felt a hand on my shoulder and then Mira and Sebby were on either side of me.

"Cookies!" Sebby said. "Rose, you have cookies."

Rose picked up the broken pieces of her tower and let them fall through her hands.

"I am rich with cookies," Rose said.

Sebby jumped up to sit on the table next to the cookie plate. Mira sat next to Rose.

"Hi, Jeremy," Sebby said.

"Hey. Hi," I said.

"Why are you sitting here?" Mira asked Rose.

"I love cookies. I can't be away from them," Rose said. She shoved three in her mouth and then spat them out at Sebby.

"Ew, woman! This means war."

"No, okay, we are not starting a food fight at homecoming," Mira said. "That would just be too iconic or something. Come on." She got up and took Sebby's hand. "'Tainted Love' is happening. We can't let eighties classics pass us by."

"Very well." Sebby let her pull him up, and he grabbed my hand, dragging me behind them.

"Have fun, Jeremy," Rose called after us.

Mira and Sebby were debating which of their elaborate dance combinations to show me. Inspired by Rose's job for the evening, they decided on Baking the Cookies, which involved pretending to be stirring a bowl of batter to the beat, then pretending to plop balls of batter down onto a baking sheet, putting the baking sheet in the oven, indicating time passing by tapping on your invisible watch, taking the tray out of the oven, and eating one of the cookies.

I did the best I could, trying to copy their moves, although

Sebby's favorite thing to do was spin both of us at the same time, and I was starting to feel dizzy. I had lost track of how I had gotten here. I arrived at the gym. I ate a cookie. What about before that? And now? The three of us laughing and spinning as if this was the way that it was supposed to be. As if anything about this was normal.

The song changed and Sebby started doing dramatic moves of framing his face and dropping himself to the floor.

"When Sebby starts vogueing, I need to take a break," Mira said in my ear. "I'm gonna go get some fresh air."

She said something to Sebby and he nodded, and she left us there alone together. Sebby smiled at me and grabbed my hand.

"Do you know ballroom?" he said.

I was suddenly very aware of the presence of other people around us, remembered my own fear about the unstructured nature of this night.

I felt myself hesitate, but Sebby pulled me toward him so our torsos were touching. We were almost the same height, his hair dusty blond to my very brown, his defined edges in places where my face had stayed insistently round, but somehow looking into his eyes felt like a mirror. As if that was the reflection of myself that I wanted.

"You won't dance with me?" he said, smiling.

My hands were sweating. I didn't know what to say. I had arrived at the gym . . . I had eaten a cookie . . .

He whispered in my ear. "No one cares," he said. "And if they do, then fuck 'em."

I took a deep breath and nodded, tried to smile, and then he dipped me to the floor and I fell backward and I was laughing too hard to care anymore. Fuck 'em. Yes, that was right. That was it exactly.

MIRA

Mira made her way out the back door of the gym. She looked back to see Sebby with his arm around Jeremy, dipping him to the floor.

"Be gentle with shy boy," she had whispered in Sebby's ear. He wasn't listening to her, of course.

Outside in the parking lot the night seemed to have taken an unfortunate turn. Molly Stern was leaning against a Jeep, loudly throwing up any food she had eaten that day, or possibly anytime that week. Rose was standing next to her, nobly taking on the job of holding Molly's hair back for her, while Sarah and Anna looked on disapprovingly from a distance. And in the middle of it all was chaperone Peter Sprenger. Mira almost turned back around and went inside, but her curiosity got the better of her when Talia pushed past her clutching a cup of water, nearly spilling it in her eagerness to bring it to Peter.

"Molly, why don't you drink some water, okay?" Peter said.

Molly, temporarily done vomiting, lifted her head and tried to stand up straight.

"She just came over to the cookie table and barfed on my shoes," Rose said. "I got her outside as fast as I could, but I think she left a trail."

"I thought I should have . . . something to eat," Molly said between choking sobs.

Talia tried to help her sip from the cup of water.

"She can hold the cup herself, Talia," Rose said. "I'm pretty sure her arms still work."

Talia glared at Rose as Molly sipped the water and tried to stop crying.

Peter looked over at Sarah and Anna. "May I speak to you girls?" he said.

Sarah hesitated, and for a moment it seemed like she might actually say no, but then she gave in and Anna followed her over.

"Were you with Molly before the dance?" Peter asked.

Sarah shrugged. "Maybe."

"Maybe? Or yes?"

Sarah and Anna looked at each other.

"Yes," Sarah said.

"And what exactly were you doing?"

"Nothing," Sarah said, making a drunken effort to stand up straighter, readying for a fight.

Peter let a tense pause go by before saying, "All right. There are two ways that we can do this. The first is that you tell me exactly what Molly has been drinking or consuming in any other ways, and we see that she is able to get the proper help. The second is that I assume you're all high and drank a full bottle of vodka each and I call your parents and tell them my suspicions."

Sarah glared at him, hating to lose a power play, even with a teacher.

"Just wine coolers," she mumbled. "She had, like, five or something. She probably didn't eat anything today and that's why she got sick."

"Looks like she ate something," Rose said.

Molly attempted to say something in her defense, but the effort just got her started again, and Rose grabbed at her hair to keep it out of the way.

Sarah scowled in disgust.

"Can we go now?"

"You girls have a ride home?" Peter asked.

"My mom's coming to get us later," Anna said.

"I suggest that you call her now."

Anna nodded, more easily intimidated than her friend.

"You have a phone?" Peter asked.

"Yes."

"Then take it out and call your mother to come get you. Now."

Sarah stood with her arms folded as Anna did what she was told. Molly had stopped throwing up again but was crying now, trying to say something through her tears about having a sensitive stomach.

"Rose and Talia, why don't you take Molly into the bathroom and help her get cleaned up."

"I'm supposed to be at the refreshment table," Rose said. "There's probably chaos breaking out over the cookies."

"Talia then," Peter said. "You can help her?"

"Of course," Talia said, leading a crying Molly to the gym door. Peter followed behind. Rose and Mira watched them go.

"Bitch barfed on my shoes," Rose said to Mira. "She can clean herself up."

"Poor Molly," Mira said.

"How about poor me?" Rose said. "The one day I get to wear my shit kickers at school and they get barfed on."

Mira looked down at Rose's impressive combat boots.

"Probably makes them more authentic," Mira said.

"Yeah, right," Rose said. "I better get back in there. You coming?"

Mira looked around the parking lot, streetlamps illuminating patches of concrete in the dark. Clusters of older kids were sneaking cigarettes behind cars.

"I'm just going to chill out here for a little bit."

"Letting the boys dance?" Rose said, looking back at the open double doors. Sebby and Jeremy were still in the middle of the dance floor, now doing an improvised version of the electric slide.

"Yeah, something like that," Mira said.

"Generous of you to share him," Rose said.

"He's his own person."

"Still," Rose said.

Mira shrugged.

"All right," Rose said. "See you later."

"See ya."

"We're probably going to go to the diner after," Rose said as she walked back toward the door. "Everyone goes."

"Okay, cool."

Mira watched Rose go back inside and then started to walk around the perimeter of the parking lot. Something sad and sinister had been creeping up on her ever since the phone conversation with her sister, and she was finding it difficult to shake. She sat down on the curb and took her phone out of her dress pocket, opened her messages, and started typing to Julie.

You kind of hurt my feelings before, she wrote, and then immediately deleted it. She watched some seniors smoking nearby. The smell of pot floated over to her.

Do you even care about what's been happening to me for the past year or do you just think I'm a fat mess? She stared at that one for a minute. She could feel the pressure behind her eyes. It always started there. Then moved down to her heart, her stomach. *Don't cry. Don't cry. Don't cry.*

She looked down at her dress. The elastic around the waist was a little too tight, pinching her between her stomach and the extra roll of fat that inevitably appeared when she sat down. She suddenly felt like it was cutting off her circulation. Why had she picked this outfit? Why had she even come here tonight?

She stood up, dusted off the back of her dress, and put her phone back in her pocket. She looked over at the kids smoking. One of them glared at her, then looked away. Yes, of course Julie was right. She was a fat mess. She didn't try hard enough. She wasn't good enough. Her parents probably regretted even having a second child. They should have just stuck with the one and everything would have been fine. Then their mother could have gotten a new job instead of deciding to spend all of her time attempting to cure the incurable.

Mira walked toward the gym door, trying her best to take in deep breaths of the nighttime air. When she was in the hospital they had taught her to breathe with intention, a mission to fill her lungs and then empty them again, as if her body might forget. It had to be reminded. *In and out. Nothing's wrong. Try to remember that nothing's wrong.*

She almost walked into Peter without seeing him. He was standing by the door, watching out over the parking lot.

"Hi, Mira," he said when he saw her.

"Hey," she said.

"You doing okay?" he asked.

"Oh yeah. Sure."

"No wine coolers for you tonight?"

"I'm more of a whiskey girl, myself," she said.

Peter smiled. "Let me guess. Jack Daniels, neat?"

"On the rocks," Mira said.

He nodded. "Nice."

His face was half illuminated by the light coming from the

gym, and Mira couldn't help noticing that he looked so much younger out of his button-down shirt and tie.

"How's Molly?" Mira asked, suddenly feeling self-conscious about this half-lit conversation.

"She'll be okay." He shook his head. "It's a shame. Molly's a smart girl, you know? Smarter than that."

"Is she going to get in trouble?"

He shook his head. "Everyone makes stupid mistakes when they're young."

"I guess."

"And I wouldn't want her to get suspended for something like this. She learned enough of a lesson tonight already."

"Yeah, but Sarah and Anna sure didn't."

"You know what, Mira? Girls like Sarah are probably never going to learn much of anything in their lives. Until they're maybe forty-five, going through a second divorce and questioning why they always feel so alone and for what reason they could possibly have been put on this planet other than to take up space and get their nails done."

Mira looked at him. He was completely serious.

"Of course," he added, "I'm not saying that Sarah's even going to make it to the point of that much enlightenment."

Mira smiled, and he smiled back. This was Peter out of dress code then. Jeans and a T-shirt. A real person.

"I like your dress," he said. "Very 'alternative school spirit.'"

"That's what I was going for. Early eighties moody cheerleader realness."

"And you know a lot about the early eighties?"

Mira laughed. "I've seen it in movies," she said. She looked down at her dress. "Why, do you remember it differently?"

"I wasn't born in the early eighties," Peter said.

"You weren't?"

Peter smiled. "How old do you think I am?"

"I don't know. I guess you just look like a grown-up."

"Hmmm. Thanks, I think."

The truth was that he didn't look like a grown-up at all. Not tonight. He could have been mistaken for a senior, or someone's older brother, visiting from college for the sake of nostalgia.

Mira's phone buzzed in her pocket. She took it out and saw that she had two texts. The first was from Sebby: Come meet us in the art room. This dance is OVER.

The second was from her sister: I don't even know what you're talking about. You're being a huge baby right now.

"Everything okay?" Peter asked.

Mira scrolled back in her messages.

"Oh, no," she muttered. The last thing she had written to Julie had sent without her meaning for it to: Do you even care about what's been happening to me for the past year or do you just think I'm a fat mess?

"Oh, no. Oh, shit."

"Mira? You okay?"

She could feel the tears coming now. There was no holding them back. She shoved her phone into her pocket.

"Yeah, yes, sorry. I just have to go."

She went inside and walked quickly through the gym to the main hallway, keeping her head down as she passed people. Why hadn't she deleted that message? Why was she such an idiot?

She made her way down the empty hall to the art studio. The lights were off inside, but she could see Sebby and Jeremy through the window in the door. They were sitting next to each other at one of the tables in the dark, shoulders nearly touching. She saw Sebby smile at Jeremy, then turn back to whatever they were looking at.

She felt suddenly like she couldn't breathe. Like if she sat down on the floor she would never get up again. She had to get out of there.

She made her way outside, walked down to sit on the bench at the bottom of the hill. She took out her phone and hit the number for home, tried to make her voice sound as normal as possible when she asked her mom to please come and pick her up now.

JEREMY

When the music at the dance took a turn toward the "unaccept-able" (according to Sebby), he decided that we should reconvene at our regular home base of the art studio.

"Do you think it's open?" he asked.

"I have a key, actually," I said.

"Okay, that's hot."

I unlocked the door and we walked into the empty room. It felt a little ghostly, with all of the noise drifting down the hall from the gym, as if the building's spirits had shut themselves in there in order to get some quiet.

"Are you going to show me your etchings?" Sebby said.

"I have sketches," I said.

"Good enough."

I got my portfolio down from my shelf in the closet. It was stuffed full of all the classwork I had done in the past year, plus all the things that I had done instead of doing my classwork. I laid them out on one of the drafting tables.

"Who's this?" Sebby asked, picking up a paper with multiple views of a man in a tiny bathing suit.

"He's this guy who likes to sunbathe on the beach near our summer house. He comes out every day at noon for exactly half an hour. That Speedo is pink—I didn't have any colored pencils. But it's always pink."

"Where's your summer house?"

"Provincetown. It's in Massachusetts. Cape Cod."

Sebby looked up from the drawings.

"I've been there," he said. "Mira and I went once."

"I've been going to Ptown every summer since I was a kid. We have a fisherman's shack that my dad converted into a little house."

"Nice," Sebby said. He put down the drawing.

"Can you see?" I asked. "I can turn on the light."

"That's okay," he said. "I like the dark." He flashed me a grin. I tried to distract myself by going through another stack of papers, looking to see if there was anything else worth showing.

"You draw a lot, huh?" he said.

"Yeah. I kind of do it without thinking," I said.

"Who's this?" Sebby asked, holding up another drawing.

I looked up to see. It was a portrait of a woman with a shy smile and straight hair pulled up into a high ponytail. I had forgotten it was in there.

"That's my mom," I said, looking away.

Sebby examined the portrait. "She looks like you," he said.

"I did that from a photo. She's not around. Anymore."

"Dead?" Sebby said. "Mine's dead."

"Oh. No," I said. "I'm sorry."

"It's okay," he said. "Long time ago."

"Mine's just gone," I said.

Sebby nodded.

The door opened and Rose stuck her head into the room.

"You texted?" she said to Sebby.

"Yeah, let's get out of here," he said.

"Diner?" she said. "I'll drive."

Sebby looked at me.

"Shall we?" he said.

"Sure, let me just put this stuff away."

He helped me gather the drawings together and put them back in my portfolio.

"You're really good," he said. "At drawing."

"Thanks," I said. "I just do it a lot, so I get better. Anybody could do it."

"No. You have a style. Like, I can feel how you feel when I look at them."

I tied the ribbon on the portfolio and put it back on the shelf.

"I don't think you want to feel how I feel," I said.

"Why not?" Sebby said.

Rose stuck her head in the door again.

"Let's get a move on, ladies," she called.

"Have you seen Mira?" Sebby asked her.

"She was out in the parking lot with Molly the incredible barfing woman," Rose said.

"Ew."

"It was very ew. Text her to meet us. I need to get out of this place."

Sebby walked toward the door, looked back at me.

"You coming?" he asked.

I nodded.

"Yes," I said. "Of course."

MIRA

Alone in her room was the safest place for Mira in moments like this, comforted by the womb of things crafted to protect her against the outside world. Protect against the inside one too, the places in her head that did not have her best interests in mind. She collected things like hoarded rations, her overflowing closet, her scarves and hats and jewelry, stocking her own emotional fallout shelter.

But her room only really provided a safe space to fall apart. The falling apart was inevitable. With the door closed against the outside world she could stop pretending that she was any good at basic functioning. She and life didn't always seem to like each other much. It was nice to be able to admit it.

This was how easy it was to fade away, then, with something pulling hard on a string attached to her heart. It was a familiar sensation, her mind turning in on itself, turning away from the world because it didn't want to be seen. This feeling was an old friend. It had been a while, though, since its last visit. She hadn't been expecting it.

What did it feel like now? It was good to name it. A pressure in her head. A desire to crawl out of her skin. Like some part of her needed to be removed. Some part was poisoned. Like her body and brain had always been enemies. Like only one would survive this night.

When it got this bad, she would do anything to make it stop, and that's where the danger was. The feeling itself had no patience. It did not want to sit and wait. And so it made her believe that she couldn't survive as long as it was there with her. She would destroy herself in order to destroy it.

She wanted to climb underneath her bed, crawl in with old shoes that had lost their partners, socks pushed off feet in the middle of the night. A box of things that used to mean something to her. Back when she was a person and not an empty shell filled with violent static. She couldn't fit under the bed anymore. Maybe a long time ago.

She had pills for this now, to be taken "only as needed," but her mother had them stashed away safely in her room. Because she might have taken too many. So she would have to tell her mom. And that was not an option. She had managed to keep it together during the car ride home, managed to make it up to the safety of her room without arousing suspicion. And now admitting what was happening would be too much of a defeat. She couldn't have the shame of failure on top of all of this. To see her mother's look of disappointment. Because this was who she really was. She was just kidding herself when she was walking around, going through her day like a normal person. What a funny joke that all was. A practical joke played on her by her. How funny.

There were no scissors in her room. Still. Still there were only table knives in the drawer downstairs. Her father kept the real knives in a locked cabinet. Only safety razors in the bathroom. After all this time. Because she needed to feel anything else in that moment. Even a different kind of pain. And she had learned the terrible lesson that if she gave the demon a tiny taste of destruction, she could call its bluff. Let it know that she was still in control.

It was no one else's job to save her.

Please don't let this happen again. Don't let this be happening.

What is wrong with me something is wrong with me.

There was cold medicine in the bathroom cabinet from when her mother was sick last month. There was one dose left.

Take it. Take it so you can survive this night. So you can sleep.

Take it and tell yourself these words over and over: It will end it will end I promise I promise it will end.

JEREMY

I had never experienced the after-dance diner phenomenon since I had never stayed at a school function for more than an hour before, but it seemed that migration to the twenty-four-hour diner down the street from St. F was a mandatory part of the evening. The place was filled with most of our classmates, yelling and laughing between tables, carrying on dramas that still had the entire night ahead of them to unfold completely.

Rose, who had a learner's permit and exclusive use of one of her family's cars, drove me and Sebby there, and we found a booth open in the back and staked our claim. Sebby had been texting Mira, and as soon as we got there, he left to go call her.

"Drama with the wife," Rose said when he left.

Before I could respond, the waitress, a girl with bleached-white cropped hair and piercings running down her left ear, came over to our table.

"I am in no mood tonight, so if you want more than coffee

and fries you better move to someone else's section," she said, looking at Rose.

"Jeremy, this is Ali, my ex," Rose said.

"You wish," the girl said. Her hair and piercings looked strange next to her crisp white waitress shirt and black apron. "So, what'll it be?"

"Coffee and fries, please," Rose said. "Jeremy?"

"Coffee, sure," I said.

Ali wrote down our order and moved on to the next table.

"She is my ex," Rose said. "She just doesn't like to admit it."

Rose pulled something out of her bag and set it on the table. It was a small metal flask. Sebby slid into the booth next to me.

"Everything okay?" Rose asked.

He shook his head. "She'll be okay," he said. "She does this sometimes."

He reached for Rose's flask.

"May I?"

"Help yourself, my friend," she said.

Ali delivered our coffees, and a tall boy in oversized aviators with messy black hair followed her over to our table and slid into the booth next to Rose.

"Nick's here," Ali said to Rose.

The boy put his arm around Rose's shoulder.

"Rosewood," he said. "How goes it?"

"Worse now that you're here, Nick," Rose said, shrugging off his arm.

"More coffee?" Ali turned to Sebby. "Coffee for you?"

"Yes, please, gorgeous," Sebby said.

Ali smiled.

"Nothing for me," Nick said. "I'm here on business."

Ali left to get another coffee.

"Nick, this is Jeremy and Sebby," Rose said. "Nick is Ali's friend."

Nick propped his aviators on the top of his head and grinned at us.

"Pleasure," he said.

"I've seen you before," Sebby said.

"Possible," Nick said. "I get around."

"You go to West Pleasant High."

"Sometimes," Nick said. "You go there?"

"Yeah," Sebby said. "Sometimes."

"Maybe I'll see you around then," Nick said. He put his aviators back down. "Anything I can get for you kids tonight?"

"Get away, Nick," Rose said. "This table has a strict alcohol-based culture."

She poured some of the contents of her flask into her coffee, poured some into mine.

"All right then," Nick said. "Nice to meet you, Sebby. See you in class."

Nick got up and approached a table of football players at the front of the room.

"Creep," Rose muttered.

Ali came back with another coffee and fries covered in melted cheese. Rose tugged on her sleeve.

"Come sit with us," she said, making a sad puppy-dog face.

"I get off at four, stalker," Ali said, walking away.

"I'll get *you* off at four," Rose countered, deadpan.

Sebby cackled and poured the remains of the flask into his coffee.

The rest of the night was a blur of noise, kids jockeying between tables, Rose flirting with Ali, Nick maneuvering among social groups, then periodically coming back to bother Rose. At a certain point I took out my sketchbook just to have something to do. I opened it to a blank page and started doodling.

"Here," Sebby said, taking the pencil out of my hand. "I can draw a turkey."

He placed my hand flat on the page and traced it with the pencil, slowly.

"There. A turkey!" he said.

I laughed. He had finished his laced coffee by this point, and mine too, since I had no idea why anyone would want to drink coffee at midnight.

Sebby turned my hand over so my palm lay facing up on the paper. He took his finger and traced along a curved line.

"Long life," he said. "Tentative. Gains strength around the middle."

I smiled at him, not sure what else to do.

"The turkey needs a wattle," he said.

I took the pencil from him and attempted to make the turkey more realistic looking as Rose said something and Sebby laughed and the room filled with noise and I heard none of it because the world had gone quiet when he touched me, and nothing else mattered.

MIRA

Morning came aggressively, glaring at Mira through the space between the curtains. She had slept, at least. And now she was awake. That was the way that it was supposed to happen.

Surviving herself was a bittersweet victory. It meant that some part of her had lost. The ugliness had settled down into a small smoldering lump deep in her stomach. It wasn't gone completely. It would never be gone.

She got out of bed, pulled a sweater over her pajamas, and went downstairs, following the smell of coffee.

Her mother was sitting at the kitchen table, doing the crossword puzzle.

"Lost puppy waiting for you on the front stoop," she said.

Mira poured two cups of coffee and went outside.

"Hey," Sebby said as she came out the front door.

"Hey," she said, handing him a mug.

"Thanks."

"What are you doing out here?"

"Waiting for you."

She sat down on the steps next to him.

"You could have woken me up."

"I wanted to just sit for a little while. It's been a noisy morning."

"Already?"

"Well, the babies started screaming around five. Then Stephanie woke up and threw a fit about how no one's paying attention to the fact that she needs her beauty sleep or something. And that got Daniel and Connor started."

"Sounds exciting."

"It's a fucking circus over there."

"You should come live here. It's all passive-aggressive crosswords and food control all the time."

"At least it's quiet."

"Oh, it's quiet, all right."

She took a sip of coffee. It tasted better than usual. As if she had forgotten that things could taste good. As if the real world was calling out to her from the other side of coffee.

"I wish you had come out with us last night," he said.

She shook her head.

"I was just freaking out," she said. "It's okay. You didn't want me around."

"You don't know what I want," he said.

"I know you don't want to have crazy there while you're putting the moves on Jeremy."

"First of all no one was putting any moves on anyone. And second of all you better not try to pretend to the boy who was in the psych ward with you for three weeks of our lives that you're the only crazy person sitting here."

She smiled.

"I don't know," she said. "It was a stupid moment to get upset. I just wanted to come home."

"Just tell me what's going on, okay?" he said. "Don't disappear like that."

"I said I was okay when you called me."

"Yeah, but I knew that you weren't."

She looked out over the quiet, green stretch of her block. A few kids on bikes were headed to the park with baseball gear strapped to their backs, holding out against the protest of the cooling weather.

"So what's happening?" Sebby said. "Talk to me."

Mira watched a breeze rustle the turning leaves of the oak tree in the yard, looked for something that would tell her what to say to make it better. Maybe if she believed in signs she would see more of them.

"Remember in the hospital," she said, "they talked about how when we left we would have to get used to all of these things again, all of the demands that don't exist in there?"

"Yeah."

"I feel like that never really ended for me. I just forget about it sometimes. I forget that I don't know how to do this, and then suddenly I remember."

"Do which part?"

"All of it."

"Well, you have me convinced."

"I talked to my sister yesterday," she said.

"Oh god," he said. "Why would you do such a thing?"

"She was looking for my dad. She wasn't even calling to talk to me and she just immediately managed to make me feel like the worst person in the world."

"She's got a talent."

"And then at the dance I was still mad about it and I accidentally sent her a text telling her I was mad and it just made it worse. She thinks I'm this pathetic mess. She's probably right."

"You're not pathetic."

"I'm not like her."

"You're not supposed to be like her. I wouldn't be friends with you if you were."

She pulled her sweater over her knees. He stretched his legs down the steps next to her, leaned back on his elbows.

"Do you ever feel like it could come back?" she said.

"What?"

"All of it. Wanting to give up."

"Yeah. Sure."

"And this time maybe you wouldn't survive it."

"We would. We are."

"I guess."

He sat up and put his arm around her shoulder.

"What can we do?" he asked.

"I don't know. There's nothing to do."

He shook his head. "A ceremony."

She smiled.

"Maybe," she said.

"Without a doubt. An offering up to the gods."

"Okay," she said. "When?"

"Tonight."

"Where?"

"Here."

"We'll need some stuff."

"I'll take care of it."

"Don't steal it all, Sebs."

"No. Just some."

He stood up.

"Be ready at eight," he said.

"Okay."

He kissed her on the cheek. "Wear your wings," he said.

JEREMY

I showed up at Mira's front door after being summoned by a text from Sebby. He was standing on her porch when I got there, wearing blue sparkly wings that made him look like a defiant nighttime butterfly.

"Did you bring anything?" he asked.

I opened the plastic bag that I was carrying. A bag of popcorn, a pound bag of M&Ms, and a box of fruit roll-ups.

"My dad's a secret junk-food eater," I said.

"Great," he said. He rang the bell.

Mira came to the door in a sheer pink dress with a large collar and tiny clear plastic buttons that looked like glass if you squinted. A lacy slip was peeking out from the bottom. She was wearing purple wings that matched Sebby's.

"Jeremy," Mira said. It was a statement, not a greeting.

"Hey," I said. "Hi, Mira."

"I think he can help," Sebby said.

"Really?"

Sebby nodded.

Mira seemed to make some quick decisions about a few things. "Okay," she said, finally.

The house was dark except for strings of Christmas lights lining the stairs. We stepped inside and closed the door behind us.

"Beautiful." Sebby said, adjusting Mira's wings. "From one fairy to another."

"I convinced my parents to go on a date night by doing my best impression of my bossy sister."

"Well done," Sebby said.

We went upstairs to Mira's room. Vintage scarves were tied together into a long garland that was threaded throughout the room, ending in a canopy over her bed. Her closet was overflowing with piles of shoes and belts and rejected outfit options. A few dresses hung in places of honor on hooks on the wall. In the corner a small table with a sewing machine on it was partially covered with scraps of fabric and strewn spools of thread.

"Wow," I said.

"Sorry about the mess," she said.

"No, I just didn't know you had . . . all of this."

"She's a hoarder," Sebby said.

"There's more in the basement, unfortunately," she said.

"She's going to be, like, on the show *Hoarders*. About hoarders."

"Shut up, Sebby."

Mira had decorated any part of her room that wasn't already covered in things with silver and blue hanging ornaments for the occasion.

"From our Christmukkah tree," Mira said. "Mom lets us have a tree but it has to be in all Hanukkah colors, or else her Jewish guilt sets in and she starts force-feeding us rugelach."

She had covered her dresser with tiny tea lights and incense, and she and Sebby lit them until the air was thick with smoke. I breathed it all in, worried that at any moment they would realize that they had made a mistake in allowing me to be there. But Sebby had taken my hand at the diner the night before, and it seemed to mean that he knew me now. That I was permitted to witness this.

We sat in a circle on the floor and presented our offerings. The bag of snacks from me, a container of glittery gel and a pint of whiskey from Sebby.

"You're not much of a fairy without wings," Sebby said to me. "We'll have to make do."

He opened the jar of glitter and dipped his fingers in it, holding it out for Mira to do the same.

"You must prove yourself worthy of the gods' attention," he said.

"Close your eyes, Jeremy," Mira said to me.

I closed them and felt their fingers on my eyelids, cold glitter spreading out down the sides of my face.

"Perfect," Mira said.

I opened my eyes and watched them put glitter on each

other's faces, as we became three of a kind. Tiny tribe.

Sebby opened the whiskey and held it up in a toast.

"We are here to draw out the demons," he declared.

He passed the bottle to Mira.

"Drink," he said, "and speak the name of that which you must defeat."

She smiled and sipped from the bottle.

"Depression with a side of chronic fatigue syndrome," she said.

"Mira," Sebby said. "More poetic."

She took another drink and thought about it.

"The demons of sadness," she said. "The aches of daily life. The reasons not to live."

"Good. Jeremy?"

Mira passed the bottle to me.

"What do I say?"

"Your own thing, if you want," she said.

I took a sip. The whiskey burned going down. "I don't know," I said.

"Something you would give anything to get rid of," she said.

I took another sip.

"Being afraid," I said. A tiny part of me, like a knot in the back of my throat, wanted to cry when I said it. But something stronger held it back. Something that knew that in this moment I wasn't afraid.

"Good," Mira said. "That's really good, Jeremy."

I handed the bottle to Sebby.

He contemplated it for a moment, then said, "Being alone," and drank.

It was only much later that I would understand what Sebby meant by this, how the presence of other people could not be counted on to protect him. And that even though you could touch someone, it did not always mean that they were really there.

"And now," he said, taking our right hands and placing them on the bottle, "we have to replace it with something good. The life we wish for ourselves."

He looked at each of us.

"How about one where I'm allowed to eat pizza?" Mira said.

"The demons have made you think too small." He closed his eyes as we sat in that circle, all of us holding the bottle together, the warm burn of the alcohol feeding something that was growing inside each of us, an energy joining where our fingers touched.

"May we live impossibly," Sebby said when he opened his eyes. "Against all odds. May people look at us and wonder how such jewels can sparkle in the sad desert of the world. May we live the impossible life."

Sebby waved incense over the snacks to bless them, and we lay on the floor and ate and passed the bottle around until we gave ourselves stomachaches.

When the incense burned down, Sebby lit a new stick and pointed it at Mira's bed.

"The demon lives in here!" He got on her bed and waved the smoke around it. "Why do you keep my best friend prisoner in your comfy folds? Don't you know she needs to be out at the mall with me?"

Mira climbed on the bed with him and laughed. "Don't yell at my bed," she said. "It's not Bed's fault."

"Lie down," he commanded. "Close your eyes. I feel the gods are here with us now."

She did as she was told, and I watched from the floor as Sebby swirled the incense around her limbs, letting a smoky outline of her dissolve into the air.

"Better," he whispered. "They have heard our calls for help."

He leaned over and kissed her on the forehead, then on the mouth. The smoke from the incense hovered around them as I watched him lie down next to her, curl his body around hers, breathe deep into the space between her neck and the pillow. She played with his hair, letting her legs entwine with his, as if their bodies were meant to fit together. An ache formed down in the bottom of my lungs as I watched them.

Mira looked over at me.

"He looks lovely in glitter, Sebs," she said.

Sebby looked up and smiled. Mira held out her hand to me.

"Come here, Jeremy."

She pulled me onto the bed next to her, the three of us lying there in the smoke, my body pressed against hers.

"You have to kiss him, Sebby," she said. "To make the gods happy."

Sebby smiled, leaned himself up on his elbow, and looked at me, his eyes sparkling like real magic there in Mira's candle-lit bedroom. A breeze was creeping in through the half-open window. The ornaments hanging from the ceiling fan swayed gently.

"She says we have to," he said.

He leaned toward me and something, some boldness that to this day remains a mystery to me, brought me to him, Mira lying between us as we met in the space over her. And then his lips were on mine and the universe fell into a perfect white heat. I had been nothing before that moment, and one day I would be nothing again. But there and then my life was real. With his lips, and his lovely mouth.

He pulled away and Mira curled her body around his, turning away from me.

"Good," she said. "The spell's complete."

JEREMY

I felt myself panicking before I even woke up the next morning, my barely conscious brain already taking stock of the events of the night before. This was the part of me that knew that no matter how happy I had been with Mira and Sebby in that moment, I was sure that I had embarrassed myself. I had been too bold in thinking that I had the right to be there with them, and now I would be punished with my own signature style of self-shaming.

I hid under my blanket at the memory of Sebby's kiss, Mira's body between us, and felt a stirring in my stomach, the kind of desire that could only lead to more opportunities for me to do and say the wrong thing. Other people were not a good idea for me. I had always known this. What did I think I was doing?

I looked at my phone on my nightstand. One new text message. It was from Mira.

Meet us at the bus stop on Bloomfield and Ridge. 3pm.

They were sitting in the bus shelter when I pulled up on my bike.

"Excellent," Mira said. "You made it."

"Where are we going?"

"Arc's," Sebby said. He turned to Mira. "Or Goodwill?"

"Goodwill's closed on Sundays."

"Arc's it is," Sebby said. "We have to thrift immediately in order to solidify our good moods. We have no patience for those who insist on observing the Lord's Day with a somber lack of activity."

I locked up my bike.

"We're going to a thrift store?"

"We are going to a place of former victories," he said. "No reason to get overconfident, but Arc's has literally never failed us."

"Plus I'm wearing my lucky one-dollar outfit," Mira said. "One-dollar dress, one-dollar coat, one-dollar boots."

She stood up to show me. It was a vaguely nautical navy-blue dress with tiny white polka dots and white piping along a boat-neck collar. A navy fitted trench coat flared out at her hips. Battered brown cowboy boots finished up the ensemble.

"Nice," I said. "Really only a dollar?"

"Technically the boots were two dollars, but I figure they were a dollar each, so it still counts."

The bus pulled up, and we got on and made our way to the higher seats in the back.

"How far is it?" I asked.

"This is a pilgrimage, Jeremy," Sebby said. "It should take years of your life. You must prove yourself worthy of the gifts that are to be bestowed upon you once you reach the promised land."

"Twenty minutes," Mira said.

Arc's was an unremarkable-looking storefront in a strip mall off the highway, flanked by a craft store on one side and a pawn shop on the other. Mira immediately started rummaging through a rack of coats outside next to the front door.

"Heavenly," Sebby said, looking at the sign declaring HALF OFF ALL RED TAGGED ITEMS ON SUNDAYS, HALF OFF BLUE TAGGED ITEMS ON MONDAYS.

He pulled me inside, a bell on the door announcing our entrance to an uninterested populace. Rows of racks of clothes filled the store lengthwise to capacity, with a section for shoes at the front and toys and books at the back. Large women in sweatpants pushed shopping carts from row to row, examining floral nightgowns and used children's Halloween costumes before replacing them on the rack. There was no décor beyond what was needed for the purposes of display. This was a place with a mission. No need to sugarcoat it. These were the castoffs of a disposable society, semiorganized for those with either the patience to sift through it or the financial need to find a bargain.

"Are we looking for something specific?" I asked.

"You haven't thrifted before, have you?" Sebby said.

I shook my head.

"We are looking for everything and nothing. We are looking"—he picked up a giant red platform shoe with palm trees painted on the heel—"for inspiration."

Mira came in the door behind us and immediately disappeared to the back of the store.

"Best to give her the first half hour alone," Sebby said. "She doesn't really like to talk until she's got a good pile going."

"You guys do this a lot?"

"Mira more than me. She's obsessed." He put down the platform shoe. "Unfortunately not my size," he said.

Sebby took me to the men's section and picked out some T-shirts and sweaters for me to try on. For himself he found a leather motorcycle jacket with a skull painted on the back by someone who didn't seem to have much familiarity with human anatomy, and insisted on wearing it around the store.

"So none of these badasses will mess with us," he said, eyeing an old lady with a blender in her shopping cart.

We met up with Mira at the fitting rooms, three tiny stalls in the corner with swinging saloon-style doors that exposed your feet at the bottom and your head and shoulders at the top. Mira had an armful of dresses and some belts slung over her shoulder.

"Fashion show," she said.

I took the room next to her while Sebby raided the rack of accessories nearby, attaching as many clip-on earrings to his ears as he could.

"Okay, this has potential I think," Mira said. She pushed

open the doors of her fitting room and stepped out wearing a purple lacy prom dress with a poufy skirt. The back zipper was open, showing the latch of her bra.

"Too small on the top," she said, "but I could cut it off at the waist and make it into a skirt."

"You know how to do that?" I said.

"She's handy with a needle and thread," Sebby said. He wrapped a few scarves around his neck. "Mira used to do the costumes for the illustrious Mountain View Players. Her Pippin was very daring."

"You did?"

"Just some stuff for the plays at my middle school. It was dumb."

"That sounds cool."

She shrugged.

"It was nothing."

I pulled on one of the cardigans Sebby had picked out for me. It was blue with brown buttons down the front.

"It's good," Sebby said.

"But will he wear it?" Mira said.

"Will you wear it?" Sebby asked me.

I turned around to look at myself in the mirror. The sweater looked like something we might have found when we cleaned out my grandfather's closet after he died, fussy and a little ratty. But Sebby had picked it out for me. And that made me want to wear it every day for the rest of my life.

"Thrifting's no good if you just accumulate things with

good intentions," Mira said.

"Yeah, that's how you end up with a closet like Mira's," Sebby said.

"I have a plan for everything I get," she said.

"You collect projects that you don't do," Sebby said.

"Yes, fine, some projects later seem less worthwhile. But it's not my fault. Stupid school uniforms have taken all of the fun out of things."

She looked at herself in the mirror.

"But this I'll work on, I think."

"You think?" Sebby said.

"Yes, Sebby, don't be such a nag," she said, heading back through her swinging doors. "I'll decide once we've seen everything. Jeremy, you're getting that sweater."

"I will wear it," I said.

"Of course you will," Sebby said. "It looks great on you."

Two hours later Mira had decided to pass on the purple and go with a hand-sewn, forties-style black-and-white dress and an original Girl Scout Scoutmaster's uniform, complete with patches and troop number. Sebby returned the fifteen-dollar leather skull jacket to the rack, explaining that "nothing at Arc's should ever cost more than ten, not even this exquisite work of art."

I bought the cardigan and a distressed brown leather belt that Mira picked out for me. We were almost out the door when she stopped at a rack of men's accessories.

"Look at this." She picked up a tie, navy with lines of white script and white sketched flowers on it.

"What does it say?" I asked.

"It's Shakespeare quotes," she said. "'To thine own self be true.' 'To sleep, perchance to dream.'"

Sebby examined it. "Totally random Shakespeare quotes."

"We should get this for Peter," Mira said, turning to me.

"Peter Sprenger?" I said.

"Yeah."

"Why?"

"Doesn't it scream 'English teacher' to you? A tie with flowers and random Shakespeare quotes?" She turned it over to look at the price tag. "It's only fifty cents. I'm getting it."

Back on the bus we reviewed our purchases.

"You didn't get anything," I said to Sebby.

"I'm just the wingman today," he said. "Plus my room is a little crowded at the moment with tiaras that surprisingly don't belong to me."

"I thought Tilly promised you a closet," Mira said.

"I don't think she even remembers that I live there."

"Who's Tilly?" I asked.

"Otherwise known as Big Momma," Sebby said. "She runs the brothel where I work."

"His foster mom," Mira said.

"Oh," I said.

"It's true," Sebby said, holding up Mira's new Scoutmaster uniform to see if it would fit him. "I am a ward of the state. Pretty sexy, right?"

"You don't have, um . . ." I wasn't sure what to ask.

"Dead mom, as you know. Nobody else. Joined a brothel." He folded the dress carefully and put it back in Mira's bag. "Share room with fellow tiara-obsessed prostitute."

"Probably not great to call a nine-year-old a prostitute," Mira said.

"Fine. Filthy whore, then."

Mira rolled her eyes and pulled out the tie that she bought for Peter.

"Do we know when Peter's birthday is?"

"We have to give it to him today," Sebby said. "So he can share in the joy of discovery."

"He won't be at school on a Sunday," Mira said.

A minute went by before I decided to say, "I know where he lives."

Peter lived a few blocks from the school, in half of a two-family house that St. F owned, with a neglected backyard and a peeling paint job. He answered the door in cutoff jean shorts and a white T-shirt and stared at the three of us standing on his front stoop like underprepared but expectant trick-or-treaters.

"Hello there," he said, looking bemused as always, as if

one of us had just said something insightful about *The Sun Also Rises*.

"We brought you something," Mira said.

"A present," Sebby said.

"Hold on a second." He went back inside. The door fell open a little and we could see him gathering up some bottles in the living room, letting them clank into a recycling bin in the kitchen.

"Come on in," he said when he came back, pulling the door all the way open.

His living room looked the same as I remembered it from the last time I had been there, a little messier since he hadn't been expecting anyone. A basket of unfolded laundry lay on a lumpy futon couch next to a beat-up recliner. A large flat-screen TV had a football game on mute. A stack of student essays lay on the coffee table next to red and blue pens.

"Aren't you supposed to have *the guys* over to watch the game, Peter?" Sebby asked, making himself comfortable next to the laundry.

"What? A man can't sit folding his laundry alone on a Sunday evening and not be seen as pathetic?"

"You said it, not me," Sebby said.

"I'm starting to regret inviting you in."

Mira sat down on the futon next to Sebby.

"We do actually have something for you," she said. She took the tie out of the bag and handed it to Peter. "Literary neckwear."

Peter examined it. "'Neither a borrower nor a lender be,'" he read.

"Shakespeare," Sebby said with authority.

"I see that."

"We saw it at the thrift store and thought you would like it," Mira said.

"I do." Peter smiled. "I love it, thank you."

"You're very welcome," Sebby said.

Peter's kitchen was separated from the living room by a counter with some uncomfortable-looking stools, as if breakfast should only be eaten while perched on the edge of the day's possibilities. He went to the fridge.

"Can I get you guys something? I have juice, I think."

"I'll have a Diet Dr Pepper with a lime twist," Sebby said.

"Like I said, I have juice."

"We're good," Mira said.

I was standing by the window, looking out at the porch that led to Peter's backyard. I was worried that I might have betrayed some kind of secret trust between me and Peter by leading Sebby and Mira here. Or else visiting him with no reason other than to bring him a present could be a way of saying thank you for how he had helped me. It was difficult to find a way to say thank you for something like that.

"This is the Patriots?" Sebby said, watching the TV.

"Yeah. I just have it on for background noise while I'm grading," Peter said. "I'm more of a basketball guy."

"WNBA?" Sebby said. "That is some hot action right there."

"Peter is actually our teacher," Mira said, "so if you could avoid talking about 'hot action' with him, that would be great."

"Listen, this is man stuff," Sebby said. "You wouldn't get it."

Peter came and sat down in the recliner.

"Am I right, dude?" Sebby held out a fist for a fist bump. Peter met him halfway.

"Totally, bro," he said.

Mira rolled her eyes.

I felt awkward suddenly. The memories of this place were something that I felt needed to be processed in private before I could act like it was normal that Sebby and Mira were here in Peter's living room with me, making jokes and demonstrating in some way to Peter that yes, maybe things had gotten better for me. Maybe I would have friends after all and not continue to be that boy from last spring who he needed to look out for. But it was all so new. The dance had only happened two days before, and I felt sure in this moment that it couldn't last. I was already anticipating my own shame at an inevitable future when Peter would ask why he never saw me with Mira and Sebby anymore.

"I need to use the bathroom," I said, and headed to the stairs by the front door.

"You know where it is," Peter said.

"Me too," Sebby said, getting up and following me up the stairs.

On the second floor the bathroom was on the left and Peter's bedroom was on the right, the door open to an unmade bed and a dresser with clothes spilling out of it.

"He's messy, huh?" Sebby said, going into the room.

"I guess when you live alone it doesn't matter," I said.

Sebby sat down on the bed, making himself comfortable.

"What do we think about Peter? No girlfriend? No boyfriend?"

"I know he had a serious girlfriend in college," I said. "They went backpacking around Europe together the year after they graduated. She didn't want to come home and he did. So they broke up."

Sebby was leaning back on the bed, studying the room, the messy sheets twisted around him. My mind suddenly formed a picture of the two of us in that bed, imagining that Sebby and I had been the ones to tumble those sheets into a knot.

"You know a lot about him, huh?" Sebby said.

"I guess so. Yeah."

"And you've been here before?"

"Uh-huh. Last spring. This thing happened at school—"

"Your locker," Sebby said.

"You heard about it?"

He nodded. "Word gets around."

I was leaning in the doorway watching him, not quite willing to step over the threshold.

"I thought you had to pee," he said.

I shook my head. "Not really. Just, uh . . ."

"Looking for some alone time?"

"Sort of."

"Some alone time in Peter's bedroom? Yeah, I get it." He smiled, teasing.

I was blushing now.

"No. Not like that."

"Come here," he said.

"I don't think we should be in here."

"No, it's okay. I want to show you something."

My heart jumped a little as I stepped toward him, as if preparing itself either to run or to stay and fight my own stupid ways of sabotaging every interaction, every attempt to live in a world that involved anything more than my own private visions. I sat down next to him on the bed.

He lifted up his shirt.

"See that?" he said.

A large red scar ran lengthwise along his torso.

"Yes," I said. I resisted the urge to touch it.

He put his shirt down.

"That's two weeks in the hospital after these ape-men from my school basically kicked my stomach in."

"Are you serious?"

"Oh yeah."

"What happened?"

"Some assholes from the football team just didn't like the looks of me."

"You knew them?"

"Barely." He leaned back on his elbows. "And the real shame

of it all is I really do like football."

"But you were okay?" I said. "I mean, you are okay?"

He nodded. "Yeah, sure. It was almost a year ago. You know. Get over it, right? What's the other option?"

"I don't know," I said.

We were quiet for a minute. My hand was near his on the bed.

"I've never gotten hit by someone," I said. "I can't imagine it."

"It sucks. And I can throw a punch, you know? But this was two against one. I didn't stand a chance."

"Two weeks in the hospital?"

"Um-hm. Two surgeries. It shouldn't have been such a big deal, but there were complications with the first one. My doctor dropped his cigarette in my abdomen or something."

"What happened to those guys? Did they get in trouble?"

"I think they got suspended for a little while. I don't know. Things got complicated after that. They were kind of the last thing on my mind."

"Was your foster mom upset?"

He leaned back on his elbows.

"You mean did she rush to my side like the loving parental figure she's supposed to be? No."

"So who took care of you? After it happened?"

He pushed off his shoes and brought his feet up onto the bed.

"Mira," he said. "Mira did."

He took my hand then, like he had two nights before at the

diner. I tried to hold still while he ran his finger along the lines of my palm, tracing some kind of secret message.

"Peter took care of me," I said finally. "I guess. Last spring. That's why I was here."

"I'm glad you had him," he said.

"Yeah," I said. "Me too."

MIRA

Looking around Peter's house, Mira felt a little bad for him that the school couldn't have provided something nicer.

"So do you like it here?" she asked him.

"It's all right," he said. "Serves its purpose. And a lovely screaming newborn lives in the other half of the house, so that's fun."

"Yeah, I didn't think that giant minivan in the driveway was yours."

"No, I leave my car at school. I walk there every day anyway."

Mira got up from the couch and went over to the fridge, examined its contents.

"Wow, you really do only have juice in here, don't you?"

"Yup," Peter said.

"And beer."

"And that is not for sharing with my underage students."

Mira picked up the bottle of juice. "What is this? Cran-Apple? Are you five years old?"

A car commercial was on, showing a red convertible zooming through impossible desert rock formations. Peter turned the TV off.

"I'm not sure I appreciate the level of judgment that has been brought into my normally peaceful home this evening."

"Sorry." Mira sat back down on the couch. "Cran-Apple is great."

He smiled at her. The trademark Peter Smile. Mira felt herself blush, tried to recover.

"Do you really like the tie?" she asked.

"It's great," Peter said. "You go to thrift stores a lot?"

She nodded. "It cheers me up. In a really good thrift store you feel like you're in a room with all of these stories, and it's up to you to go and find the stories that you want to bring home with you." She stopped, suddenly feeling embarrassed. "That sounds silly, right?"

"I love it. A room full of stories."

"And then when you wear the clothes, they help you tell a new story, but they're bringing that old part with them and with you and you're benefiting from that in a way that you can't even really understand."

He smiled.

"That's a beautiful thought, Mira."

She looked at the woven throw pillow on the couch next to her.

"It's why I hate those school uniforms so much," she said.

"They're designed to not have a story," he said.

"Exactly."

"That's their whole purpose."

"Right. That's exactly it."

He nodded. "I get it."

She pulled at a string on the pillow.

"Here," he said. "Come see the backyard. I have a special 'sit and stare at the place where I should put a garden but I have no patience for growing things' spot."

She followed him out onto the back deck. It was dusk now. The yard was a mess of weeds.

"Wow," Mira said. "That's pretty bad."

"Try to imagine it." Peter sat down in one of the rusted metal chairs. "Maybe a vegetable garden over there, and then some rosebushes, and a . . . what's it called? A trellis."

"A trellis. Nice."

"Maybe a little pond with some goldfish."

Mira sat down next to him. "Well, you're dreaming big, and that's what's important."

They sat for a moment looking out over the yard.

"So you needed some cheering up today?" Peter said.

"What?"

"You said going to thrift stores cheers you up. Is that why you went today?"

"I guess." She let a moment go by before saying, "Sometimes I have these weird spells. My mom calls them that. I would never call them that. It makes me sound like some kind of delicate Southern lady."

Peter laughed.

"But I have these moments when I just get overwhelmed," she said. "And I feel kind of invisible. Like I don't exist. Or maybe I wish I didn't? Do you know what I mean?"

"Sure," he said. "I think so."

"When it's over it all feels so silly. Like, why couldn't I just relax? But when it's happening it feels like I won't ever be able to relax again."

"You seemed upset at the dance," Peter said.

"Yeah. That was because of my sister. She has this amazing way of making me feel terrible about myself."

"Siblings can be good for that."

"Sometimes I really think she's doing it on purpose. Like, she thinks she needs to break me down or something before I'll get better."

"And what are you supposed to be getting better at?"

"Everything. I mean, Julie does everything perfectly. In high school she was captain of the girls' softball team, class president, ran the newspaper. And now she's at Harvard. Prelaw. She's basically my parents' dream come true."

"And what does that make you?"

"Their nightmare." Mira made a face.

Peter smiled. "I doubt that," he said.

"Ever since Julie left for college, it's felt like they've been slowly realizing that I am not exactly the daughter they would have chosen for themselves."

"You think your parents expect you to be like your sister?"

"I know that they do. They're both just like her. And they all believe that if someone isn't successful, it means they just aren't trying hard enough."

"And what do you believe?"

"I guess I believe that some people just aren't good at some things."

"Maybe they're good at other things."

She shrugged.

"And you think these spells have something to do with all of this?" Peter asked.

"I just know they started when Julie left for school and I started freshman year at Mountain View. And they kept getting worse. Until I just stopped going to school and then I didn't have to worry about what I was good or bad at anymore."

"But now you're back in school."

"Yup. Now I'm back."

They looked out over the yard together. It was getting dark.

"Do you mind if I say something about what you're telling me?" Peter asked.

"Yeah. No. I don't mind."

"Well, in my own life, when I've had emotions that seemed mysterious or unreasonable, it usually meant that I was hiding a part of myself. That there was something in me that I was afraid to show other people. And I needed to find a place of strength to look inside and figure out what was trying to get out, and then, you know, embrace it. Be myself."

"Hmm."

"Yeah, sounds simple, right?"

"So what were you hiding?"

"Well, I was in a relationship with someone who had a lot of very grand ideas about life. She wanted to travel the world and live out of a suitcase and have these big adventures. And I wanted to believe that I could be like her, and keep up with her. But actually I was resenting her and resenting myself for not just admitting that I wasn't that person. I like to travel and see the world, but at the end I want to come home and have a quiet life where I wake up at the same time every day and go to the same place and get to feel like I'm doing something worthwhile."

"Teaching makes you feel like that?"

"I know it's not glamorous, but I'm not a glamorous guy. And if I can feel like I make a difference in my students' lives, that's the best feeling in the world."

Mira smiled.

"What?" he said. "You're laughing at my unbridled optimism?"

"I just can't believe I somehow got tricked into a therapy session in Peter Sprenger's backyard."

"It is true that these are my trick-people-into-therapy chairs. Did I not mention that?"

Mira laughed. "No, you didn't."

"Well, we better go back inside then, before I provide any

more insights into mental health."

They both stood up.

"Okay, one more thing, Mister Armchair Therapist," she said.

"Yes?"

"What's my thing that I'm hiding?"

"Unfortunately the whole point is that you have to figure it out for yourself."

"Yeah, I had a feeling you were going to say that."

JEREMY

We left Peter's house together, Sebby and Mira walking me back to the bus stop where my bike was locked up. I knew that I would see Mira at school the next morning, but I found it difficult to leave them. That weekend had started something. Two and a half days spent together, time compressed and then expanding in the way that it does when something in your life is opening to accept a new phase. A new version of you is being born and you must be patient with it. I felt anything but patient. I thought that if I lost sight of the two of them, I would never see them again. It would be as if none of it had ever happened.

I rode home on my bike away from them, feeling like a cord that connected us was stretching thinner the harder I pedaled. And that was it. As of that weekend, my heart was no longer my own.

PART 2

SEBBY

The day that you were released from the hospital last December, you were driven home in an ambulance because Tilly wasn't able to come pick you up. The driver made you sit in the back alone, as if you were keeping watch over an invisible body. You felt like a ghost haunting yourself.

The ambulance pulled up in front of Tilly's house and the driver came around and opened the back doors and you got out, holding a plastic bag with your few personal items in it. Then he closed up the doors again and drove off. You watched him go. There was something unnerving about a quiet ambulance.

You looked at the house. Small faces were peering out at you from the front window. Stephanie opened the door and the faces disappeared.

"Did you get in an accident?" Stephanie asked.

"Something like that," you said.

You walked to the door and she moved aside to let you in.

"Did you get hurt?" she asked.

"Yeah, I did," you said. "Where's Tilly?"

"In the kitchen."

You went to the kitchen, where Tilly was sitting at the table with Daniel and Connor. There were coloring books open on the table, crayons everywhere. The boys stared up at you.

"I'm home," you said to Tilly's back.

She let a moment go by before she turned to look at you. When she did, her eyes didn't meet yours.

"Good," she said.

She turned back to the coloring books. The boys kept staring.

You went to your room, where Jonathan was lying on his bed, reading *Sports Illustrated*. You closed the door behind you a little too hard, threw your stuff on your bed.

"Look who's back," Jonathan said.

"Missed me?"

"No," he said. "It was nice to have the room to myself."

"Thanks a lot."

Jonathan sat up on his bed.

"You talk to Tilly?" he asked.

"Doesn't seem like she has much to say to me."

"Yeah, I think she's pretty pissed."

You sat down on your bed.

"What does she have to be pissed about? I'm the one who just spent six weeks in the fucking hospital," you said. "Thanks

146

for visiting, by the way."

"The school told her you were hooking up with some guy in the locker room or something. That's why you got beat up."

"What?"

"She completely freaked out. Kept asking me if I knew anything about it. She spent a whole week saying I'm probably gay too."

"Are you kidding me?"

Jonathan shook his head.

"No, man," he said. "Look, you have to be more careful. Tilly's a religious woman. She's not going to be okay with that kind of thing in her house."

"It wasn't in her house," you said. "And I wasn't hooking up with anyone."

"She said they put you in the loony bin for it, too. That's why you were gone so long."

You put your head in your hands.

"Jesus," you said.

"You're okay now though, right?" he asked.

"I'm still gay, if that's what you're asking."

"No, I mean, did you really get hurt?"

"Yeah," you said. "I did really get hurt."

"That sucks."

"Yeah, thanks."

You got up and went to your dresser to find a new hoodie to put on. This one smelled like the hospital.

"Listen, you have to try to make it up to Tilly, though,"

Jonathan said. "She's talking about having Family Services come pick you up."

"Great."

You pulled out a gray hoodie and put it on, throwing the dirty one in the corner.

"And if you were really in the loony bin, they're probably gonna send you to that place in West Valley for the fucked-up kids."

"What, a group home?"

"Yeah, I knew a guy who ended up there. He was schizo or some shit, so no one could deal with him, and they sent him to West Valley and he said it was fucking rough. Like kids off their rocker screaming all night. He used to sleep with a knife under his pillow so no one would fuck with him."

"I'm not going to a group home," you said.

"You're not gonna have much of a choice if Tilly doesn't want you here."

You pulled your phone out of the bag of your stuff from the hospital and plugged it in to charge it. When it turned on, there was a text from Mira:

Are you out yet? Tomorrow's my birthday. Sweet sixteen not so sweet

"Tilly doesn't control my life," you said, throwing the phone and charger back in the bag.

"Look, just put in some hours at church, make up a fake

girlfriend, and you'll be fine. You just gotta ride it out for a couple more years, buddy."

"I don't have to do anything," you said. You picked up the bag and went to the door. "Thanks, Jonathan, it's good to see you."

"Yeah," he said. "I'm glad you're okay, kid."

You closed the door to your shared bedroom and went out, past Stephanie in the living room looking at you with her big eyes, past Daniel and Connor and Tilly with her passive-aggressive crayons in the kitchen, back out the front door into the cold December afternoon.

You took out your phone and wrote a quick text before the battery died again.

Let's run away.

JEREMY

Over the next couple of weeks I decided to pretend that there was nothing unusual about the fact that I now seemed to have friends. It was easier to act like my father's amazement at my requests to hang out at the mall on a Saturday or go over to Mira's house to watch a movie was not an accurate reflection of how alone I had been before. Of course I was even more amazed than he was, but if I allowed myself to think about it too much, I would start to panic, sure that it couldn't last.

Mira and Rose and I now sat together at lunch, the two of them finally abandoning the Molly/Sarah/Anna table, where all talk had permanently turned to the internal politics of the JV cheerleading squad. I left my life of solitude in Peter's office behind, and the three of us claimed a regular spot at a table in the corner of the cafeteria.

Our current lunch topic was the fact that the school had given us permission to have an Art Club exhibit by the library in the spring, much to Talia's satisfaction. They were just giving us a hallway, one mostly used by students who needed to print out something on the computers, but it still felt exciting to know that it wouldn't have happened if we hadn't started the club.

Most of the club members had decided on their projects already. Rose was the most ambitious, planning to craft an over-sized Jenga tower out of 3D cardboard pieces inscribed with quotes from Freud.

"Every viewer takes a piece, and it's finished when it falls over," she informed us.

Mira was having trouble coming up with an idea, and I was worried that she would stop coming to the meetings. Keeping her in the club suddenly felt important to me, as if her leaving would be some kind of personal rejection.

"There's nothing you want to make?" I asked her.

"I'm not an artist," she said. "I just joined the club because you asked me to."

"Who knew Jeremy had such pull with the ladies?" Rose was dissecting an unappealing-looking square of cherry-chocolate cake. "Chocolate should not be tarnished by the abomination of fruit," she explained.

"But what about your clothes?" I insisted.

"What about them?" Mira said. "It's just thrift-store stuff."

"Yeah, but you sew. You have all of those projects."

"Those aren't art."

"They could be," I said. "If Rose can make some weird Jenga tower, you can make anything."

"The tower is not the art," Rose insisted. "The art will be the moment the tower collapses."

"What about when the librarian knocks it over by accident?" Mira said. "Will that be art?"

"I know you're teasing me, but that's a good point. Maybe we could put a velvet rope up around it. Or caution tape. Like it's a crime scene."

"No one will knock it over until you want them to knock it over," I said.

"The whole point is that I'm giving up control." She went back to dissecting her chocolate cake, and Mira rolled her eyes. I tried not to laugh.

"I'm just saying that it doesn't have to be a painting or anything like that," I said to Mira. I pulled an art book from my bag. It was Nick Cave's *Meet Me at the Center of the Earth*, the one that she had taken from me that day back in September when I had first spoken to her, when she had signed the club petition. It was filled with photographs of figures covered in hair and sticks and fabric. She took it from me and flipped through the pages.

"You could make something like that," I said.

She smiled.

"Maybe," she said.

My attempts at persuasion succeeded, and Mira announced at the next meeting that she was going to make a piece of "wearable art" for the show.

After that, Rose and Mira and I started staying after school in the studio to work on our projects. Sebby came by most afternoons to help, declaring that all good artists needed a studio assistant. Peter found a sewing dummy and got permission for Mira to set it up in the corner. She brought in some of the clothing that she had purchased with ambitious intentions and then inevitably shoved into the back of her closet, and began to slowly piece together an idea.

"They look happy to be out and about," she said, sifting through the giant tote bag of abandoned apparel. She would sit for hours cutting out small patches of fabric and arranging them on one of the drafting tables, staring at them for a while, then rearranging them. Sebby would try to distract her with suggestions.

"Aren't you going to make a pattern?"

"This isn't *Project Runway*, Sebby."

He stood up very straight for his best Tim Gunn impression.

"Make it work, Mira."

"Thank you, Tim," she said in a voice that I came to understand meant "Leave me alone. I'm thinking."

Then Sebby would give up and inevitably demand that I draw elaborate Sharpie tattoos on his arms for him.

"I want a pirate ship with a merman attacking it."

"I have my own project to work on, you know."

"Why do you people even have a studio assistant if you're just going to ignore him?"

I would hold his arm while I drew, turned over to the soft skin on the underside, the marker like a conduit of something still indefinable running between us.

I couldn't really work on my own project when they were there. When they left I would go out with them, closing up the room behind us. Some afternoons we would all go together to the diner, but on days when we had too much homework we would say good-bye to each other at our lockers. Mira headed to the late bus or got a ride with Rose and Sebby in Rose's car, and I would secretly go back to the studio. I kept the lights off so the janitor wouldn't know that I was staying even later than was allowed. Then I would go into the back of the supply closet and pull out my canvas, three feet by five feet, stretched myself. The biggest I had ever done. I set it up on an easel by the window for light, although as the weeks went by and the evening light got dimmer, I had to rely on a small desk lamp, shining back and forth from the paint palate to the canvas, hoping it wouldn't be noticed from the hallway.

At this point there were still things that we didn't know about each other. Secrets that we had to protect. It would be a while before it was all out in the open, the messy and difficult and unmanageable truth of our individual lives. But we were starting to learn.

Rose's secret was that her family had money. A lot of it. Most of the students at St. F came from upper-upper-middle-class families, but Rose's family was just undeniably rich. They had made a fortune generations earlier from an old-school manufacturing empire that literally made nuts and bolts and now resided in what could only be called a castle, built by an early Manhattan adopter of New Jersey as a nice place for a robber baron to have a country home. It was hidden down a private road behind a brick wall that made the Victorian mansions of Mountain View look like they were trying too hard to be noticed. Real wealth hid itself tastefully on multiple acres.

Rose was the middle child, with an older sister and younger brother, and somehow she had gained a reputation in the family for being the low-maintenance one, which just meant that she was better at keeping her bad behavior to herself. When she started high school she convinced her parents that she could be trusted to move into a section of the house that had its own entrance, a round turret with two floors and a separate bathroom. The arrangement worked out well for all of them. Rose pretended that she was behaving herself and they pretended to believe her.

Sebby and Mira and I were summoned to Rose's private apartment for the first time one Friday early in November. Halloween had passed without much fanfare the week before. Sebby said Halloween was for "con artist children."

"It's not respectable to beg for candy," he said. "One must earn one's candy. Or steal one's candy."

Rose invited us over after acting grumpy at school all week. She refused to drive us to the diner, claiming that it was "a hostile environment," instead asking us to come over and help her dye her hair. We made a quick stop at the mall for bleach, developer, and blue Manic Panic. Then Mira and I found ourselves lounging on Rose's plush bedroom rug, flipping through magazines and eating all the snacks that we could find across the way in the kitchen of the main house, while Sebby and Rose mixed the bleach in the bathroom.

"It smells disgusting," Mira said.

Sebby stuck his head out of the bathroom. The plastic gloves on his hands were covered in white goo.

"I think I'm getting brain damage," he said.

"It's worth it!" Rose yelled from her perch on the toilet.

"We should all get brain damage so you can go Technicolor?" Mira said.

"I am in need of a major life change, and the only thing I can change about my stupid life is my stupid hair," Rose said. "And if we don't do it tonight I'm going to continue to be a huge bitch to be around."

"And that will be different from normal, how?" Sebby asked.

Rose turned around in her towel and tried to swat at him. He held his gloved hands in front of him for protection.

"You do that, you get your mouth bleached, lady."

Rose turned back to the mirror and looked at herself.

"Really, we could do my mustache while we're at it."

"Gross!" Mira yelled from the other room. I took a pen and started drawing mustaches on the models in *Allure*. Mira snickered.

"Look, little Miss Perfect Skin, some of us are pale, pasty, white people with disgusting black hair growing in places that it shouldn't be, okay?"

"Pay attention," Sebby demanded. "Or we won't even make it to the blue tonight."

"At least close the bathroom door," Mira said. "It smells terrible."

Sebby kicked the door shut.

"What is Rose so upset about?" I asked Mira.

"I don't know," she said. "But if she's banning us from the diner, I'm sure it has something to do with Ali."

Rose had become increasingly sullen during our recent diner trips, one time even refusing to talk to any of us for the rest of the night when Ali was too busy to wait on us and asked another waitress to take our table.

"Maybe Ali told her not to come by anymore," I said.

I had crafted a small mountain out of Wheat Thins and Easy Cheese, and Mira and I were slowly making our way through it.

"Maybe," she said. She put another Wheat Thins sandwich in her mouth.

"Oh my god, why is terrible food so delicious?" she said.

"I'm guessing that Easy Cheese isn't an approved part of your elimination diet?"

She shook her head. "Nope. Not supposed to be adding in dairy for another month."

I picked up the can of Easy Cheese and looked at the ingredients.

"I really doubt that this has any actual dairy in it, if that helps."

"It doesn't, but thanks."

Sebby came out of the bathroom, taking off his gloves.

"Ze surgery vass a success," he said in his best German

accent. "But ze patient now hass ze head of a donkey. And ze ass of an ass. Vhat I'm telling you is zat she's an animal."

"I'm setting the timer," Rose called from the bathroom. "How long?"

"Forty minutes for albino white," he said.

Rose came out of the bathroom.

"Is it normal that my head is burning?"

"Yes," Sebby said.

"How about that my eyes are burning?"

"Probably."

MIRA

Mira and Rose sent the boys to go forage for more snacks in the kitchen while they waited for Rose's shower capped hair to transition from white to blue. They were sprawled on the rug, Mira looking through a copy of *Glamour* magazine.

"See, this is why I can only read European magazines," Mira said. "I mean, what is this? 'Give your man pleasure like he's never felt before'? That is some serious patriarchal bullshit."

"Preach, sister," Rose said. "They're my mom's. She uses them to torture herself so she'll have something to talk to her life coach about."

Rose picked up a remote control and pressed some buttons, aiming it toward a speaker in the wall. A Tegan and Sara song started playing.

"Is that your stereo?" Mira asked.

"Yeah. It's this crazy wireless sound system my dad had

installed," Rose said. "Like I live in a creepy bachelor pad or something."

"It's cool, though," Mira said.

"Is it?" Rose said. "I don't mean to sound ungrateful, but people come to install things in this room more often than my parents come visit me."

"I thought you liked living separate from them."

"Sure, I mean, it just gets a little lonely, I guess. When Ali and I were together over the summer, she stayed here every night for almost a month. It was the first time I felt like, okay, there's a reason why I live like this."

"So what happened with you two?"

"She comes from this really conservative Korean family, and she acts like she doesn't care what they think, but of course she actually does. She didn't tell them about me, but they assumed she was with someone when she didn't come home for a month. That was bad enough. If they knew Ali was a lesbian they would completely lose their shit. So eventually she was just, like, 'I need to go home, my parents are freaking out.' She never said that it meant that we were breaking up. But in retrospect she had never said that we were really together."

"If she lived in your room for a month, that seems pretty together," Mira said.

"I know," Rose said. "That's what I thought." She flipped absently through the pages of a magazine. "She's only a year and a half older than me, but she does this *you don't understand* thing with me. Like, *You don't understand that two people can spend every minute of an entire month together and then just stop."*

"It sounds like it's more about her family than you."

"Well, she also started hanging out with Nick around the same time, and I kind of feel like it has something to do with him too."

"You think he likes her?"

"Yeah, kind of. I don't think she would go for it or anything. I think it's more of that 'straight guy who thinks it's cool to hang out with a lesbian' thing."

"Is that a thing?"

"Oh man, that is totally a thing. They think that we're, like, their weird alterna world doppelgängers or something. Or else they just think lesbian sex is hot. And it's hard to blame them for that."

"So Nick probably wants to sleep with both of you," Mira said, laughing.

"So gross, right? I don't know what he wants. I just don't trust him. And I can't help thinking that he talked Ali out of wanting to be with me. Like he probably thinks I'm not cool enough for her or something."

Rose lay down on the floor, the shower cap crunching under her head.

"How could he think that?" Mira said. "You're the coolest person I know."

Rose smiled. "Well, you go to St. F. You have a terrible frame of reference."

Mira closed the magazine she had been flipping through

and tossed it into a corner.

"Listen," she said. "If Ali is so weak that she can't make decisions for herself about her life, then she's not the right person for you."

"Yeah, I know that in theory. And then I remember what it was like to be with her and I feel like I just need to remind her and she'll remember how great it was. So I end up sitting in the diner for hours, staring at her, waiting for her to remember. And the stupid truth is that maybe she just doesn't want to be with me."

"But now you'll be super cool with your blue hair," Mira said.

"I know, irresistible, right?"

Rose got up, went back in the bathroom, and lifted a section of the shower cap to check her hair's progress.

"No, I mean the blue hair is more to say fuck it," Rose said. "If she doesn't like me, so be it. I don't care. "

"That's such a lie," Mira said. "You totally care."

"Yeah, but wouldn't it be nice to pretend that I'm someone who doesn't?"

The boys came in from the main house with armfuls of snacks. Sebby had decided to add streaks to his own hair, and he now had twists of tin foil standing up like antennae on his head.

"Your kitchen is like a grocery store, Rose," he said, handing Mira a bag of Oreos.

"Oh no, evil!" Mira said, dropping the Oreos like they were on fire. "Why do you do this to me?"

Jeremy sat down next to her, depositing the rest of the snacks in the middle of the rug. Sebby went into the bathroom, where Rose was removing her shower cap.

"Is it ready?" he asked.

"Holy shit, that's blue," Rose said, looking in the mirror.

"They're going to freak at school on Monday," Mira said. "That is definitely not 'within the spirit of the dress code.'"

"Good." Rose came back into the room and turned up the music. She started doing a crazy dance, banging around her newly blue hair that was plastered to her head like a sticky helmet.

"Freak out at the dyke rejecting your heteronormative arbitrary beauty standards!" She picked up the copy of *Glamour* and rubbed it on her body. "I got your glamour right here, bitch!"

Sebby started laughing and came out of the bathroom to flip his hair antenna in solidarity. Mira pretended to be embarrassed by both of them and hid her face in the carpet, and Jeremy drew blue hair on Gwyneth Paltrow on the cover of the *Allure*.

JEREMY

Sebby pulled me into the bathroom with the excuse of giving me a makeover after he had finished washing the blue dye out of his new streaks. I sat on the toilet lid while he ran a handful of mousse through my hair.

"Hold still," he said.

I closed my eyes, feeling his fingers on my scalp.

"You have good hair," he said.

"I do?"

"You should do something more fun with it. You always have it brushed down like this."

"I didn't know there was anything else to do."

He held up a hand mirror for me to see when he was done.

"Fauxhawk," he said. "I think it suits you."

He had gelled my hair to a point in the middle of my head.

"I look ridiculous," I said, studying myself in the mirror.

"Fashion is supposed to be ridiculous," he said. "Just look at the stuff Mira wears."

I smiled and handed him the mirror. He took it and examined his new blue streaks.

"We look good together," Sebby said. "Very *nouveau punk*."

The bathroom door was closed. We could hear the girls talking in the other room, and the fact of our aloneness suddenly felt significant. He turned back to me, touched the point of my hair with his finger. Then he leaned down and kissed me. I held very still, as if he were an animal that I didn't want to scare away. He stood back and looked down at me.

"That's okay, right?" he said.

I could feel my heart beating faster. I didn't know what to say.

"Yeah," I said. "I want you. I mean, I want to."

Nice, Jeremy. Smooth.

He sat down on the edge of the tub, his knees touching mine. He smiled.

"What are you going to do about it?" he said.

I laughed. He laughed too. I leaned toward him and then we were kissing again.

His hands found the back of my head and something in me felt bold enough to reach for his waist, gather the fabric of his worn T-shirt in my hands. He felt real, there in Rose's bathroom. Our first kiss alone. It felt like something real.

MIRA

For the first time in the history of their family, Mira's mother had decided to cook Thanksgiving dinner. Her excuse was that she wanted to make sure that there were enough options for Mira to eat that fit her meal plan. Mira wanted to point out that it would have been easier to just bring some gluten-free bread with them to her aunt's house, but by that time her mother was already making multiple shopping lists.

Mira suspected that her mother's secret motivation was to put on a good show for the extended family. The past year had not been the best one for them, and maybe she thought that if she could craft the perfect holiday dinner, everyone would see that they were doing okay.

The kitchen was a disaster for the entire week before Thanksgiving. Mira didn't even understand how there could be so much to do, but every day when she got home from school, her mother looked a little more desperate.

Julie arrived the night before Thanksgiving to a hero's welcome.

"Thank goodness you're here," their mom said, greeting her at the door. "Nothing's done."

Of course Julie immediately took charge, rewriting the to-do lists so that they were color coded by family member.

"This is completely disorganized, Mom," she said, tying on an apron.

Mira stayed up with them cutting vegetables and listening to Julie's incessant talk about Harvard.

Her sister hadn't changed much. She had cut her hair short when she first left for college, but now it was growing long again, and she looked even more like her old self. She and Mira had matching hair as children, unruly curls that Julie had tried to straighten for a while, finally giving in to the inevitability of nature. Sometimes Mira would just look at her sister's hair when she talked, trying to focus on what little proof she had that the two of them had come from the same place.

Around ten Mira got tired of chopping and excused herself to go to bed. Their dad still wasn't home. He always had to work later around holidays to make up for missed time. Mira was walking to the upstairs bathroom when she heard her mom and Julie talking downstairs, heard them mention her name. She looked down the stairs. They were sitting in the dining room, aprons still on, each of them holding a glass of wine.

"She's much better, I think," her mom was saying. "The new school seems to have helped a lot."

Mira sat down at the top of the stairs where they couldn't see her.

"She hasn't been having any of her episodes?" Julie asked.

"No. This whole food-allergy thing seems to be working."

"You have to be tough with her. You guys let her get away with too much."

"I'm just trying to keep her on track, make sure she takes care of herself."

"Yeah, but are you taking care of yourself, Mom?"

"I'm fine."

"Don't you get bored being at home so much?"

"There's enough to do with helping your sister. I'll go back to work eventually."

The front door opened and Mira heard her dad come in. Julie yelled, "Daddy!" as if she were a little kid, running into her father's arms. Mira got up and went to the bathroom.

At noon the next day, Mira's grandparents and aunts and uncles and cousins arrived, fifteen people in all, and somehow Julie and their mom managed to actually pull together food for all of them.

Mira spent the meal trying not think about the "special plate" her mother insisted on preparing for her, which meant she was not permitted to serve herself from what had been put on the table, a luxury even her seven-year-old cousin was allowed. She tried not to focus on the fact that her aunt had hugged her for too long and whispered in her ear, "I pray for you every day." Or that her grandparents had not asked her one question about what was going on in her life, but beamed more happily every time Julie uttered the word *Harvard*.

Sebby showed up as her mom and Julie were preparing dessert. The younger kids had begun running in circles through the house, periodically screaming for effect. Mira had an urge to join them. Sebby let himself in the front door, and she nearly knocked him over with joy when she saw him.

"I'm in hell," she said.

She squeezed him too tightly and he laughed.

"Oh really?" he said. "I've just come from an epic Thanksgiving potluck in the basement of Tilly's church, where her priest informed me over Jell-O salad that by not attending church regularly I am spitting in the eye of the generous saint who has allowed me to live with her."

"It's not fair. You always win," Mira said, releasing him.

"Will your mom let you leave?" he asked.

She looked into the kitchen, where her mother was cursing over a half-burned pie, while Julie attempted to fan away the smoke.

"I think so," she said.

JEREMY

I got the text from Mira around five. Dave liked to make his epic seven-course meal last most of the day, and we were just about to sit down for dessert. People had been stopping by earlier in the afternoon, my aunt, some neighbors, a few of my dad's coworkers, but none of them had made it this far.

"Amateurs!" Dad liked to taunt people whenever they insisted that they had to leave before Dave forced another perfectly crafted entrée on them.

I was lying on the couch in the living room with Dolly Parton the Cat, attempting to will my stomach to make room for Dave's famous pies, when my phone vibrated.

can we come over???? the text read. we are desperate you must rescue us from our lives

I read it again. They wanted to come over? I had talked about Mira and Sebby to Dad and Dave, but they were still an abstract idea to them. Presenting two actual humans felt like a big step. And then there was the fact that I hadn't had a friend over in years, especially not since last spring. But of course I was excited that they wanted to come, that I could be the one to rescue them.

"Hey, Dad?" I called into the kitchen where my dad was hand whipping the bowl of cream that Dave had placed in front of him.

"Come in here," he called back. "Don't yell through the house like an animal."

"Do animals yell?" I said, coming into the kitchen.

"May I help you?"

"Sebby and Mira were wondering if they could come over."

"Do they want pie?"

"I don't know."

"They're probably going to want pie. Dave?" He called into the dining room, where Dave was clearing the plates from the previous course. "Is there enough pie for Jeremy's friends?"

"Okay, now you're yelling, Dad."

"Of course," Dave said, bringing the plates into the kitchen. "The more the merrier."

I texted Mira the address and they were at the front door in fifteen minutes. I made introductions and we sat and ate Dave's amazing pies and Dad asked Dad-type questions and I sat there nearly silent, not knowing how to participate. This was new territory. Dad and Dave and Sebby and Mira. And me.

After dessert we helped Dave clean up and then went upstairs to my room. Sebby closed the door behind us and stood leaning against it as if someone might try to barge in, eyes wide in shock.

"What?" I said.

"So that's your dad," he said.

"Yes."

"And Dave is . . ."

"My other dad."

"You have two dads?"

"Yeah," I said. "Yes."

"Gay dads? Two gay dads?" he said.

"Yes. My dads are gay."

Mira was shaking her head.

"What?" I said.

"How could you not tell us, Jeremy?" she said.

"This is literally the coolest thing I have ever heard," Sebby said, still barricading the door.

"It's not a big deal," I said.

"It's a huge deal and we're furious with you," Mira said.

"Why didn't you tell us?" Sebby asked.

I didn't say, "Because I need to protect them, and protect us, even from you."

I didn't say that every day when I left the house, I imagined words spray-painted across our garage instead of my locker. That Dad and Dave lived in a carefully crafted world, one designed to keep us safe, to keep things normal, and that I had already done enough damage.

"Start at the beginning," Sebby said, leaving the doorway

to come sit between us on the bed. "I need to know absolutely everything about this situation."

"My mom and my dad got divorced right after I was born," I said. "She moved away and left me with my dad. Dave moved in when I was two. He's been my second dad ever since. They got married last spring."

Last spring before the incident. There had been a picture of them in the local paper along with a wedding announcement. The two of them smiling side by side, Dad's head tilted a little in Dave's direction. "Announcing the marriage of David Martinez and James Worth." They had wanted me to be in the picture with them. I didn't want to do it. But the announcement mentioned me: "The couple have a son, Jeremy Worth, who is a freshman at St. Francis Preparatory School."

Mira looked at Sebby, both of them shaking their heads.

"Unbelievable," she said.

"They're just dads. They're not cool or anything," I said. "Dave is obsessed with Martha Stewart."

"When your gay dads do anything, it's cool," Sebby said.

I shook my head.

"Believe me. It's really not."

Dave's Martha Stewart obsession was a running joke in our house. He had a special shelf where he saved her magazines in pristine condition. He would photocopy pages at work rather than tear them out for recipes or instructions on how to make the perfect handwoven rattan Christmas wreath. Dave's job was running the administrative end of the county's sanitation department. Dad was a court clerk, and they had met when someone had tried to sue Dave's department. Dad always said he had never seen a neater-looking garbage man.

So because Dave thought about garbage all day, he made sure that at the end of it he got to return to a spotless, perfect fantasy of a home.

"You certainly are a nester," my dad would tease him whenever another elaborate holiday centerpiece was revealed.

Before the incident at school, my biological dad had always been the one trying to push me out of the nest, to convince me to go out into the world. But when I would come home early from another school event that my father forced me to attend, it was always Dave who was ready with freshly baked cookies in the kitchen, who would sit up with me as we made our way through the batch, dunking them in tall glasses of cold milk.

"I hated high school too," he would say.

It was only after the incident that my dad stopped pushing me. As if he had started to understand that my high school experience might be different from his. And that if my life was going to be difficult, he might not be the one who would be able to fix it.

And now, sitting on my bed with two very real, tangible friends, I could only imagine the conversation that Dad and Dave were currently having downstairs. I wondered if they had suspected that I'd made Mira and Sebby up.

The three of us sprawled out on my twin bed and watched

Miracle on 34th Street on my little TV. By the time it was over we were ready for more pie.

The full story of what had happened the previous spring was not something that anyone would ever know except for me and Peter. And even Peter didn't know just how wrong it all went.

It was early May. Peter had assigned *The Great Gatsby* as the final book of the year in his freshman English class. After all my worrying, my first year of high school hadn't actually been so bad. I didn't have many friends, but it hadn't been the epic move into adulthood that had so terrified me back when I was at St. F Middle School. Eighth grade had seemed so final back then. The end of a childhood that I wasn't sure I was so ready to leave. But the move to high school had just been a change of buildings. The same kids I had known forever were still there. And, new haircuts aside, we were still the same people we always had been.

There was a reckless feeling in the air in Peter's class on the day we were supposed to discuss *Gatsby*. It was a Friday and he had opened the windows wide to the spring air. It took a while for him to get the class to even focus on the book, and then the conversation was mostly about the idea of the unreliable narrator.

"Doesn't he end up in a mental institution or something?" was Sarah's contribution.

"In the movie," Peter said. "We did all read the book and not just watch the movie, right?"

The conversation eventually turned to the mysterious end of Chapter Two, after Nick Carraway ends up in a drunken apartment party in New York with Tom Buchanan and his mistress and the neighbors.

"They have this big party in Myrtle's apartment and then Nick and Mr. McKee end up downstairs, like, in his bedroom and then he doesn't say what happens," Anna said. "It's like, dot dot dot."

"An ellipsis," Talia said. "It's called an ellipsis."

"Then it just goes to Nick alone in the train station."

"Yeah, that part was weird," Sarah said.

"Well, okay," Peter said, smiling, always smiling, "what do you guys think that's about?"

He looked around the room and no one responded. Not even Talia. Talia, who always knew everything. She looked down at the book in front of her, flipped to the page that we were talking about.

"I mean, I think it's kind of obvious," I said. Because it was. It was obvious to me, and why was no one going to say it?

"Great," Peter said. "Tell us what you think, Jeremy."

"I mean, uh . . ." I doubted myself for a moment, thought better of it, but then thought no. Peter was asking me. There was no reason not to respond.

"Well, there's that part where the guy says, 'keep your hands off the lever,' that seems like a kind of euphemism," I said.

"For what?" Sarah asked.

"For, you know, hooking up. They're drunk and maybe Nick

doesn't remember so then he can't narrate it, or maybe Fitzgerald didn't want to spell it out like that, or maybe he couldn't. I mean, you couldn't really say stuff like that then. So he just kind of fast-forwards to after."

I looked around the room. No one said anything. Talia's head was still in her book.

"Hook up?" Anna finally said. "Nick and Mr. McKee?"

"Yeah," I said. "I mean, they're alone in Mr. McKee's bedroom, and Mr. McKee's in bed in his underwear. It seems pretty obvious."

There was what felt like a full minute of silence before Sarah just started laughing.

"Okay, thank you, Jeremy," Peter said, but it was too late to save this moment from the direction in which it was now headed.

Anna joined Sarah in laughing hysterically. "Yeah, obviously there's a gay sex scene in *The Great Gatsby*. Are you crazy?"

The boy who always sat next to Sarah, a jock named Tommy, had his head in his hands.

"That's just Jeremy's wishful thinking, that everything would be gay," he said, as if this were the most predictable thing in the world.

"And you think 'the lever' is a penis?" Anna sounded horrified.

"I'm not the first person to have this idea," I said. "If you look online . . ."

"So you're just going online and searching '*Great Gatsby* gay stuff'?" Sarah said. "Maybe you've been reading some kind of fan fiction or something."

Tommy leaned over to Sarah and I thought I heard him say, "something something dads," and Sarah laughed, and Peter started to say something but it was the bell finally that ended it, everyone rushing for the door even as Peter said, "This is not the end of this conversation!"

But of course it was the end, because it was Friday, and then it was the weekend. And there was plenty of time for anyone who had not been in that room to hear about what I had said. And plenty of time for anyone in school for sports practice over the weekend to sneak over to the unsupervised locker aisles with a can of spray paint. Plenty of time for me to think that this had just been an embarrassing moment in English class and that was it. That my only lesson would be to think twice about speaking up next time.

Monday morning I got to school early. Before the buses had arrived. So I was the first person to see it, my locker tucked away in a back corner of one of the aisles, not visible to anyone passing by in the main hallway. And Talia was the second.

Jeremy ♡s 2 suk dix.

The heart was actually kind of sweet, round and girlish, a few drips of paint hanging down from the bottom. Bleeding heart.

"Oh my god," Talia said, the two of us standing in that aisle that we had shared all year.

And then the noise of the buses arriving, the students

streaming in through the front doors. Talia grabbed my arm and pulled me toward the dean's office before they descended.

The dean called my dad and they had me wait for him in the teachers' lounge so that I wouldn't have to see anyone, except for Talia, who waited with me. We sat in silence at a table as the noise of the hallway streamed by outside. I tried not to hear what anyone was saying.

When Dad got there, he talked to the dean alone for an hour. Then he came and got me from the teachers' lounge. He looked pale and angry. He put his arm around my shoulder and walked me to the car. I could feel the school watching us go.

Dave was there when we got home. We sat at the dining-room table and let Dad rage around the house, pacing through rooms, threatening to sue the school, to put the entire county court on the case.

Dave got up and made tea while Dad ranted. He came back and put a mug in front of me.

"Jeremy," he said quietly, when Dad had finally tired himself out. "Do you think that these kids are assuming things about you because of us?"

I stared at the steam coming off the cup of tea. I shook my head.

"I mean," I said, "I think that I probably am gay."

This was not the way that I wanted to have this conversation. But this was not the way that I wanted any of this to go, so who cared at that point.

"Do you really think that's true?" Dave asked. "Or are you

just reacting to what other people think of you?"

"I think it's true," I said. That was when I started crying.

Dad came and sat next to me and put his hand on my back. But he let Dave continue to do the talking. He knew Dave was better with things like this. This did not need ranting, or even charm. This needed Dave's gentleness.

"You know, people used to assume I was gay in high school too," Dave said. "And I knew that I was gay, but somehow everyone else knew before me. It's a strange position to be in, because it doesn't let you decide how you feel about it on your own time. And the kids in school just tortured me for it. That's when I really started drinking."

Dave had been in AA since before he and Dad had gotten together. He went to meetings every Wednesday night.

"But the thing is," Dave said, "there was also something liberating about it all being out in the open. There was no opportunity for me to hide, so there were no choices to make. The kids who wanted to torture people were going to torture me because I was an easy target, but at least I knew who my real friends were. And those people were very important to me because they were kind, good people."

"I don't think I have real friends," I said. I wiped at the tears on my cheeks with the back of my hand. I had never felt more like a little kid. Dad was rubbing my back in circles now, like he used to when I was young and had trouble falling asleep.

"You will," Dave said.

"I was a jerk in high school," Dad said. He let out a little laugh.

"You were?" I said.

"I mean, I wasn't mean to anyone, but I hung out with people who were and I didn't say anything about it. I guess I was scared that they would find out who I really was. And that lasted until, well, after you were born." He squeezed my shoulder. "I don't know what I would have done without you, kiddo. But some people got hurt along the way, and I think I could have avoided that if I had been truthful with myself."

"You mean my mom?"

He nodded. "Sure. And her family. And my family. There were a lot of people involved when I finally realized some things about myself."

"You're a strong kid," Dave said. "And you're going to be even stronger because this happened to you."

I wanted to say, "I'm not." I wanted to ask if I could just move far away from here and call it a day. That's what my mother did. I was her child too, after all, and I had it in me to run.

But I was learning not to say what I was thinking. So I went to my room and I stayed there and let everyone else figure out what they were going to do.

Peter called the next day and asked if I wanted to stop by his house after school to pick up my homework assignments. That started a week of afternoons spent with him, sitting on his back porch with glasses of lemonade sweating in our hands, watching things sprouting into their summer glory in his jungle of a yard, talking it all out. Everything, about my mom, my dads, his life before he came to St. F. And on the last day he convinced me that I should try to go back. He said I couldn't let this beat me, couldn't let other people's stupidity control how I lived my life.

I did try. It was the middle of the next week when I decided to stop by in the afternoon, in the middle of a period. I had some library books in my locker that were due, so I figured I would drop them off and at least see how it felt to be there. Maybe Peter was right. Maybe it wasn't a big deal after all. Just one stupid day of someone doing something stupid.

The halls were empty when I got there. Everyone was in class. I made my way to my locker. I could smell the fresh paint before I even got to it. The other lockers hadn't been painted in years, so mine now stood out as a slightly lighter color. I tried not to look too closely at it, wondering how many coats it had taken to cover up the black spray paint.

I opened the combination on the locker, let the door swing open. There was a folded piece of paper stuck in the slot at the top of the inside of the door. I pulled it out.

I had thought, just for a second, that it might be something nice. Maybe a note of concern from one of my "sort of" friends. And then I unfolded it.

It was a photocopy of Dad and Dave's wedding announcement from the paper, their two smiling faces, Dad's head tilted just slightly toward Dave. Someone had drawn in the rest of their bodies under the picture, cartoon pants with open flies and crudely drawn penises sticking out, with a figure on its knees in front of them. My name had been circled in the announcement ("The couple have a son, Jeremy Worth, who is a freshman at St. Francis Preparatory") with an arrow pointing to the drawn figure.

I looked into my locker and saw a pile of folded notes at the bottom that had been shoved in the slots in the door. I picked up another one and unfolded it. It was another photocopy of the announcement. This one said, "DIE, FAGGOT FAMILY" on the top of the page.

I stared helplessly at my locker for a minute, then slammed it shut and ran. Down the hallway, out the front door, down the hill, into town. I didn't stop running until I had to, until I felt like either my heart was going to explode or I was going to throw up.

I was in the middle of town when I finally stopped on a side street and bent over in a doorway to catch my breath. I wanted to set the school on fire. I wanted it to not exist anymore. There wasn't enough paint in the world to paint over this bullshit.

Next to me on the street was an old pay phone. I stared at it as my breathing started to go back to normal. I wasn't thinking. I just knew that I had to do something.

It seemed impossible that the pay phone actually worked, but when I picked it up there was a dial tone. I found two quarters in my wallet, put them in the slot. I dialed information. My hands were shaking.

"St. Francis Preparatory Academy," I said, watching the

street to make sure no one was walking by. I pressed the button to have them dial for me, put in another two quarters.

"St. Francis Prep, how can I help you?" It was Denise in the office. Denise, who was always nice to me.

I almost hung up. But then I didn't.

"There's a bomb in the school," I said, making my voice low. I hung up.

I walked the rest of the way home quickly with my head down.

The only thing that really happens with a bomb threat is that everyone gets to go home early. The police come with special bomb-sniffing dogs and search the entire building. That's it. So really everyone should have thanked me.

The problem was that there was one other person home from school that day, one other student with a reason to make a prank call like that. Tommy, who had muttered under his breath about me in class, who had been at school for sports practice over that weekend, who had already been under suspicion for the spray paint on my locker and had spent the previous week defending himself in the dean's office. But Tommy was a scholarship kid. And there was only so much that the school was willing to take from a scholarship kid. And unfortunately for him, Tommy had called in sick that morning. So when they traced the call to a pay phone near his house, and Denise in the office said she thought that the voice on the phone had sounded vaguely like his, that was a good enough reason to expel him for good.

Maybe I thought that if Tommy had been the one to deface my locker, then he deserved to be expelled anyway. But I didn't know for sure that it was him. If I had turned myself in, I might have been okay. There would have been consequences, but I wouldn't have been expelled. My parents paid full tuition, after all. It wouldn't have ruined my life. Any more than it was already ruined.

After that I knew that I was someone who was capable of doing something shameful and then running away. And I didn't like knowing that about myself. And I didn't like myself much at all anymore.

JEREMY

Mira's birthday was the week before winter break, and Sebby was determined to plan something exciting to mark the occasion.

"All I want is pizza," she said in Art Club that week. The meeting was over and we were all staying after to work on our projects. Mira's dress form was starting to have an actual form on it, as she meticulously sewed together tiny squares of fabric.

"Yes, but we could do anything," Sebby insisted as he sat there cutting more squares for her. "Secret picnic at the top of the Empire State Building? Hot-air balloon ride along the Delaware Water Gap?"

"First of all, you know I'm afraid of heights," Mira said, "Second of all, my parents have been very happy with my lack of drama recently and I would like to keep it that way."

"If you were better at lying to them, we could have a lot more fun," Sebby said.

"So what do you want to do?" I asked.

"Just pizza," she said. "Literally only pizza."

"The woman knows what she wants," Rose said from her hot-glue-gun station.

So the day of Mira's birthday the four of us headed to the cheapest, greasiest pizza place in Mountain View and ordered four large pies, one for each of us.

"This is disgusting," Mira said, obviously delighted, when we set her personalized pie down in front of her. One quarter pepperoni, one quarter mushrooms, and half mushrooms with pepperoni, for all possible flavor combinations of her favorite toppings.

We were each only two slices in (Sebby was insisting that we had to finish at least half while sitting there or else the evening would be a failure) when a car pulled up to the sidewalk in front and Talia got out.

"Look out," Rose said. "Art Club reunion about to happen."

We all turned to look through the window. Talia was leaning into the car saying something to the person driving.

"That's Peter's car," I said.

"Are you serious?" Rose said.

As Talia stepped away from the car, we could see Peter in the driver's seat.

"She's coming in," Mira said.

The bell on the front door jingled, and Talia came in and headed to the counter.

"I'm picking up a large margherita," she said to the man at the register. He went to check on her order, and she turned and saw us.

"Oh, hello, everyone!" she said. I had never seen her so cheerful before.

"Hey," Mira said. "Hi, Talia."

"Having some pizza?" she asked.

"Yup," Sebby said. "Just having some pizza. At the pizza place."

"Wonderful." Talia nodded.

"How about you?" Rose said.

"I'm picking up," Talia said.

"Large margherita to go," the guy at the counter called. Talia went over to pay.

"What. The. Fuck?" Sebby whispered under his breath. Mira kicked him under the table.

"Well, see you all later. Have a wonderful evening," Talia said, holding the pizza box.

"Yeah, see you later," Rose said.

Talia practically skipped out the door and got back into Peter's car, and they drove off.

"Okay, what the fuck?" Sebby said, no longer whispering.

"What the actual fuck," Rose agreed.

"Maybe they're having a meeting or something?" I said. "Or she's helping him with something?"

"Yeah, I think we know what she's helping him with," Sebby

said. He stuck his tongue in his cheek and moved it around. Mira kicked him again.

"He's our teacher!" Mira said.

"I've seen the man's bedroom," Sebby said. "He's basically a teenager."

"You've been in his bedroom?" Rose said. "What were you doing in his bedroom?"

"That's between me and Jeremy," Sebby said.

"Ew, you guys hooked up in Peter's bedroom? That is sick."

"We did! We totally hooked up in Peter's bedroom. Right, Jeremy?"

I conveniently already had pizza in my mouth and couldn't respond. Rose and Sebby egging each other on was something I couldn't quite keep up with.

"This is weird," Mira said. "I feel weird about this. Did you see how happy she was? I've never seen that girl so happy."

"I'm sure there's a reasonable explanation," I said.

"Only one way to find out," Sebby said.

"What?" Mira said. "What sick plan is your twisted brain crafting right now?"

"Just eat your birthday pizza," Sebby said. "Then we'll go for a walk."

It was dark and freezing outside by the time we finished the dictated halves of our pizzas. We combined the rest into two boxes that I was now carrying as we made our way back toward St. F.

"Does Peter live at school?" Rose said.

"Right down the street," I said. "The school owns the building and he rents it from them."

"And what, you guys hang out there?" Rose said.

"Jeremy does," Mira said.

"I did last spring," I said. "Sometimes. Guys, why are we doing this?"

"We're not doing anything," Sebby said. "We're walking off our extravagant dinner. And if we happen to walk by Peter's house and happen to see if he and Talia are having a very intimate pizza party, then so be it."

"I'm with Jeremy," Mira said. "This is creepy."

"Listen," Rose said. "We were sitting in a public place when we were literally assaulted by the sight of Talia experiencing some kind of joy aneurysm. We need to make sure she's okay. Plus it is completely unfair that everyone else in the world other than me has seen where Peter lives."

So Mira and I followed dutifully behind as we passed St. F, the lights of the empty cafeteria glowing from the second floor as the janitors made their way through.

"Are you having a good birthday?" I asked Mira.

"You know I'm going to eat the rest of that pizza before I go home," Mira said. "So the answer is yes."

"Your mom wouldn't even allow sometimes pizza? Birthday pizza?"

She shook her head. "It would interfere with my allergy-elimination diet."

"Have you found out what you're allergic to?"

She smiled. "Difficult to determine when I keep sneaking pizza," she said.

"Oh my goodness," Sebby said, in a voice of mock amazement. "How weird. Look, we're right outside Peter's house."

We were standing across the street from it. The light was on in the downstairs living-room window.

"That's it?" Rose said. "What a shithole."

We all stood for a minute watching.

"Okay, it's really cold out," Mira said. "What are we doing?"

Just then we saw Peter walk past the window. We all instinctively ducked.

"Is he alone?" Rose said.

"He looks alone," Sebby said.

"Guys, this is super creepy," Mira said.

"Fine," Sebby said. He straightened up and walked across the street.

"Sebby!" Mira whisper-shouted at him, but he was already ringing the bell.

Peter answered the door.

"Neighborhood watch," Sebby declared.

Peter looked across the street at the rest of us standing there sheepishly.

"Hello," he said.

Rose and Mira and I made our way over to the door.

Sebby held up a tiny birthday candle.

"It's Mira's birthday. We need something to stick this in," he said, grinning.

"Hmm . . ." Peter smiled. "I might have a muffin."

He moved away from the door and we went inside.

"I'm going to stick this in Peter's muffin for you," Sebby whispered to Mira. Rose laughed and Mira pushed him.

We followed Peter into his little kitchen. I set our pizza boxes on the table.

"You brought a whole party?" Peter said, rummaging through his fridge.

"We ate at Anthony's," Rose said. She let a pause go by before saying, "We saw Talia there." Another pause. "Picking up a pizza."

Peter emerged from the fridge with a blueberry muffin.

"Talia was just here," he said.

Rose gave Sebby a meaningful look.

"Did you have an Art Club meeting without us?" Sebby said. "Your favorite members of Art Club?"

Peter put the muffin on a plate.

"I'm always here when a student needs to talk," he said.

"Or needs a muffin," Sebby said, sticking the candle in.

We sang "Happy Birthday" to Mira over the muffin candle and she blew it out. Then we sat in Peter's living room and ate the rest of the pizza.

At one point Rose, determined to see Peter's bedroom,

followed Sebby upstairs to "see where the bathroom was," leaving me and Mira alone with Peter.

"This has certainly been an unexpectedly eventful evening," Peter said.

"Is Talia okay?" I asked.

"Yeah, sure," he said. "Everyone just needs someone to talk to sometimes."

"She certainly isn't going to talk to us," Mira said.

"What do you mean?" I said.

"She's really weird with us," Mira said.

"I think she has some trouble with people her own age," Peter said. "She's an old soul."

"She's a weird soul," Mira said.

Peter smiled. "Possibly."

There was an awkward pause, broken by Rose and Sebby coming back downstairs.

"Top-notch medicine cabinet, Peter," Sebby said. "Don't worry. We only took a handful of Viagra."

"Aaaand it is officially time for my students to leave," Peter said, standing up.

"Sebby, too far," Rose said.

"Shoot," Sebby said. "I never know."

Peter showed us out the front door and we made our way back to the school. Mira's mom had offered to pick us up.

"That," Rose said as we walked, "was awesome."

"I know, right?" Sebby said.

Mira and I were walking behind again. I looked at her in the dark. She looked back and half smiled.

"Good birthday?" I said.

"Sure," she said. "Good birthday."

SEBBY

The Christmases that you spent at Tilly's were always a study in chaos. The perfectly trimmed tree never had many presents under it, but the ones that were there were immediately ripped open by the children, played with until they broke a few hours later, and finally abandoned in a heap of youthful victory in a corner. You enjoyed watching the kids indulge so deeply in their own sugar-fueled enthusiasm. This year little Stephanie was taking up most of the middle of the living room with a human-size Barbie head with hair made for styling, while the boys ran toy trucks in circles around her.

Neighbors and families from Tilly's church stopped by, ate from the never-ending cookie plate that Tilly refilled throughout the day, dropped off fruitcakes and hand-me-downs for the babies, remarked on the beautiful tree and the happy children and the lovely holiday and God bless us every one.

You were expected to stay until the end of the festivities,

but there was enough activity that you could sneak out every once in a while to smoke a cigarette from the secret pack that you kept for emergencies, to the tiny backyard where Tilly had installed a secondhand swing set and playhouse. The grass was covered in a light frost and you wrapped your hoodie tightly around yourself to stay warm. You had the Waitresses' "Christmas Wrapping" stuck in your head.

Merry Christmas, Merry Christmas
But I think I'll miss this one this year

By six o'clock the visitors were gone, the cookie supply had finally been exhausted, and the children had collapsed in their rooms, storing up for a second wind. You were sitting in your regular chair in the corner reading one of Daniel's new comic books, enjoying the temporary quiet.

"Sebastian, can you clean up all that wrapping paper?" Tilly called from the kitchen.

You put the comic back in the pile of the kids' gifts on the floor where you had found it, got up, and went into the kitchen. Tilly was standing over the sink scrubbing dishes. The babies were asleep in their portable playpen in the corner.

"Yeah," you said. "Where are the garbage bags?"

"Bottom drawer on the left," she said. "I guess it's been a while since you've taken out the garbage."

You grabbed a bag and went back into the living room, picked up the paper that the kids had ripped to shreds in their enthusiasm that morning, tied up the bag, and brought it outside to the curb.

When you came back inside, Tilly was sitting in the living room, looking at the tree.

"Thank you," she said.

"You're welcome."

"Seems like I haven't sat down all day," she said.

"You haven't."

You started to go to your room, where Stephanie would inevitably be found snoring in the corner, clutching her giant Barbie head, when Tilly stopped you.

"Have you heard from Jonathan?" she said.

You turned back to her, looked at her sitting there in the overstuffed armchair, her apron still on, a cup of tea in her hand.

"Why would I have heard from Jonathan?" you said.

"I don't know," she said. "I just thought, maybe, because it's Christmas."

You had been thinking about Jonathan on this day too, as you watched the holiday chaos unfold around you. For the past two years he had been the one sitting in the corner with you, the one who would sneak outside for a cigarette with you. And now he was gone.

The day that he left, you came home from hanging out with Mira to Tilly sitting alone in the dark in the living room, a cop show on mute on the TV.

"Jonathan left," she said.

She sounded tired and sad. Like she had been crying. You

realized that you had never seen Tilly cry. She had always seemed too busy with the kids for something as self-indulgent as crying. You thought in that moment that Tilly had probably done a lot of crying before you knew her. Maybe she had done all of her crying when she lost her husband, and then decided that was enough.

"Do you know where he went?" you asked.

"No," Tilly said. "But he's allowed to go." She said it as if she were trying to remind herself.

You started to go to your room.

"There's cake," she said. "I made him a birthday cake. He didn't have any."

"Okay," you said.

That was four months ago now. And it seemed that you and Tilly had been thinking the same thing, that if he was ever going to walk through that door again, it would have happened today.

Tilly took a sip of her tea.

"I haven't heard from him," you said.

"Well," Tilly said, "I hope he's having a nice Christmas."

You nodded and turned to go.

"You'll leave here when you turn eighteen too," she said.

You looked at her.

"That's true," you said, not sure where this was going. If Tilly drank, you could have written this off as sentimental holiday overindulgence talk, but she just sipped more of her tea.

"Until then you're going to have to follow my rules, though," she said.

"Okay," you said.

The two of you stared each other down for a minute, as if she expected you to say something. Finally she said, "I know that you're not going to school."

Ah.

"I go sometimes," you said.

"The school called me. They said you're not going."

"Maybe they were confused."

"You need to be going to school, Sebastian. I don't even understand where you are all day if you're not at school."

You didn't say anything.

"I have a feeling that I don't want to know," she said. "I gave you a second chance a year ago. You got yourself into trouble, and then you pulled that whole running-away stunt, but I gave you a second chance. Now, if you are getting into trouble again, I can't risk you bringing that back here to this house. I have other children to worry about."

"I'm not getting into trouble," you said. "I'm not bringing anything here."

"If you're going to continue to live here, you need to be in school. Do you understand me?"

You took a deep breath. You needed another cigarette.

"Yes," you said.

"Good," she said.

"Is that all?"

She turned to the tree again.

"Did you have a nice Christmas?" she asked.

"Yeah. Yes. Thank you."

"You're welcome," she said.

You started to go to your room and then thought better of it, headed toward the front door.

"I'm going out," you said. "I'll be at Mira's."

"Fine," she said.

The front door was unlocked at Mira's house when you got there, and you let yourself in. The house was quiet, the lights lit on their Christmukkah tree in the living room.

Mira was in her room, lying on her bed reading the *Rookie Yearbook*. You lay down next to her.

"Hi," she said.

"Hi," you said.

"Merry Christmas."

"Is it?"

You rolled over onto your side and rested your head in the crook of her neck.

"Everything okay?" she asked.

"Tell me a story," you said.

"Okay," she said. "What kind of story?"

"One about how we can always run away."

She smiled. You breathed her in. She smelled like safe places. Like comfort.

"Okay," she said. "Like, one where you show up here the day before my sixteenth birthday?"

"Yes."

"And you say, 'Let's go to the beach.' And we Google 'gayest beach town in North America' and you read to me about how the Pilgrims actually didn't land at Plymouth first, but farther east. That most people don't know that because of the big Pilgrim cover-up."

"And I say, 'We are pilgrims too.'"

"And we say, 'But this time we won't lie. We will tell the truth about our explorations.'"

You curled yourself around her body as she told the rest of the story, and at some point you realized that her shoulder was wet and you knew that it was because you were crying. And you knew that she would cry with you. And that you could always run away again.

JEREMY

Dad and Dave and I went to Florida to visit my grandparents for winter break, and I spent my days there floating in their tiny backyard pool, worrying that I was missing things back home. Time spent away from Sebby and Mira or not in the art studio felt wasted. I felt as though I barely existed without them.

The highlight of any day was getting texts from them, usually among the three of us, or us and Rose. As long as I was hearing from them I would feel like I could breathe again, until the texts stopped, and I would become convinced that they had forgotten about me. Dad finally made me put my phone on silent in a drawer during dinner because I wouldn't stop compulsively checking it.

"Somebody's got a girlfriend?" my grandma would say when she saw me staring at the screen.

"Just friends, Grandma," I said.

"Time for some great-grandbabies," she said.

I got back the Friday before school started again, and texted them as soon as I walked in the door of our house, nearly tripping over poor Dolly Parton the Cat, who did not appreciate the further insult after a week and a half spent with our neighbor cat-sitting her.

"Sorry, Dolly," I said.

"I'm so glad we got him that phone, aren't you, honey?" Dad said to Dave as they carried in the suitcases from the car. "So lovely to spend your family vacation staring at a tiny screen."

Mira texted back that I should come over. She was trying to pick out more items to cut up for her Art Club project and she needed help. Sebby wrote that he would meet us later. Tilly was having him watch the kids while she took the babies to a doctor's appointment. This was accompanied by many crying-face emoji.

"I'm going to Mira's house," I said, putting my coat back on and nearly tripping over Dolly again.

Mira's room was even more of a disaster than usual. Half of the things in her closet were falling off their hangers and starting a slow leak like lava across her floor. She was on the verge of disorganized despair when I arrived, so I made her sit down on the bed while I methodically went through the mess.

"I need more fabric for the dress, but I already brought in everything expendable," she said.

"How do you even find anything in here?" I asked. Trying to go through her closet was like an archeological dig. The layers were endless.

"I like to forget about things and then let them surprise me when they turn up again," she said.

I held up a pink tutu.

"How about this?"

"No. No way," she said. "Look." She got up and slipped it on over the skirt that she was wearing. "It fits me perfectly."

"It's enormous," I said. "You can't fit through the door."

"It's vintage," she said.

"Everything in here is vintage."

"It's not, actually," she said. "Some of it is genuine crap."

"Well, can you use the crap?"

"Too crappy to use," she insisted.

"Okay, you are being impossible."

She sat back down in a heap of protest on the carpeted floor, her legs crossed under the skirt so that her bottom half seemed to be all tutu.

"Let's go out and buy new stuff for the project, Jeremy. I can't let go of my clothing babies."

"Sebby is right. You are a hoarder. 'Clothing babies'?"

"I worked so hard to get them," she said. "Look at this." She grabbed a piece of crushed velvet that was sticking out from the corner of the pile. She unbunched the dress. It was an evening gown, the top covered in black sequins.

"Too small for me," she said.

"But yet you keep it anyway."

"Here." She threw the dress at me. "Try it."

"On? Try it on?"

"Yes," she said. "I bet it'll fit you. Here, I'll find something for me. Dress-up time."

She stuck her head into the closet and rummaged through the pile. I stood for a moment holding the dress, feeling the crushed velvet and the satisfying crunch of the sequins in my fingers. Her butt was sticking out of the closet, the tutu framing it in the air.

"Put in on, Jeremy," she said, her voice muffled by the clothes.

I unbuttoned my shirt and took it off, letting it fall onto her bed. I held up the dress, trying to figure out how to get into it. There was a zipper down the back. I slid it over my head and then took off my pants awkwardly. The dress hugged my torso, the fabric smooth on the inside. Looking in the mirror, I regretted wearing boxers that day. The elastic waistband made the fabric bunch up.

Mira emerged from the closet with an armful of clothing.

"Of course it fits you perfectly," she said, looking at me. "Life is so unfair."

She zipped the zipper closed on my back and I felt encased, like the dress was holding me.

"Okay, I think this is a formal occasion," she said. "Help me pick mine."

After we had decided on a dress for her, she sat down at her vanity.

"What's the makeup look we want?" she asked, rifling through a drawer filled with half-used cosmetics.

"You are really determined to distract from the task of actually getting some of your stuff out of that closet, aren't you?" I said.

"Cat eye and a red lip?"

I was sitting on her bed, trying to keep my legs together under the narrow skirt of the dress. I watched as she applied makeup, pretending to be interested in a magazine from the pile next to her bed. She turned to me when she was done.

"What do you think? Glamorous?"

"Very," I said.

"Come here," she said. She moved over on the little bench.

"Why?" I said.

"You think you're getting away with just doing the dress?"

I scooted off the bed, feeling the strange, self-conscious freedom of having nothing between my underwear and the world, at least the world of Mira's room, and sat on the bench. She stood up and leaned her butt against the tabletop of the vanity, gathering the cosmetics into a pile next to her.

"We should give you the same look as me, I think," she said.

"I don't know about this, Mira."

"You've never worn any makeup?" she said, as if that was an absurd idea.

"I live in a house of only men. I've barely ever even seen makeup."

She opened a container of powder, dipped a brush in it, and leaned toward me.

"This is sheer with a little tint," she said. "Might look funny on you, since it's tinted for me."

She brushed it along my cheeks and forehead. I closed my eyes. It was like being tickled with a feather. Like a breeze.

"Not bad, actually," she said. She picked up a container of blush. "What's that like?" she said. "Living in a house of just men?"

I shrugged. "Seems normal to me. It's all I've ever known."

She started brushing blush on my cheeks.

"I know what you mean," she said. "Families can seem so normal and boring from the inside that you don't know you're different until someone else makes you feel different."

"Yeah," I said.

"That's how I feel about my family," she said. "There was this one time on my parents' anniversary when we were all going out to dinner together at this fancy restaurant, and my mom was running late because she was still at work. I mean, this was back when she actually had a job."

She dabbed the brush in the powder, brushed more on my cheeks.

"So my sister and I were there with my dad at a table waiting for her. It was a really big place, with lots of rooms. And my mom showed up twenty minutes late and said she was meeting her husband, and the maître d' said he must not be there yet. Because, you know, there was no white guy sitting alone waiting for his white wife. So the guy sat Mom at a table in another room, and it was only when Dad called her phone that they figured out the guy's mistake. By that time Mom was furious and she completely freaked out on the guy and we left without eating."

"Yikes."

"Yeah, I had never seen my mom lose it in public like that before. I felt a little bad for the guy, actually. We hadn't been really specific with him. Mom didn't say, 'I'm meeting my husband and two daughters, ages six and ten.' But it just hit this nerve for her. Like we had been exposed as, I don't know . . . just exposed."

"Right."

"So then you just think, *Well, if the world thinks that we're weird, then maybe we should just be weird.*"

"Dad and Dave have never been weird. I mean, maybe they were at some point, but you wouldn't know it to look at them now."

"They seem great," Mira said.

"Yeah, no. I'm lucky. I mean, I don't know how it all ended up for my mom. I assume she has another family by now."

"You don't know her at all?"

I shook my head. "She lives in Colorado. Or she did the last time Dad talked to her."

"So what happened? Why did she go so far away?"

"My dad happened, I guess."

Mira leaned forward and took my chin in her hand to steady it. She pressed the soft tip of the eyeliner against my eye. I flinched.

"Don't move," she said.

I held as still as I could as she traced along the top and bottom of my eyelids, only realizing when she was done that I had been holding on to her leg to try to steady myself.

"Pretty good," she said, examining her work. "Don't look in the mirror yet. I'm not done."

"Okay."

"So, your mom."

"My mom."

"Your dad told her he was gay, and she freaked out?"

"Yeah, that's about it," I said. "I only really know about my mom from my dad. He told me the whole story when I was ten. Before that there was just this mysterious explanation of 'Mom moved away and we don't ever get to see her.'"

"Maybe he thought she would come back someday. At least to see you."

"Maybe. But she didn't."

"Why do you think she didn't?"

I thought for a moment. I had never said any of this out loud to anyone before. Not even to Peter. "I think he broke her heart. So she needed to get as far away from him as she could. And I was a part of him too."

"Do you think you're like your dad?"

"No. He was popular in high school. Really handsome. That's who she fell in love with. Mr. All-American Dude. And then suddenly he was something else. I mean, he's still that guy. Just not the way that she thought he was."

"You're handsome," Mira said.

"What?"

"You said you're not like your dad, but you're handsome."

I could feel myself blushing under the blush.

"Well, right now maybe you look more beautiful than hand-some," she said.

"I'm not like my dad," I said.

"Maybe you're like your mom."

"Maybe."

She picked up a tube of lipstick.

"Separate your lips a little," she said.

I did it, and she leaned in, holding my chin again. I kept my eyes open and watched her eyes watching my lips. The lipstick was creamy and cool, her hand warm on my face. There was something about the feeling of her holding me, her eyes fixed on my lips, that I could feel in my stomach. Something comfort-ing and kind, with an indefinable desire hovering just around the edges. It occurred to me that she was so close to me that we were almost kissing. That if I moved toward her, my lips would be on hers. How would that feel? Lipstick on lipstick?

"Did you ever try to call her?" Mira asked. "Or write to her?"

"My mom?"

"Yeah."

I shook my head. "No. I mean, she knows where I am if she wants to talk to me."

"But you know where she is too."

"I could find out, I guess. I kind of . . ." I wasn't sure how to talk about this. "I guess I don't really want to talk to someone who doesn't want to talk to me." I shrugged. "That sounds pretty childish."

"No, it's fair. I get it," she said. She leaned back, examining her work. "Sebby never talks about his mom. I mean, he knew her. And he saw her get sick."

"When did she die?" I asked.

"He was six or seven, I think. Ovarian cancer. He literally won't talk about it."

"And he has no other family?"

She shook her head. "He doesn't even know who his dad is. He thinks his mom didn't either. Or if she did, she wanted him to believe that she didn't. That's how he ended up in foster care. Although he's been through so many places, they keep threatening to send him to a group home if he can't make this one work. Can you imagine having Sebby as your foster kid?"

"No."

"Right? I mean, these totally well-meaning people who just want to help children have that show up at their door? And you know that boy has been trouble since he was born."

She took my chin again and applied another coat of lipstick, wiping with a finger at the edges of my lips. I swallowed, suddenly feeling like I had too much saliva in my mouth.

"One day you'll forgive your mom, though," she said. "And then you'll want to talk to her."

I didn't say anything.

"You have good lips, Jeremy," she said. "You would make a great drag queen."

"Just because I'm gay I should be a drag queen?" I said, teasing.

"A little drag never hurt anyone's sense of self, believe me." She wiped her fingers on a makeup wipe. "You must always remember what RuPaul says. 'We're born naked, and the rest is drag.' Now this," she said, putting down the lipstick and sitting on the bench next to me, "this is fabulous."

We sat side by side looking in the mirror on her vanity, matching cat eyes and red lipstick, my top of black sequins on crushed velvet, Mira in silver chiffon. Our thighs touching side by side on the bench. I felt that warm tug in my stomach again, an urge to stay safe in the embrace of this dress, the incense-tinged perfume aura of her room, the unity in our matching eyes examining each other. We looked beautiful.

"Where are we going?" she asked.

"Looking like this?"

"I mean in theory."

"I don't know," I said. "A party, I guess."

"Opening night of some retro club," she said. "Where they have ironic burlesque acts and a man who eats fire tending bar."

"Yes," I said. "That sounds right."

We lay next to each other in her bed, watching out the window as the winter sunset spread along the edges of the trees. She was trying to do cat's cradle with a long string of beads.

"How did you and Sebby meet?" I asked her. I realized that I didn't know.

"Sebby never told you?" she said.

"No."

She seemed to consider for a moment. Then she tangled up the beads into a ball in her hand. "It was last December," she said, "so, a little more than a year ago. We were both in the hospital at the same time. He had to have surgery after he got in a really bad fight with these two guys. He told you about that?"

"Yeah."

"Well, when he was in recovery, he got ahold of a lot of pills, and he was going to take them. Like, all of them."

She handed the beads to me. I looked at them, felt them in my hand.

"He didn't tell you that part, did he?" she said.

"No."

"Well, they found out about it before he could do it. But a suicide threat gets moved to junior psych. So as soon as he was well enough, that's where he ended up. And that's where I was."

She pulled up the left sleeve of her dress and turned her wrist over to show me the underside. It was marked horizontally by a long, light scar that I had never noticed before.

"I had a problem with wanting to hurt myself for a little while there," she said. "It's okay now. But it got bad before it got better."

I touched the soft skin of her wrist gently.

"That's how you met," I said.

"That's how we met," she said, pulling her sleeve back down. "Cute story, huh?"

She turned toward me and propped herself up on her elbow.

"When we got out of the hospital, we ran away," she said. "Just for a day. It was my sixteenth birthday. We took my dad's car and drove to Provincetown."

I smiled.

"What?" she said.

"That's where I go. Every summer. With my dads."

"Really?"

"They own a house on the bay. Sebby told me you guys went there. But I didn't know you ran away."

"How funny," she said, lying back down. "We've been in the same place."

I laughed. "We're often in the same place."

"But it's like you were there with us. Like we already knew you."

MIRA

Sebby showed up at her front door the day that he got out of the hospital. It was December, the day before her sixteenth birthday, five weeks after she thought that she didn't want to live anymore. But she was still here. And for the first time in a while she felt like she had something worth holding on to.

He programmed their destination into the GPS of her dad's car. They did not ask to borrow it. That's not how these things were done.

Mira drove, Sebby in the passenger seat next to her, his bare feet on the dashboard, oblivious to the winter winds howling outside, the highway winding north through dark New England forests. He played his favorite Diamond Rings album turned up loud, rested his feet on the air vent, as if the heat might thaw them into a new kind of summer, one crafted from dreams of beaches and escape.

The farther out on the Cape they traveled, the closer they

seemed to be to the moon, white dunes towering above the sides of the road. Even in the dark they could tell that this place was in danger of simply being washed away.

They tried to think of magic words that would let them pass there. To prove themselves worthy. "We come in peace. We come for love." Maybe those were enough.

They reached their destination just before ten p.m., an hour after officially splitting from the mainland, and pulled up to a motel on the edge of town. Across the street from the parking lot there was only water. Mira wanted to jump into it like those polar bear people, wrapping themselves in hypothermia blankets afterward. Feel alive by almost dying.

Instead they went inside and asked for a room.

"Water view?"

The boy at the front desk was no older than they were and hardly looked up, didn't ask for ID with the credit card that Sebby gave him with the name Matilda O'Connor on it. This is how easy it was. The boy handed over two keys and a monotone "Have a nice stay, breakfast from eight to ten."

The room was on the second floor, facing out to the bay. Tiny lights of life sparkled around the scoop of land that ringed the water, asking them to make their way just a little farther. Not to stop until they found where the land ends.

They brought a single bag that they packed together. Toothbrushes and two sets of stretched nylon fairy wings that Mira had bought on sale at a costume store after Halloween, saving up for future projects.

They sat on the queen-size bed, and Mira ripped open the bag of her wings. A small cloud of glitter settled down on top of them, blessing them. Sebby tore open his plastic and now they were gold and silver sparkles, marked for beauty and greatness.

The outfit that Mira chose for this occasion was the pink fifties party dress that she got during a particularly good thrifting session over the summer. One strap was ripped when she found it and there was loose thread where a flower had joined the two sides of the giant collar. Nothing that she couldn't fix.

The night's accessories were a wide red patent-leather belt, slouchy gray boots, and a perfectly faded jean jacket from her favorite Goodwill that closed down when she was still in middle school. Back then the jacket was big on her. Now the sleeves were snug and it didn't button shut.

The past couple of years had brought this newly womanly body along with them. Mira only wore skirts now as a rule, because pants made her feel stuck into someone else's idea of a shape. And her shape often felt like a fluid thing, this way one day and something else the next. She wished that she could pin it down, the watery and unmanageable way that she was growing. She wondered if other people felt solid in their skin.

Sebby had on his traditional white T-shirt and khakis worn thin from overuse. He carried a Sharpie in his pocket at all times for moments of inspired defacement, and now he took his shirt off and laid it on the bed in front of him, spelled out the word *Twink* in wobbly block letters, finishing it with a little lopsided star. He thought this was funny. She did too.

His bare torso was so white in the dim light of that room that she thought she could see through him, see through his scars to the places where things had been fixed. She wondered what was on the other side of her scars. If there were things in her that were still broken.

The clock on the nightstand in the room clicked to 11:00 as they pulled the elastic straps of the Halloween-store wings onto each other's shoulders carefully, knowing that all they needed was a little human warmth to bring them to life, to make the humans wearing them a little less corporeal, a little more of the air.

Mira opened the door out onto the balcony to breathe in the bay wind. It froze their cheeks and made the wings flap impatiently on their backs. It was a week before Christmas, and the wind was daring these impetuous tourists to find this land hospitable. Out of respect, they crushed the delicate wings under their winter coats before they went out, tripping down the string-light-lined street with a secret under their clothes.

Earlier in the day they would have found bundled families wandering from hot chocolate to hot chocolate, children staring skyward, wishing for snow. This was beach town transformed into provincial Christmas Walk. Nothing like the sweaty crowds of summertime Commercial Street, buying their two-for-ten-dollars T-shirts, serenaded by roller-skating drag queens hawking for their shows. This was a well-crafted winter peacefulness. A Currier and Ives picture lovingly assembled through the efforts of a hundred years of gay New

Englanders, for the benefit of all.

But at close to midnight on a Wednesday this place belonged to those who did not turn to hot chocolate to keep warm on long sea-winded nights. Softly glowing windows lining the narrow streets were home to the human versions of the strange, wave-rocked formations that had washed up on the beach when there was nowhere else to go. When the only alternative was spinning out into the open sea.

The Pilgrims had unceremoniously rejected this land when they found that nothing would grow here, hoping the "great Pilgrim cover-up" would hide their rookie mistake, those fruitless months spent on a swirl of glorified sandbank, Plymouth Rock the centerpiece of an elaborate fiction crafted for posterity. But once the undesirables in the bunch began to show their true colors, they sent them back, out onto that twist of land. The outcasts would have to learn that not everything grew in the ground. Life could form on the surface, sprout up into giant, colorful shoots and twist itself around other like-minded sun seekers, holding on tight. Holding each other up.

Mira and Sebby took it all in with puffs of freezing air, gleeful in their freedom. They could go anywhere. Just try and stop them. They could do anything.

Even the bouncer at the door of the Governor Bradford seemed to sense it, looking for only a moment at their fake Hawaiian IDs before waving them in with a sigh. Sebby declared this to be their destination when he saw the sign for Drag Karaoke and the pleasing white clapboard shabbiness of the building.

Boats anchored in the harbor across the street. They imagined whiskey-starved fishermen stumbling inside.

Instead, a group of drunk, forty-something lesbians sat around the small karaoke stage. Their compatriot was serenading them with a tipsy but soulful rendition of "Constant Craving," her Red Sox cap pulled down tight over her eyes, her bulky frame rocking in her salt-stained Timberland boots.

Mira ordered two whiskey and sodas at the bar, her dad's drink, and the only one she could say with a straight face to the bearish bartender. This was her first taste of alcohol, and the inedible gasoline tang of it felt like a magic potion. Sixteen was less than an hour away, after all. It was time to learn some new things.

Dana, the drag queen host of Drag Karaoke, was done up in full Billy Idol lady glam, bleach-blond hair and combat boots with a leather mini and fishnets. She sang "White Wedding" to the delight of the assembled lesbians, Idol sneer and impressive high kicks inserted at key moments. Even at a quarter to midnight on a Wednesday in December, on the cusp of falling off the cliff of holiday spirit into the abyss of a Massachusetts winter, Dana presided over her kingdom.

Sebby responded by doing his best rendition of "Dancing with Myself," pulling Dana into his routine, not one to be stopped by the logic of the lyrics, grabbing her hand and spinning her into a twirl that he was not yet tall enough to complete.

"Happy twenty-first birthday to the prettiest girl in town," he said, pointing at Mira when the song was over. "You don't look a day over sixteen."

Dana fanned herself in a joking swoon as he handed the mic back to her.

"I didn't know the theme tonight was jailbait," she said in her best Catskills comic voice.

The lesbians laughed and sent over another round.

Mira sang "Dream a Little Dream of Me" at Sebby's insistence. Her voice faltered on the high notes, but she was feeling good on that stage in front of their friendly audience. Their only meal that day had consisted of rest-stop soggy fries and mega-size sodas that tipped the car cup holders, and she could feel the whiskey warming her from the inside out, making things feel fine in a new way. In a way that made it okay to sing in public.

Dana left for a cigarette break and Sebby threw back his drink and pulled Mira toward a thumping beat rising up from a stairwell in the back of the room. Downstairs they found disco remixes and unintelligible house music blasting through a small room of packed bodies. Men in tight T-shirts or no shirts showed off their carefully sculpted stomachs, a well-placed Santa hat here and there making an attempt at an excuse for such festivities. Those with less to show for themselves looked on from the bar.

Sebby took Mira's hand and pulled her into it, the crowd parting enough to watch these two winged fairies go by. They found a suitable spot to show off their highly original dance moves, perfected over hours of practice in the hospital. This one was called "Taking a Book Out of the Library." First put on your invisible glasses. Admire the invisible spines. Select an invisible volume.

"I like your wings."

Through the shroud of hazy improvised club lighting Mira could barely make out the features of the man shouting into Sebby's ear. Sebby flashed a grin at him, grabbed Mira, and pulled them both into the stranger. She followed his level of boldness, thrusting pelvises forward but keeping their hands to themselves, heads turning from side to side as if the last person they wanted to look at was the one right in front of them.

House transitioned back to disco, and Mira shouted to Sebby that she needed to find the bathroom. There was only one, supplied with two urinals and one stall, and she locked herself in the stall, wondering if she was expected to have stayed upstairs with the other ladies, crooning k.d. lang into the wee hours of the morning.

At the bar she decided it was time for another drink. The warm hug of her karaoke buzz was starting to wear off and she didn't want to think too much about what they were doing there.

The bartender handed over the drink with raised eyebrows.

"You better keep an eye on your little boyfriend there," he said.

She looked back to the dance floor, where their old partner was dancing behind Sebby, navigating around the wings.

"That'll be twelve dollars."

She brought Sebby the drink and he took it gratefully,

grabbing her around the waist, dispersing his fan club.

"Let's go see the water," she said in his ear.

Outside they spotted Dana in a leopard-print coat. A man in leather lit her cigarette. She inhaled and let out a grateful cloud of nicotine.

"Sleep tight, jailbait," she called after them.

They walked along the beach back to the motel, the lights of the Mid-Cape just visible along the horizon, an unwelcome reminder that there was always a path of return. In one of the houses along the bay a Christmas party was winding down. Men sang "Silent Night" in harmony on the back porch, throwing cheer to the wind.

Back in the motel room, they lay tangled in the drunken bedspread. Sebby wrapped himself in the fabric of her skirt, the wings crushed under them both like neglected moths or forgotten limbs. Mira felt like a newborn with some vague memory of reincarnation, who understood that, when it finally took its first steps, it would recognize the sensation from another lifetime.

"Do you feel older?" he asked her in the dark.

"I feel the same. I feel like I'm seven years old. Like I'm five."

"You were drunk when you were five?"

"Shut up, Sebby."

"You're mean when you're sixteen."

"I'm older than you now."

"I'll never be old. I'll sell my soul. I'll die young."

"I thought I would feel different."

"Sweet sixteen."

"I'm not so sweet."

"You're sweet to me."

"You're silly."

"I am. This is true."

"Happy birthday to me."

"Happy birthday to you, babes."

They rolled up the maps of their bodies until they were two continents of interlocking roads and rivers and dreams, and she thought, *This is how I will learn to live again.*

JEREMY

It was dark when Mira finished telling me about their night in Provincetown. Sebby had snuck in and joined us on the bed while she was talking. The lights from the vanity illuminated the room with a soft glow. He sat between our legs and listened.

"It's a good story," he said when she was done.

"What happened after that?" I asked.

"When I didn't answer my phone all night, my parents finally called the police, and they tracked the car through the GPS," Mira said. "They showed up at the motel the next morning."

"Did you get in trouble?" I asked.

"You don't steal your dad's car and then get forcibly returned to your parents by the police without getting in trouble," Mira said.

Sebby stretched himself between us and lay down on the pillow, curling a leg over Mira's leg, putting a hand on my stomach. Connecting us.

"You girls look pretty," he said.

I suddenly remembered my makeup, and unconsciously put my hand to my lips.

"What's the occasion?" Sebby said.

"We're cleaning out Mira's closet," I said.

He touched the sequins on my dress. "Looks like it's going well," he said.

SEBBY

You made your way back to school for the first time in over a year on a Monday in January, the first day back from winter break. You figured you would show up and at least get your name in for attendance, then you could use the library computer to do some research on getting your GED. Would it be possible to convince the state that you were being homeschooled? Tilly would love that. Just have you home reading Bible verses and changing diapers all day.

You passed through the metal detector at the front door to get inside. The halls were jammed with people so much tighter than Mira's school, the inevitability of bodies bumping up against each other adding to the overall sense of dread that had always permeated this place. You stuck your hands in your pockets, put your head down, and tried to forge a path through the middle, avoiding the clumps of people gathered at the lockers on either side.

What was the plan here? Head to the office first to find out what your homeroom was. Drop off the forged doctor's note you had worked on all week explaining that complications from your injuries had prevented you from attending in the fall. You handed it over in exchange for your schedule, no questions asked. They didn't have time for your problems here.

The bell for first period rang just as you were walking out of the office. Those running late forced their way past you to get to their classrooms. You looked at the piece of paper in your hand. *Chemistry*, it said. *Mr. Walters—Room 248.*

The last stragglers were dashing into closing classroom doors when you saw him.

He was bigger now. That must have helped him with his prospects on the football team. Maybe he no longer felt like a "pansy Asian kid," which was what the other guys on the team used to call him. Put on enough muscle and no one can accuse you of being weak.

That had been what he was upset about on the day that it all went down. Another day of them torturing him in practice, under the guise of hazing the freshman. All in good fun.

You had been waiting outside the gym for him to finish showering. You had the answers for the next day's history test and you had promised to deliver them to him. You both had trouble in history.

The other team members had slowly filtered out of the gym. You were sitting on the ground outside the door twisting a twig in your hand, trying to look inconspicuous. It wasn't working. Finally you gave up, tossed the twig, and went inside the locker room. Two of the bigger upperclassmen pushed past you on your way in.

"Watch it, twink," one grumbled as you grazed his shoulder.

He was in the middle locker aisle, sitting on a bench, a towel wrapped around his waist. He was alone.

"Theo?" you said.

He looked up.

"Hey, Sebby."

"I have the answers for the history test," you said.

He nodded, then looked back at his feet. This smaller version of him, his shoulder blades sticking out like pointy new wings from his back when he hunched over. His black hair hung damp in his face.

"What is it?" you said. You went over and sat next to him on the bench. You put your arm around him. "What's wrong, puddin' pop?"

He smiled in spite of himself. He found you amusing. You knew this.

"Fucking practice," he said. "It's always 'fuck up the skinny Asian kid,' you know? Like, who am I to think I can play?"

"You'll just have to prove them wrong," you said. Your arm was still around him. Damp skin. You squeezed his shoulder affectionately.

"I'm not going to get a chance if they keep fucking piling on me." He looked at the arm closest to you. There was a large bruise running down the side of it.

"Aww," you said. "Poor baby." You made a circle around the bruise with your finger. "Bruises heal," you said.

"I guess," he said. "Fucking hurts right now."

You weren't going to do it. You knew that you shouldn't. No good could come of it. Not here. And then you did it anyway. Leaned down and very lightly kissed his arm right above the bruise. Just to feel the brush of his skin on your lips. To show some tenderness. This was your method of kindness.

"What the fuck is this?" came a mocking voice from the shadows.

Someone was laughing. "Told you Theo was a fucking faggot."

Theo jumped up, pushing you away, hard.

"What the fuck?" he said loudly, to you, not to them. But he had hesitated for too long.

It was the boys you had passed on the way into the locker room. Seniors, both enormous, both born looking for a fight.

"Hey, faggots, get out of our fucking locker room," the first one said. They were emerging from the shadows now, slowly, animals stalking their prey.

"Fuck you," you said.

"Looks like the one you want to fuck is Theo," the second one said.

You could feel your heart pounding. This day had already not been going well. An F on a paper you legitimately put work into. A talking-to by another teacher about your lack of participation in class. And tonight Tilly expected you to take the kids to church study group. You were in no mood.

"Whatever," you said.

You reached into your pocket and pulled out the answers to the history test. You held them out to Theo.

"Here," you said. "Just take it."

"What's that? A love letter?" the first guy said. They were close now, the two of them standing at the edge of the bench where you had been sitting. Theo was frozen in front of you. He didn't take the paper.

"Yeah," you said, turning to the first boy. "It's for your dad. It says thanks for blowing me in your car last night."

And that was it. He was on you as soon as you got the last word out. You felt his knee in your stomach first, and then his fist connected with your face at the same time the back of your head hit the concrete floor and the fluorescent light on the ceiling above you turned to stars. You tried to hold your hands up in front of your face but the other one was holding you down. You tasted blood in your mouth, felt it running down from your nose. He was not stopping. This was not going to stop.

The last thing you saw before you blacked out was Theo, still standing there in his towel. Doing nothing.

And now here he was. And here you were. You saw him before he saw you. Standing at the other end of the hallway closing his locker and turning the combination lock. Then he looked up.

"Oh, fuck," he said.

You saw his new muscles tense under his T-shirt. You said nothing.

"What are you doing here?" he said.

You walked toward him a few feet. He moved backward, as if you were contaminated.

"I go to school here," you said.

"I thought you were gone."

You stared at him.

"Like dead?" you said. "Did you think they fucking killed me?"

"No. I knew you were okay," he said.

"I wasn't, actually," you said. "I wasn't okay at all."

Someone called to him from the stairwell.

"Look, please, uh . . ." He was looking behind him, stepping backward. "Please, just . . . don't talk to me."

"Are you kidding me?"

"No . . . just . . . pretend you don't know me, okay? It'll make things easier."

You watched in disbelief as he turned and ran to the stairwell, clambered his newly large body down to whoever had been calling him. And then you were alone. The sound of sneakers squeaking on freshly buffed floors somewhere. The smell of industrial cleaner. You felt like you were going to throw up.

You headed back through the metal detector, out the front door. Outside it was freezing. You didn't have a real winter coat. Just your hoodie and a tattered jean jacket. The wind grabbed at your eyes and did you the favor of pulling out tears so you wouldn't have to try to stop them.

Fuck this fucking place.

On the other side of the expanse of dead brown lawn, a figure was leaning on a car, smoking a cigarette.

You looked at the piece of paper still in your hand. Chemistry, it said. *Mr. Walters—Room 248.* It was a page full of fictions. *French. Mrs. Alderson. Algebra. Mr. Stein.* None of this was real.

You shoved the paper in your pocket and walked toward the figure.

"Hey, Sebby," he said when you reached him.

"Hey, Nick," you said.

He offered you a cigarette. You took it. He lit it for you, cupping the flame against the wind.

"I was wondering when I was going to see you around here," he said.

"Yeah. I can't, uh . . ." You didn't have words. There was no way to talk about any of this.

"You okay?" Nick said.

You shook your head.

Nick threw the stub of his cigarette on the ground and opened the driver's-side door.

"Come on," he said. "Let's get out of here."

You took in a deep breath of nicotine and opened the passenger side and got in. As Nick started the car, you looked back once, knowing it was the last time. Knowing that you would not be coming back.

JEREMY

Sebby showed up at my house alone one night in late January, looking glassy eyed and hungry. We had already eaten dinner, but Dad and Dave heated up leftovers for him and we sat and watched him eat like he was a lost kitten who might drown in a full saucer of milk.

He came up to my room with me after he finished. It was the first time we had been alone in a while. Alone in my bedroom.

"Are you okay?" I asked, walking into the room behind him.

"Yeah," he said, pushing off his shoes and getting on my bed. "Shut the door, okay?"

I looked out in the hallway. I could hear Dad and Dave cleaning up in the kitchen. I closed the door.

"What's up?" I said.

"Come here," he said. His eyes had a half-closed, dreamy look.

I sat next to him on the bed and he pulled me toward him, pulled my face to his, and kissed me. I could smell the unmistakable skunky odor of pot on his clothes. His hands found my back and made their way under my shirt. I followed his lead, letting my own hands find skin. Then his fingers moved to my fly. I pulled away.

"What?" he said.

"My dads."

"We'll be quiet," he said.

I shook my head.

"They could come up here," I said.

"Fine," he said, pushing his back up against the wall. There was something petulant and angry in his eyes, as if he couldn't understand why he was being denied.

"We can kiss," I said. "You can kiss me."

"Oh, can I?"

We sat for a minute in awkward silence.

"Why did you come over here?" I said.

"I was with Nick and his friends and I didn't want to go home. Why, I can't come over?"

"No, I mean, why did you come here instead of Mira's house?"

He shrugged.

"Nick, from the diner?" I asked. "Ali's friend Nick?"

"Yeah. He goes to my school."

He looked at his hands.

"You're pretty . . . high, right now," I said. "Aren't you?" *God, I sound like such a loser.*

"Yeah," he said. "Why? You want some?"

I shook my head. "No," I said. "My dads. I can't."

He seemed mesmerized by his hands for another minute and then suddenly he said, "Can I stay here tonight?"

"Uh, yeah," I said. "I mean, I have to ask."

He nodded and then looked down again. I had never seen him like this before. Unsure of himself.

Dad and Dave agreed that he could stay and we set up a sleeping bag on the floor next to my bed. He curled up in it as soon as we laid it out, so I got ready for bed early, said good night to my dads, turned out the light, and got into bed. I turned so I was facing him on the floor, watched the sleeping bag rise and fall with his breathing.

"Jeremy?" he said, rolling over to face me.

"Yeah?"

"Thanks for letting me stay."

"Yeah. Sure."

My eyes were slowly adjusting to the dark. I could make out the outline of his features.

"Are you really okay?" I asked.

He didn't answer. He unzipped the sleeping bag and got up, came over to the bed. I moved over and he lay down next to me, got under the covers.

"Yeah," he said. "I'm okay."

It was so familiar at this point, to be lying next to him. We just weren't usually alone when it happened. And the newness of his reaching for me earlier had thrown me. It had been months since we had first kissed, but I wasn't sure what it would mean to move beyond that, to have a real intimacy with him that didn't include Mira. And I wasn't sure that what he needed on this night was about me at all.

"I'm sorry about before," I said. "I was just worried . . . with other people home."

"It's okay," he said.

"It's not that I don't want to," I said. We were whispering now, our faces next to each other on the pillow. "I just haven't, uh, done much."

"Much?"

"Yeah. Anything. Much."

"I get it," he said.

"I want to," I said.

"Just not tonight."

"Yeah."

"Okay," he said.

"Okay," I said.

"Can I stay here?" he said. "Next to you?"

I nodded. He stretched a tentative hand across the blankets on top of my chest.

"Like this? This is okay?"

I laughed, tried to laugh as a whisper. "Yes, Sebby, it's okay."

He smiled and kissed me again. I tried to let myself relax, to not feel as though some forbidden dream had just manifested in my room. We fell asleep like that, holding each other in my little twin bed.

There are problems that go along with becoming a person who needs other people. Especially if you have invested most of your identity in being alone. It hadn't been a nice way to live, exactly, but I had been self-sufficient in my solitude. Now I was carrying the persistent itch of an emotion around with me, feeding it like some kind of desperate pet.

I was alone in the art studio on a Monday in early February. Mira and Rose both had papers due, so they went home after last period to work on them. Sebby had stayed at my house again the night before. He showed up after my dads were asleep, texted me to come down and let him in. He was sweating and jittery instead of glassy eyed this time. We didn't say anything to each other, and I wasn't sure if we were just being quiet so as not to disturb my dads or if there was something really wrong. He lay down in my bed with me again and I held him, his body twitching through the night. It felt like I barely slept, but I must have drifted off, because when I opened my eyes in the morning he was gone.

I had made it more than halfway through the year at this point and I was trying to avoid taking stock, counting up my gains and losses. Inventory in this moment seemed unwise. It was still too fragile.

The solution was to focus on something else. I was making progress in my painting for the exhibit. A three-by-five-foot canvas with three figures, surrounded by a wash of color. I still hadn't worked on the faces. They stared out at me, blank and inhuman, begging for completion.

Next to me, gnarled old tubes of school-supply paint lay on the table with a palate caked with years of colors, the history of every student who had tried to get something down, bring something out of their heads into the open. I was procrastinating by lining the paints up neatly next to my brushes. I looked out the window. It had snowed during the night, but it was raining now, turning the snow to dismal slush.

Talia came into the room so quietly that I didn't notice, didn't know when she spoke how long she had been there.

"That's a large canvas," she said.

I looked around. She was standing behind me.

"Oh," I said. "Yeah. I guess so."

"I was wondering what you were working on. You've kept it such a secret."

"Just wanted to wait for people to see it in the show, I guess."

She walked up to the easel, examined the faceless figures in the dim light coming in from the windows. She picked up a tube of paint.

"Pretty blue," she said.

Angel eyes blue.

"Yeah," I said.

She put the tube down, straightened it so it lined up with the others.

"You're here late," I said.

"I had Math Club. I just came in to get some drawing paper for my project."

"Still planning on doing landscapes?"

"Yes."

She went over to the shelves where the paper was kept and pulled out a few sheets. I picked up the blue tube of paint and felt the metal wrinkles of it in my hand.

"Jeremy?" she said.

"Yeah?"

"I've been meaning to say something to you."

I turned to look at her, standing next to the shelves, clutching the sheets of paper as if they might cover something shameful.

"What?"

"I should have said it before, but I didn't want to risk upsetting you. I'm not sure sometimes exactly how to say things to people."

"Okay," I said.

"It's just that . . . I'm glad that you came back. To school. After everything."

"Oh," I said. "Thanks."

"And I want you to know how much I regret that I didn't step in during class that day. With *The Great Gatsby*. If I had said something, supported you, then you wouldn't have been alone. It might not have become so . . . personal."

"Oh, Talia. I don't think it would have made a difference."

"But it might have," she said. She looked like she might start crying.

"What happened was not your fault," I said.

"I just wish it could have gone differently."

"Well, yeah, me too."

She looked down at the paper in her hands. "Peter said that I should say something to you, since it's been on my mind. He's really very insightful when it comes to matters of the human spirit."

I smiled. "That's true," I said.

She looked at the painting again.

"You seem like you're doing better," she said.

"Yeah," I said. "I guess so."

Then something changed in her face, as if she'd been snapped back into propriety. The softness that had crept in was gone.

"Anyway. I have my landscapes to work on. Peter recommended a few books for reference that should be helpful."

"I'm sure they'll be great," I said.

She turned to leave.

"Hey, Talia," I said.

"Yeah?"

"When I came to school that day and saw my locker, I was glad that you were there. I don't know what I would have done if I had been alone. So, you know, thank you."

"Oh," she said. "You're welcome."

Then I was alone in the empty room, only the sound of the hissing from the old institutional radiator disrupting the silence. I looked at my canvas. The edges could have been neater, strings hanging from the corners. I picked up the blue tube again, unscrewed the cap, and squeezed a perfect line of paint onto the palate. I wanted to leave it there like that. Wonderful in its possibility. As soon as I brushed it on the canvas, I was responsible for it, for the inevitable imperfections. My world had always been like that paint, left on a palate. That color was a passive observer. But now it wanted to make something of itself. And I was terrified.

Pick up a brush, put it in the paint, touch the canvas. That's all there was to it. I had asked to stop being afraid. And I wanted to believe that I could.

MIRA

Sunday at four p.m. the diner was nearly empty. The late-brunch crowd had finished up and it was still too early for even the most devoted early-bird special-ers. Rose had gotten Mira to join her at their regular table with the promise that she was going to "play it cool" with Ali from now on.

"I told her if she doesn't want me hanging out here, I won't hang out," Rose told Mira. "I'm not a total pathetic loser. I have other places to be."

"Liar," Mira said.

"Okay, yes, fine. Shut up."

They had been there for only half an hour when it became apparent that Rose was going to have trouble keeping her promise.

"She has been talking to them for, like, ten minutes," Rose was saying, watching Ali chat with one of the only other occupied tables from across the room.

"It's actually her job to talk to other people here, you know that, right?" Mira said.

"She doesn't have to talk to them for ten minutes. It takes, like, thirty seconds to take someone's order."

HELP save me from obsessive lesbian!!! Mira texted to Jeremy and Sebby as soon as she realized that she had been trapped.

"Hey, I've got a weird idea," Mira said. "What if you let Ali do her job and we actually get some homework done?" Their math books were lying uselessly open in front of them on the table.

"I can't think when she's over there being all cute," Rose said.

"Do I need to put blinders on you?"

"Probably."

Mira shut her textbook in defeat and went through her bag, looking to see if there was something more likely to actually get done on this afternoon. She pulled out her English notebook, opened it to a half-finished outline for yet another essay for Peter.

"I feel like Peter's trying to kill us with these papers," she said.

"I know, right?" Rose was in Peter's other American Lit class. "As if I'm going to come up with something new and super insightful to say about *Their Eyes Were Watching God* that no one's ever thought of before."

"Well, at least you don't have Talia in your class. She

basically outlines any possible paper topics just by talking, and then we're expected to come up with something she hasn't said. I think she does it on purpose."

"Oh man, Talia in Peter's class. That must be something."

"What is her story with Peter, anyway?"

They were interrupted by Ali coming over to refill their coffee cups. Rose stared at her, looking moony eyed.

"What is wrong with you?" Ali said.

"Nothing," Rose said.

Ali walked away and Rose mouthed the words "marry me" to her back. Mira threw a fry at her.

"Hey! Focus."

"What?"

"Talia and Peter. Explain."

"Oh, I don't know. She's just in love with him, I guess." She took a sip of coffee. "Talia's always been a little . . ."

"Evil?"

"No, you know, awkward. It's like there's too much going on in her brain for her to slow down and talk to us lowly normal humans. It's not worth her time. Except for Peter. I guess he's worth her time."

"Ew, can you imagine?"

"Talia's big problem is that she actually looks like she's about twelve, so he would really have to be a pedophile to go for that."

"So gross. And that night that she was over at his house . . ."

"You think Peter and Talia did it?" Rose laughed her signature cackle.

"No." Mira shook her head. "No way, right?"

"No, come on. I mean, we've been to Peter's house."

"Yeah, but it was a bunch of us."

"Listen, as fun as it is to imagine that Talia and Peter are destined to be together, I think she's just a weird girl who needs something to obsess over, and Peter's it."

"Yeah, you wouldn't know anything about that, would you?" Mira said.

Rose was already ignoring her and back to trying to get Ali's attention.

"I can see her in the kitchen," Rose said. "She's not even doing anything."

The bell on the front door jingled and Sebby came in, followed by Nick, wearing his sunglasses and trademark uninterested expression.

"Ugh," Rose said. "Why, lord, why does this afternoon need to have Nick in it?"

They slid into the booth next to Mira and Rose.

"Hey girls, what's going on?" Sebby asked, helping himself to Mira's coffee.

"Rose is stalking Ali and for some reason I have to watch," Mira said.

"I heard you like to watch," Rose said.

Mira threw another fry at her.

"Just go over there and rip her clothes off," Nick said. "Women love that."

Rose looked at Nick with disgust. "Has anyone ever told

you that your aggressive hetero man voice is really grating?"

"It's the voice God gave me. Nothing I can do about it."

"What are you even doing here?" Rose said.

"Last time I checked, this was a public place," Nick said. He grinned.

"So where's your boyfriend?" Mira asked Sebby. "I thought he might be with you."

"Who's your boyfriend?" Nick asked.

"He's not my boyfriend," Sebby said.

"Seriously, Nick, go find your own booth," Rose said. "We're doing homework here. That's something they assign to you at school." She made a face of fake concern. "Oh, I'm sorry. How can I explain school to you? It's this place where you go five days a week . . ."

"Calm down, Rosewood. I'm not here to see you. I was hanging out with Sebby," Nick said. "I do have a social life, you know. I'm not a total workaholic." He shoved some fries into his mouth. "So who's *not* your boyfriend?" he asked Sebby.

"Jeremy," Sebby said. "Jeremy is not my boyfriend."

"That kid who was here after homecoming?"

"Yes," Rose said.

Nick sat back and let out a short laugh.

"What?" Rose said. "Jeremy's great."

"Yeah, no. He seems great," Nick said, barely containing his amusement. "I just wouldn't have called that."

"What would you have called, exactly?" Rose said.

"I would have called you . . . a bitch." He laughed and got up from the table, walked toward the bathrooms in the back.

"You're an asshole and no one likes you," she called after him in a singsong voice.

"Were you really hanging out with him?" Mira asked Sebby.

"Yeah," Sebby said. "He goes to my school."

There was an awkward pause. Then Sebby stood up.

"I'll be right back," he said, and followed Nick.

Rose raised an eyebrow at Mira.

"Looks like someone's got a new buddy," she said.

Before Mira could respond, she saw Jeremy coming in the front door. She waved to him and he came over and sat down next to her.

"Hey," he said. "What's going on?"

"Literally everything," Rose said. "There is nothing that is not going on here."

"Sebby's here," Mira said.

"With Nick," Rose said, making a face.

"He seems okay," Jeremy said.

"He's a jerk," Rose said.

The three of them sat and ate fries while Jeremy drew and Mira made another futile attempt at getting some work done. Finally she pushed away her notebook, annoyed.

"Where is Sebby?" she said.

"Back there somewhere," Rose said, pointing behind them.

Mira got up.

"They're probably in the bathroom," Rose said.

Mira walked to the back of the diner where the bathrooms

were, walked to the men's-room door and listened. She could hear Sebby talking inside. She pushed open the door and walked in.

He was sitting on the sink and Nick was using one of the urinals, facing away from her.

"Girl in the boys' room," Sebby said.

"Came for a free show?" Nick said.

"You've been in here for almost half an hour," Mira said.

Nick finished and zipped up his fly.

"A man's allowed to take his time in the bathroom, darlin'," he said. He walked past them and pushed the door open, went back into the other room.

"Ew, do guys really not wash their hands?"

"I do, but I'm very neat," Sebby said. "Bodily fluids have their time and place."

He hopped off the sink.

"What were you doing in here?" Mira said.

"Nothing," Sebby said. "Just hanging out."

"With Nick?"

Sebby turned on the water, started washing his hands.

"Yes. What's wrong with that?" he asked.

"I just don't know him."

"That doesn't mean there's something wrong with him."

Sebby hit the air blower and held his hands underneath to dry them.

"Is everything okay with you?" Mira yelled over the sound of the air.

Sebby waited until it turned off to answer.

"Yeah, of course," he said. "Why wouldn't things be okay?"

"You're just acting weird."

The door opened suddenly and a man started to come in, looked at Mira and apologized, embarrassed, then looked again at the sign on the door.

"She was just leaving," Sebby said to the man, taking Mira's hand and pushing past him.

"Sebby," Mira said, stopping him outside the bathroom door, "I'm serious."

"I'm fine," Sebby said.

"Would you tell me if you weren't?"

"How could I avoid it?" He started walking back to the table.

"That isn't an answer," Mira said, following him.

When they got back to the table, Nick stood up.

"I gotta get out of here," he said to Sebby. "You coming?"

"Yeah, sure," Sebby said. He turned to the table. "See you guys later."

Mira sat down in her spot next to Jeremy and they watched through the window as Nick and Sebby got into Nick's car.

"Everything okay?" Jeremy asked.

"Yeah," Mira said. "Sure. Everything's okay."

JEREMY

It was Dave's idea to invite Sebby and Mira to come and stay with us at the house in Ptown for part of the summer. My dad's general hatred of winter usually meant that he started talking about our summer plans in February, and this year was no exception.

"I've got that extra vacation time coming, and I just think we should get up there as soon as we can," he was saying.

"It's still three months away, Dad," I said.

"Yes, but if we spend the next three months planning the summer, the time will go by so much more quickly."

"Somehow I don't think that's true."

"I should go up after you so we overlap a little and Jeremy can have more time up there," Dave said. "Unless your sister wants to come and stay again."

"I can stay alone at the house," I said. "You don't have to plan to be there with me."

"No you can't," my dad said.

"I don't need Aunt Patty babysitting me."

"I think Pat is happy for the vacation," Dad said. "And if you want to stay up longer, you're going to need company. You already spend all of your time alone during the day up there. You're not going home to an empty house."

What I couldn't say was that being away from Mira and Sebby for only ten days over Christmas had felt unbearable. I couldn't imagine not seeing them for most of the summer. But to say this to my dads would be unfair. I was lucky that we had a place to go for the summer. Was I that ungrateful to say that I would rather be with my friends than at the beach?

"I'll just come back when you guys do," I said, hoping that I was being subtle. "I don't need to stay there longer."

"What about if your friends come up?" Dave said.

I looked up from my plate.

"Really?"

Dave looked at Dad.

"Pat would still have to stay with you," Dave said. "We're not leaving you without an adult. But there's no reason why the kids can't use the extra bedroom."

Dad looked at me.

"Would you like that?"

I couldn't believe it. They were so excited by the idea of me having friends that they were willing to hand over the summer house to us.

"Are you serious?" I said.

"Sure," Dad said. "Why not?"

"Yeah," I said. "Yes. Um, I'll ask them."

I had too much homework to do after dinner to go over to Mira's, and I felt this was news that had to be told in person, so I sent her and Sebby a cryptic text and said we had to meet at her house after school the next day.

Part of me was worried that they wouldn't be as excited as I was about the idea. Maybe I was blowing it up into something bigger than it was. I couldn't help but think that it would act as a kind of symbolic solidification of our friendship if I could bring them back to the place where they had gone together.

It was nearly ten o'clock and I was sitting on my bed drawing sketches for my painting when my dad walked by the door of my room. The faint sounds of the TV were floating up from downstairs, where Dave was getting his nightly fix of Judge Judy.

"Hey," Dad said, stopping in my doorway.

"Hey," I said.

"Do you like that idea about your friends coming to the house?"

"Yeah," I said. "It would be fun."

He glanced down at my sketchbook, where many versions of a boy's face were looking up at me.

"So, are you and Sebby . . . an item?" he asked.

"An item?"

"You know what I mean. Are you going out? Is he your boyfriend?"

I shook my head.

"I don't think he's my boyfriend," I said.

"You don't think?"

"No," I said. "He's just . . . He's Sebby."

"Well, if you ever have anything you want to talk about . . ."

"I don't, Dad," I said.

"Okay. Sorry. Forget I said anything." He backed away from the door making joking peace signs with his hands.

The next afternoon in Mira's room I told her and Sebby about Dave's idea. It was just the three of us alone together, something that was becoming increasingly rare. These days when we were together we were in the art studio, or at the diner with Rose. And nights at the diner usually ended with Nick arriving and Sebby leaving with him soon after.

Sebby was staying over at my house two or three nights a week now, always texting me around one a.m. to come and let him in, always gone before I woke up in the morning. The last time he'd stayed he had been even more jittery than usual, could barely lie still in the bed next to me. This was a different boy from the one who appeared in the daytime, the person that he was around Mira. And I didn't know what to do with the fact that his visits seemed to implicitly ask for my continued silence. I was keeping his secrets now, too.

But with the three of us together things felt back to normal. We could come back to the way that it was supposed to be.

I brought them a picture of the beach and the house, in case they needed convincing. They didn't.

"For real?" Mira said.

"It's not a big house or anything," I said, looking at the picture, "but it's right by the bay."

Sebby got up and did a dance on the bed.

"Summer in Ptown!"

"Do you think you could go?" Mira asked him.

"Yeah, what is Tilly going to do?" he said. "Force me to stay and ferry the kids to church camp?"

"She could try."

Sebby rolled his eyes. "I am master of my own destiny."

"Do you think you could come?" I asked Mira.

"I think so," she said. "At least for part of the summer. It would be really fun."

"First stop is the Governor Bradford," Sebby said. "I have so many new songs to debut."

MIRA

Mira's dad was home for a rare family dinner the next night, and Mira was making a good show of helping her mom set the table, getting the food out of the oven, filling the water glasses. She needed them in a good mood if she was going to bring up the summer.

Talk over dinner predictably turned to the topic of Julie and some new professor she had this semester who they felt wasn't giving her a fair grade.

"She'll be fine," Mira said. "It'll probably be good for her to get a B. It'll help her build character."

"Of course she should get a B if she's doing B-level work," her dad said, "but I've read her papers for the class and those are A papers."

Mira tried her best not to roll her eyes. She couldn't believe her sister still emailed their parents her papers, as if they were finger paintings from kindergarten and she was a little kid announcing, "Look what I can do!"

"She should just speak to the professor," her mom said.

"It's an insult that she should have to," her dad said. "She's obviously too advanced for that class and the professor feels threatened by her."

Julie was a nice, safe topic for her parents. They both thought that she was amazing, so the only thing up for debate was how the rest of the world was or was not adequately agreeing with them.

Mira waited for an appropriate lull in the Julie lovefest to bring up the summer. "So. Jeremy invited me to go to his family's beach house with him this summer," she said. "I guess they have a nice place by a bay."

Her mom looked at her dad.

"Well. That was very generous of him," her mother said.

Her father cleared his throat. He always did this when he was getting ready to say something significant. Mira had never seen him in action in the courtroom, but she imagined that there must be a lot of throat clearing.

"We've actually been meaning to talk to you about the summer," he said. "We were thinking you might want to spend some time catching up with the rest of your class."

"What do you mean, catching up?"

"Well, if you make up classes for the next two summers, you might be able to graduate when you were supposed to," her mom said.

"You mean go to summer school?"

Her mother looked a little nervous, as if they might be missing the opportunity to make this sound like a great idea.

"If you want to get into a top college, you're going to have to show them that you worked hard to make up for all that lost time last year," her dad said.

Mira looked down at her dinner plate. Tonight's offering was flavorless fish with flavorless vegetables and plain rice. A dietary-restrictions special. Her stomach suddenly started churning.

"So you've already planned my next two summers?"

"I know college seems like a long time away, but you have to start thinking about these things now," her mom said. "And you're doing so well. We just want to see you continue to move in the right direction."

"But I don't care about all of that."

"Well, I assume you want to go to at least a good liberal arts school," her dad said, "and with your record, getting into anything other than a state school is going to be difficult. St. Francis can help with college guidance, but keep in mind that you're now in competition with everyone at St. Francis for those same schools. They can only take so many people from each prep school. Some people are of the mind that it's actually more difficult to get into the top schools from a private school for that very reason."

"So then why didn't I stay at MouVi? If college is the most important thing?"

"You tell us, Mira," her father said, his lawyer voice now

fully engaged. His I-have-something-to-prove voice.

"Okay, let's just take a minute here," her mother said, sensing that the conversation was not quite going as planned.

"And what if I don't want to go to a liberal arts school? Maybe I want to go to art school."

"Art school?" her father said. "No. Absolutely not. If you want to study art you can do it in liberal arts. You're too young to be deciding those things anyway. You can't be limiting yourself at this point in your life."

"I bet you didn't say that to Julie when she said she wanted to be a lawyer when she was, like, twelve."

"Art school is not an option, Mira," he said. "End of discussion. You will spend the summer catching up so that you will be in a strong position to apply to colleges."

Mira stared at her plate. Why did he always do this? Act like she didn't have a say in her own life? She could feel the tears starting behind her eyes.

"I don't understand what you want from me," Mira said. "I'm doing okay. So I'm going to be punished by having my summers taken away from me? I should be able to have a fun summer."

"I think you probably had enough fun when you spent nine months not going to school," her dad said.

"You think that was fun?" Mira said in disbelief. "You think depression was, like, a laugh riot?"

"I think getting to spend all your time doing nothing with your friends is probably something that's very easy to get used to, and that's not going to be acceptable anymore."

"Maybe there's some room for negotiation here," her mom said. "I'm sure there's a weekend when you could visit Jeremy."

Mira stood up. She had to get away from the table.

"This is so unfair," she said.

"No. This is not unfair," her father said. "We have been very patient with you, and now that you are better, you are going to need to deal with the consequences of that missed time."

Mira looked at him in disbelief.

"Consequences? Seriously? You realize you are basically punishing me for something that I have no control over."

"Obviously you have some control over it," her father said.

"Mira . . ." Her mom tried to stop her, but she was already out of the room, up the stairs, and in her bed.

"Mira!"

She could hear her mother calling her from downstairs. She put a pillow over her head so she wouldn't have to listen anymore.

Mira hadn't been on the roof in years. She could climb out her bedroom window and get out onto the lip over the garage. Her mom used to let her do this, and then at some point she decided it was too dangerous. Maybe as Mira got bigger. She lost that dexterity of childhood. An ability to adapt to different surfaces. Why, now, would it be harder to catch herself? Broken bones fuse back together quickly on children. Evolution wants them to survive.

Now it was two a.m. and she was perched on the sloped shingles, arms around her knees. Her parents' bedroom was on the other side of the house. They wouldn't see her out here. It was cold, but she wrapped herself in the oversized sweater coat that had been her favorite in sixth grade. She used to put the hood up in class and hide inside it. She brought it out here now to ask it some questions. It was the past, and the clear night sky and bracing cold felt an awful lot like the future. She wondered if she could get them to come to some kind of a consensus on things.

She knew her dad didn't believe that there was anything wrong with her. He thought depression was for people without real problems who didn't understand the value of hard work. He was the first one in his family to go to college, his parents taking multiple jobs to make sure he had enough money to make it through. Mira had all the opportunities that they had worked so hard for, and she was squandering them.

But wasn't the story more complicated than that? Her father had a younger brother who killed himself after high school. No one ever talked about that. What if that was a legacy too? A kind of cellular depression passed down through the ages. Maybe her father was so scared that she was the same way that he wouldn't even consider it. Or else he thought his brother had been weak too.

Mira couldn't stop feeling like she was the thing rotting away at the center of this family.

She had been home from the hospital for only a week when she and Sebby ran away. Her dad had been so careful with her during that week. Her mother was fussing over everything, but he seemed to have decided that he was going to be the calm one. The level-headed one. He was at dinner every night. After they ate, they would watch old movies together in the family room. Mira would fall asleep on the couch, and he would carry her up to her bed like she was a little kid again. And then she ran away with Sebby, and when she got back everything was different.

It was her mother who met the state troopers halfway and drove Mira and Sebby back in silence, her dad's car pulled by a tow truck behind them. It was days before Mira even saw her father after that. He seemed to be needed at work until almost midnight every night that week. And when she did see him he was distant, no longer casual, kind dad. He seemed to be angry with her for not rewarding his patience. For not recognizing that "casual, kind dad" did not come easily to him. Her running away had been a betrayal of their attempt to try to put their family back together. She had abandoned them in a moment when they needed to be reassured that she was okay, that she would not try to hurt herself again.

After that, her parents had fallen into these new roles, which seemed to have now solidified into their new life. Mom as fussing caretaker, Dad as distant disapprover. They did not make her go back to Mountain View. She was allowed to spend her time with Sebby. But even that felt like a result of them giving up on her, or at least needing a break from trying to force her to be who they needed her to be. Going to St. F in the fall had been a kind of test, to see if she really was a lost cause after all or if this was just a phase. And unfortunately, passing the test meant to them that she should be doing more. That it was safe for them to start pushing her again.

She knew as soon as Jeremy invited her and Sebby that it wasn't going to happen. She hadn't even bothered mentioning where this house was located. A return trip to Ptown, unsupervised by her parents, would not be in the cards.

So did this mean the boys would go without her? Would they really leave her like that? She gathered the sweater tighter around her. Could she survive a summer alone, knowing that they were together?

Everything was feeling up in the air again, and this was not a place where her brain did well. She had always been afraid of the dark, her mind racing to try to stay one step ahead of the inevitable, invisible thing lurking out there. As if a person was walking behind her too closely, breath she could feel on the back of her neck.

This late at night was when she got her best ideas. Thinking about her project, she wanted to write down all of her secret fears and tuck them into the sewn pockets so that they dragged on the ground behind her, picking up dirt and earth as she went. She could sit in her sewing corner in her room and work on it, give up on sleeping for the night and give in to the idea that this restless energy wanted her to use it. But then she remembered that she could work all night and the dawn would bring with it the reality that none of it mattered. She was foolish to think that it did.

This was the essence of the depression. If nothing meant anything, there were no choices. When she fell into the depths of tiredness she was deep inside a lack of possibility. She felt like a heap of meat tied to this planet for no reason. A foggy dream of a future where she could spend all her time doing something that she loved, rather than fulfilling duties out of obligation, was nothing more than a fantasy.

She pulled the hood of the sweater around her face and asked for a sign. She remembered in the hospital the girl who thought that she was being sent messages through her soup, her cereal—anything that came with a spoon had to be examined for spiritual content before she would eat it. She was insane, of course. But what if she was just tuned to the wrong frequency? Buddhist monks adjust their brains like radios to the waves of the universe. What if the insane are too raw to know which stations are real and which are just confused static?

She and Sebby were supposed to keep each other tuned to the right frequency, like twin receptors, each receiving noise that only made sense when combined. But when the rest of the world imposed, it got harder to hear any of it. She could feel him pulling away. Keeping secrets. That wasn't how this was supposed to go.

Late at night she sometimes felt that she could hear the messages on her own, something telling her that, if she just listened hard enough, she could do anything. That it could be important.

Her little life. The things that she had to offer. She could hear the night sky telling her that she was not small, she was as big as the whole universe. Maybe the universe itself was a sign. It was trying to tell her that she was it too.

JEREMY

Two days after I told them about Ptown, Mira texted me and
Sebby. Meet me at St. F bench in an hour. Wear butch shoes.

It was a Saturday, and the school was quiet except for the
sounds of preseason baseball practice coming from one of the
fields in the back. Sebby was sitting on the bench when I got
there. I hadn't seen him in a few days. We could see Mira making her way down the block.

"Hi," I said to Sebby.

"Hi," he said.

"What's going on?" I asked.

"I don't know," he said. "I got the same text as you."

I sat down on the bench next to him, looked at my hands. I
felt awkward suddenly. How was that possible? Wasn't this the
same boy who slept next to me? My tiny twin bed somehow
now felt too big when he wasn't there.

"Are you okay?" I asked Sebby.

But Mira was there before he could answer. Close up we saw that she was wearing some unstylish hiking boots that were caked with mud.

"Those are definitely butch," Sebby said. He and I were both wearing sneakers.

"They're my sister's. From some rainforest trek or something. Come on." She started walking away from the school and we followed her.

At the end of the street that St. F was on, past Peter's house and before it crossed over into the next town, there was the entrance to the nature reserve, a winding path that led up a hill into a county park.

It took us almost an hour to follow the path up to the top, Sebby complaining most of the way that we should have just made Rose drive us.

"We have to earn it," Mira said.

At the top we were rewarded with the view. It was the highest point between there and the city, and on a clear day you could see the entire Manhattan skyline. In the spring, warring bridal parties jockeyed for the best spots for pictures along the low stone wall. But on this day it was sparsely populated. Only the most committed dog walkers and joggers were braving the late-winter chill.

Mira put a quarter in one of the viewers and looked through. The wind whipped her blue coat around her. Sebby leaned out on the wall, looking below us.

"What do you see?" I asked Mira.

"People," she said. "People who have escaped."

"You can't really see people," Sebby said.

"I can," she said. "And I can see the future. Oh look. I see us. There we are. We look great."

She stepped back from the viewer, away from the edge.

"Come on," she said.

She led us away from the trail, away from the parked cars and dog walkers and panoramic view, into the woods. The dead branches and leaves crunched under our feet, as we trekked through this place that was left to what little true nature still existed out here.

"How far are we going?" Sebby asked.

"Just a little farther," Mira said.

We watched her make her way through the brush ahead of us. Then she stopped.

"Here," she said when we reached her.

It was a round patch of dirt and leaves surrounded by sections of fallen trees. We stood on either side of her and looked at the ground.

"What are we going to do?" I asked.

She thought for a minute, then said, "Help me clear it off."

We watched her get down on her hands and knees, instantly dirtying the skirt she was wearing, and start pushing aside dead leaves and sticks with her gloved hands.

"Are you serious?" Sebby said.

"Yes," Mira said, looking up at him.

We watched her for another minute. Then Sebby and I got

down on the ground and helped her. We worked until we had a smooth patch of dirt in front of us.

"Now what?" Sebby said.

Mira looked at me. "You have to cast a spell for us, Jeremy," she said.

"Me?"

"Draw us. The three of us together. This summer."

I looked at Sebby. He nodded at me.

I went back into the woods behind us and found a sharp stick, came back, and knelt down next to the two of them in the dirt. I drew three figures sitting on the dock, the water, and the beach, and another figure lying on a towel.

"Who's that?" Sebby asked.

"The man in the pink Speedo," I said.

I drew long curly hair on one of the figures on the dock. Short hair on the other two.

I turned to Mira. "How's that?" I said.

She examined the drawing. It looked like something a cave-man might have carved into stone.

"It's good," she said.

"Now what?" Sebby said.

"Now we make it come true," she said. She lay down in the dirt next to the drawing. The sun was getting lower and rays angled down into our tiny clearing. Sebby lay with his head on her stomach and motioned for me to complete the circle. I got down and rested my head on his chest, making sure to keep the drawing in the triangle of dirt between the three of us. Sebby's hand found the top of my head and he left it there. I closed my eyes, feeling him breathing under me.

The three of us stayed like that for hours, until the sun had dipped so low that I was worried about finding our way back.

"Maybe we'll just stay at your summer house forever," Mira was saying. "We'll live there and eat saltwater taffy and ride our bikes down the street in the middle of the night when everyone is sleeping."

"It gets too cold in the winter," I said.

"Not in my fantasy," she said. "Always summer."

"Eternal summer," Sebby said.

The sun's departure felt like the promise of spring fading away. But lying there with them in the cold, I thought I could feel the ground softening under us, waking up to the call of our spell.

We were three bodies that didn't know the end of each other, breathing together. We knew that we would have to go back. Kick off the leaves and become three separate people who would go off into the world, forced to breathe on our own. But not yet. Not quite yet.

SEBBY

It was early, six a.m., when you woke up in Jeremy's room, lifted his hand off your chest gently, and let yourself out from under the covers. The sun was coming up earlier on these spring days, and hints of the sunrise were creeping in along the edges of the shade on the window. You glanced back at Jeremy still sleeping before you left the room. You were always amazed at how peaceful he looked. You were jealous of that peace.

You closed the bedroom door quietly behind you. His dads always left a light on downstairs, so the hallway was brighter. You made your way to the stairs, feeling a little shaky. Nick took you to a party last night and you did more than you were used to. But you liked feeling that testing those limits was within your control. You got to decide how much.

These days you often found yourself thinking about the hospital, about lying in bed after the first surgery, when they hadn't yet realized that something was wrong and they would need to go back in. Remembering how you would cry in pain through the night, ringing the buzzer for the nurse so many times that one of them finally took it away from you. They would not give you more morphine. Well, now you got to make the call. Of how much you needed.

It was after the second surgery that you were done. You understood all too well by that point that no one there was on your side. There was no one sitting and keeping watch through the night in a chair while your roommate's TV blared on. When you did sleep, you saw your mother in your dreams. You thought you heard her say that she would forgive you. That you had suffered enough.

So you bribed an orderly, offered him whatever he wanted in exchange for enough Percocet to just end it once and for all. But a vigilant nurse saw that the pills were missing and the boy said you blackmailed him, hoping to save his job. It was close enough to the truth. Didn't really matter at that point.

"Yes, I wanted the pills," you told them. "Yes, I want to kill myself. Yes, I understand what I'm saying."

It took them a while to believe that you weren't kidding. You had always been so amusing.

The irony was that they had great drugs in psych. Beautiful hazy drugs that dulled your brain and made you stop caring about any pain that was left. You would have stayed there if you could, ridden out the years until eighteen on a lovely cloud of sedation. But it was only a temporary reprieve. Out here in the real world you were expected to be awake. To deal with things.

And that was where the coke came in. Pot was lovely but coke made you feel capable, like it was all possible again. Like you weren't fucking up absolutely everything.

You told yourself that you kept coming to Jeremy's after these nights with Nick because you didn't want Tilly to hear you coming in the house so late. But you knew the truth was that the same part of you that could have stayed in that hospital forever wanted someone calm to bring you back down. And he would let you in, no questions asked.

As early as it was on this morning, you usually tried to be gone before this. Tilly didn't expect to see you before bed at night since she was asleep by nine thirty, but if you weren't there in the morning, she would start asking questions, and that was the last thing that you needed right now.

You made your way down the stairs, careful to avoid the spots that creaked, and headed toward the front door. As you passed the kitchen you saw another light on. Dave was sitting at the table, a cup of coffee in front of him. You stopped.

"Hi, Sebby," he said.

"Oh, hi," you said. "Jeremy let me crash last night. I hope that's okay."

"Sure," Dave said. "You want some coffee?"

You thought about just going, but it seemed better to try to pretend that this was a normal moment, Dave catching you sneaking out of his kid's room at six a.m.

"Okay," you said.

He nodded and got up, poured you a cup.

"Black is fine," you said.

He put the mug down on the little breakfast table across from him. You went to it and sat down in the chair.

"You doing okay, Sebby?" Dave asked.

"Everyone's always asking me that," you said. You tried to smile, make it a joke. Your head hurt a little too much to make it convincing.

"Isn't it better than people not asking?"

"I guess." You took a sip of coffee. It was good. It helped.

"So?" Dave said.

"I'm fine," you said.

"Everything okay at home?"

"Home is . . ." You tried to think of something clever. It was not coming easily today. "Fine. Home is fine."

"You've been staying over here a lot, haven't you?"

You looked up from your mug. Caught.

"I'm a light sleeper," Dave said. "It's all right. You don't have to sneak around. We would rather know that you're here."

"Okay," you said.

Dave took a sip of coffee.

"I've been wanting to talk to you, actually," he said.

"Okay," you said again.

"Did Jeremy tell you that I'm an alcoholic?" he said.

You shook your head.

"I'm in AA. I've been sober for twenty-two years now. I started drinking in high school."

"Okay." You only seemed to have one word today and this was it.

Dave took another sip of his coffee before continuing.

"I just want you to know that I'm here to talk about anything," he said. "If you ever need someone to talk to."

Your head was starting to hurt again. You stood up.

"I need to go," you said.

"Okay," Dave said.

"Sorry," you said. "I'm fine, though."

You left him sitting there at the table with the two coffee cups, went out the front door. It banged shut behind you. No point in trying to be quiet now.

The sun was up. Stephanie was probably awake and would notice that you weren't in your bed, so you would have to make up some lie about going for an early-morning run. Would Tilly believe you were on a fitness kick all of a sudden?

You started running just to back up your story. It felt terrible and then you liked how terrible it felt and then you went faster, as fast as you could pound your feet down onto the pavement across town, back to your neighborhood, where you were going to spend the next two years lying any way you knew how. Lying like breathing, because those were the only two things allowing you to survive.

JEREMY

Molly Stern's parents were going out of town the first weekend in May, leaving their house in the care of their children, and Molly had decided to throw the "biggest, baddest party" St. Francis had ever seen.

"There is no way that we are missing this party," Rose informed us. We were all working in the art studio after school. I had convinced the janitor that we could be trusted to stay late, Sebby brought us coffee, and we were holed up with the intention of finishing our projects so we could install the exhibit the next week and have it up for the last month of school.

"If homecoming was any indication of what that girl is capable of, then this is going to be the show of the century." Rose said. She was hot-gluing her many cardboard pieces together, periodically crying out in pain as she accidentally glued her fingers instead.

"It's just going to be Sarah and Anna throwing themselves

at upper-classman boys who will go anywhere there's alcohol," Mira said.

"And you don't think that has any entertainment value?"

"Yeah, if your goal is to see JV cheerleaders flash their boobs."

"Are you just hoping to see some boobs, Rose?" Sebby asked. "Is that what this is about?"

"Oh yeah," Rose said. "I've got a one-track mind and it's all about JV boobs."

"Dirty, dirty girl," Sebby said. He rolled some of Mira's extra fabric into two balls and shoved them into his T-shirt. "How about these?"

"You're not really my type, hon. No offense. And anyway, this party is going to be hilarious."

"We'll be the only ones who show up," Mira said. "We'll end up playing Twister with Molly all night."

"Awesome," Rose said. "I love Twister."

"I'll go," Sebby said. "Molly and I are total BFFs."

"Excellent. Jeremy?" Rose turned to me. I was sitting at a drafting table sketching, thinking about the details I still had to add to my hidden painting.

"What?"

"You coming?"

I looked at Sebby. He was wrapping a piece of red silk around his neck.

"Does this look ghastly?" He turned to Mira. "Do I look very ghastly right now?"

"You always look ghastly," she said.

I hadn't seen Sebby in a couple of days, since the last night he'd stayed at my house. He had shown up later than usual. It was almost three when I got his text and went downstairs to let him in. He lay down with me, but an hour later I woke to hearing him in the bathroom down the hall, throwing up. I wanted to go to him but I was afraid to make any more noise, afraid for my dads to hear more than one person walking around. When he came back to bed, he was shaking, and I held him while he sweated through his clothes, neither of us sleeping much.

He hadn't been responding to my texts since then. And now here he was with us again in the art studio, acting like nothing was wrong.

"Jeremy?" Rose said.

"What?"

"Molly's party. In or out?"

"I'll go if you guys are going," I said, looking at Mira.

Mira looked at Sebby. "You really want to go?"

"Yeah, why not? I missed out on seeing Molly barf at homecoming."

Mira sighed in defeat. "All right. I'll go. But I'm not going to like it."

"You better be careful with those self-fulfilling prophecies, Mira," Rose said, setting a finished piece on top of her cardboard tower.

Peter came in to check on all of us before he left for the day and to go over some of the details of the exhibit with me.

"I haven't seen your project yet, Jeremy," he said.

"I want it to be a surprise," I said.

"Well, I think it's really going to be a great show. If you guys finish up, we can start installing it next week."

"I'm not going to finish in time," Mira said. "I have a terrible assistant."

"The worst," Sebby said, making himself a turban out of some fabric. "You should fire him."

"I was thinking," Peter said, "we could have a little gallery opening. I can get some sparkling apple cider, cheese, and crackers."

"Fun!" Rose said.

"You guys can invite your families," Peter said.

Mira rolled her eyes.

"Or not," Peter said.

"Families are lame, Peter," Sebby said.

"Well, either way," he said. "I'm really proud of you all. This looks great."

We worked for another hour after Peter left us, until the janitor finally came in and said he had to close up the building. The girls went to their lockers to get their stuff and I headed outside with Sebby. Rose was going to drive us all to the diner.

Sebby leaned up against Rose's car and took out a pack of cigarettes. He lit one, inhaled deeply.

"You're smoking?" I said. I had never seen him with a cigarette before.

"I am, in this moment," he said, his voice cold.

Why was it always like this with him? Why did it always go back to this? As if suddenly I had done something wrong and just needed to wait things out until I was forgiven.

"Do you really want to go to Molly's party?" I asked him, hoping a change of subject would help.

"Sure," he said. "Why not?"

There was a moment of awkward silence. I looked to see if the girls were coming.

"Did you say something to Dave about me?" Sebby said suddenly.

I turned to him.

"What? No. What do you mean?"

"He talked to me. The last time I left your place. He was already up. He knows I've been staying there."

"I didn't tell him," I said.

"He seemed to know some other stuff too."

I shook my head. "We haven't talked about anything."

"No?"

"No. Why, what did he say?"

Sebby took a long drag off his cigarette.

"Nothing," he said finally.

The girls came out the back door then, school bags in tow.

"All right," Rose said. "Operation Make My Ex Go to Molly's Party with Me begins!"

"Oh no, is that why we're going to the diner?" Mira said.

"Also fries," Rose said. "I can multitask."

MIRA

Mira got dressed for Molly's party on Saturday night, carefully picking out her ensemble. It was almost warm enough to not wear leggings. The transition from leggings season to leg warmers and knee-highs season to bare-legs season was always exciting.

For a high school party, an ironic nod to authority might be nice. She picked out a green plaid dress that looked like something a kindergarten teacher might have worn in 1985. She would take a risk with the weather and go for the leg warmers. Finish the ensemble with a gold belt and her lucky one-dollar cowboy boots.

Jeremy was coming to walk over to the party with her. He had offered to pick her up and cryptically mentioned that he "needed to talk" to her. Mira had a feeling that it was about Sebby. Something was off with him, and she wasn't sure what to do to make things better. Magic words and ceremonies had always been their solution before, to fix their unfixable problems. What else did they have?

For a boy who never seemed to stop talking, she knew that Sebby did not want to talk about these things. She hated how he could turn himself off when he wanted to, that he could so easily make her feel like she was on the wrong side.

She sat down at her vanity to fix her hair, looked at her face in the mirror. It had been a long time since she had really looked at herself. She looked too alone, suddenly. She wished that Sebby was here now. That they could be together before facing the rest of the world. That was how it was supposed to be. Recharging their batteries.

In the hospital they used to spend their time lying in one bed, sitting squished into one chair in the rec room. The other patients called them the Siamese Twins.

She put her head in her hands and tried not to cry.

Don't let this be a thing, Mira. This doesn't have to be a thing tonight. Just have a nice time like a normal teenager.

She looked up at herself again, picked up some bobby pins.

Jeremy would be there soon. She wasn't alone. It would be okay.

JEREMY

Mira was waiting on the front porch for me when I got to her house. She had put her hair up in a mess of curls on the top of her head, and she had on her lucky one-dollar blue coat and cowboy boots.

"Hey," I said. "You look nice."

"Thanks," she said.

I suddenly felt like I was picking her up for a date.

"So, Sebby and Rose are meeting us there, I guess," I said.

"Yeah," she said. "It's this way."

We started walking down the sidewalk in the direction of Molly's house.

"Should we take bets on whether Rose finally convinced Ali to come?" she said.

"I'm going to say no," I said.

"You're such a pessimist, Jeremy," she said. "Don't you believe in true love?"

"I believe that Rose comes on a little strong."

"Maybe Ali secretly likes that," Mira said. "Or else we need to find someone else for Rose to obsess over."

"Not a lot of options for her at St. F," I said.

"Poor Rose. The only lesbian in the village."

We walked the rest of that block in silence. I had rehearsed what I wanted to say on my way over, but now it all sounded so stupid in my head.

"Did you want to talk to me about something?" Mira said finally.

"Yeah," I said. "Yes."

"About Sebby?"

I stopped and turned to her.

"Something's wrong," I said.

"I know," she said.

"He's been staying at my house. He comes over after he's with Nick. And he's been . . . kind of messed up lately. And I guess the other morning Dave said something to him. I don't know what, but I think maybe Dave heard him throwing up."

Mira shook her head.

"I don't know what to do," I said.

"There's nothing we can do tonight," she said. "We're not going to stage an intervention at Molly's party."

"Maybe I'm making a big deal out of nothing," I said.

"No," she said. "You're not."

We kept walking, finally reaching Molly's block, where it was immediately obvious which house was hers. She had made sure to get the word out that one of her older brothers would be buying alcohol in bulk from Costco for the event, and people were now streaming in the front door.

Mira and I stood in the driveway for a minute. She looked at me.

"We'll figure it out," she said. "Okay? We just have to keep him close to us."

"Okay," I said.

Inside the front hall we found Molly wearing a tight black dress with an oval cutout between her boobs.

"Omigod, Mira!" She squealed and pulled Mira into a giant hug as if they hadn't seen each other in years. "I'm so glad you came." She turned to some uninterested upper classmen lounging on the stairs behind her and declared, "Mira lives right down the street," as if it were the most amazing thing imaginable.

"Looks like a pretty successful party so far," Mira said.

"So fun." Molly was teetering on her stilettos, so excited to be the most popular girl in school for one night that she was overdosing on joy. She was also about five shots ahead of everyone else.

"And you know Jeremy," Mira said.

"Oh, yeah, hi!" Molly said, awkwardly hugging me.

"Hi, Molly," I said.

"Drinks in the kitchen," Molly instructed us and a few people who had come in behind us. "My brother went crazy at Costco."

The island in the middle of the kitchen looked like it

belonged to an alcoholic giant. Oversized bottles of whatever Molly's brother could get ahold of were interspersed with gallon jugs of soda and juice. Tequila, vodka, Bailey's, gin—he had played his own version of supermarket sweep. If you can get out of the store before the cashier guesses that you're buying for a hundred underage drinkers, you get to keep it.

Mira turned to me.

"What'll you have?" she asked.

"Whatever," I said.

"Bartender," she said to an invisible person, "a Jeremy special." She grabbed two plastic cups. "Coming right up," she replied to herself.

The Jeremy special ended up being an elaborate mix of fruit juices and vodka, and wasn't half bad.

"I think you have a successful bartending career ahead of you," I said as we made our way into the living room.

"Later I'll make you the Sebby special," she said. "It's used to remove paint from cars."

Some of the girls had started an impromptu dance floor in the corner of the living room, sending flirty looks at a group of boys from the football team. Sarah was holding court on the couch, watching over them.

"Let's say hi to Sarah," Mira said to me.

"Really?" I said.

"If we're going to do this party right, we have to mingle with cheerleaders," Mira said. "I believe I saw it in a John Hughes movie."

She went and sat down next to Sarah on the couch. I followed reluctantly.

"Hey, Sarah," Mira said. "How's it going?"

Sarah was perched on the edge of the couch, her legs crossed under a silver miniskirt.

"Fine," she said.

"Hi, Sarah," I said.

"Hi," she said.

"No dancing for you?" Mira asked. Anna was enthusiastically attempting to make a duet with a lamp look sexy.

"Molly has the absolute worst taste in music," Sarah said. She was holding a real wine glass, not a red plastic cup from the stack in the kitchen.

"Where did you get that?" Mira asked.

"Molly's dad always leaves the liquor cabinet open," she said. "I think he does it on purpose. Maybe he thinks it'll chill her out or something if she drinks. Fat chance." She took a sip.

"You don't seem like you're having fun," Mira said.

"Oh, no. Loads of fun." Sarah plastered on a smile and raised her glass in the direction of the football players, who were now watching her instead of Anna.

Mira's phone beeped. She took it out of her pocket and checked it.

"They're running late," she said to me. "Should we just go?"

"I don't know," I said.

"If you leave now you'll miss everything," Sarah said. "This party's just getting started."

Mira raised an eyebrow at me.

"How can we say no to that?" she said.

We distracted ourselves by making another drink in the kitchen. This one involved some elaborate parsley garnish that Mira found in the fridge.

"Let's call it . . ." She thought for a minute. "The Peter."

"Isn't that kind of dirty?" I said.

"It is dirty—I put olive juice in it."

I laughed.

"Isn't that weird?" she said. "To have your name be Peter? Like, 'Hi, I'm Peter, meet my peter.'"

Drink number one had gone down a little too easily, and tipsiness was setting in quickly. We were finding ourselves to be much more amusing than anyone else would.

"I do not want to meet Peter's peter," I said.

"No?" Mira smiled. "You and Peter never had 'special time' at his place?"

"No. Come on."

"Listen, Peter's cute," she said. "No one would blame you."

"You think he's cute?" I asked, sipping my second drink.

"Of course I do. That's, like, a fact. There's no debate about that. I mean, I don't think he's cute the way that Talia thinks he's cute, because that would be psycho, but yeah, he's a cutie."

Suddenly she froze and looked behind me. I turned and saw Talia standing there, just having emerged from the hallway. Her face was completely white.

"Oh, hi, Talia," I said awkwardly.

She pushed past us, past the other people in the kitchen, and ran out the front door.

Mira looked at me.

"Shit," she said. "She heard all of that, didn't she?"

"It seems like it."

"Oh, shit. What should I do?"

"I don't know."

"I mean, she knows everyone knows that she loves Peter. It's not like it's a big secret."

"I guess."

Mira put her drink down. "Okay, well, I'll just apologize when I see her at school. Oh man, I'm such an idiot. But who expected that girl to come to a party like this?"

"Well, no one would expect to see us at a party like this," I said, "so I guess anything's possible."

We downed our second drinks quickly in an attempt to forget the stricken look on Talia's face, and started working on our third concoction when the front door opened, and in walked Sebby, Rose, and Ali.

Mira hit me in the arm.

"Ali!" she whispered.

"No way," I said.

The three of them were being attacked by Molly, who was squealing in delight when Nick walked in the door behind them.

"Oh no," Mira said. "Nick."

Sebby managed to extricate himself from Molly's enthusiasm and led the girls into the kitchen. Nick went off into another room.

"Hi, pretty ladies," Sebby said. He gave us each a kiss on the cheek.

Rose and Ali came in behind him. Rose immediately grabbed two cups and poured giant helpings of vodka.

"Ali, you know Mira," Sebby said.

"Yeah, I see you guys at the diner, like, three times a week," Ali said.

Sebby, ignoring her, turned to me.

"And this is my boyfriend, Jeremy."

"Boyfriend?" Rose looked up from her cup.

Sebby put his arm around me.

"You don't mind if I call you that, do you, my darling?"

He was already drunk. I could tell. But I was on my way there. I could at least match him on this night, not be the sober caretaker to his recklessness.

"I like it," I said.

He kissed me. A long kiss. A few other kids in the room made goofy whooping noises. If I had been sober, I might have worried, might have thought they sounded more like a warning than encouragement. But with two and a half drinks in me I didn't care. He was kissing me in front of people. He had called me his boyfriend. That was all that mattered. Sebby released me and I took a long drink from my cup. I needed this feeling to last.

After that we found ourselves on the floor in the corner

of the living room for a while. The music was too loud to hear anything and no one seemed to be saying anything anyway. Just a lot of shouting and Rose trying to get Ali to dance with her, and me and Sebby and Mira piled together in the corner. Next to us some boys had cracked a window open in an attempt to send the smoke from a joint outside, instead of twirling up to the smoke alarm.

The more we drank, the farther Sebby's hand crept down my back, until it rested in the waistband of my jeans, inside the top of the elastic of my underwear. My boyfriend. My boyfriend touching me.

Nick appeared again after a while, came over, and whispered something in Sebby's ear.

"I'll be back," Sebby said, disentangling himself from us.

Mira gave me a look as the two of them made their way across the room.

Whatever went wrong between Rose and Ali happened quickly, because neither of us saw it. All of a sudden there was yelling and Ali was out the front door and Rose was running after her. We saw them on the lawn out the window. Rose was saying something to Ali and Ali was crying. Then Ali yelled something and went off down the driveway.

"Uh-oh," Mira said. She got up and I followed.

I had become undeniably drunk while sitting down, and I was now forced to struggle with the more strenuous activity of getting across the room. We pushed our way across the dance floor, past Molly falling on one of the boys who had been passing the joint before. Somewhere in the back of my mind I tried dully to calculate what time it was, and wondered if it was an amateur move for us all to be this wasted before midnight.

Outside Rose was blowing puffs of smoke from a cigarette at the place where Ali had been standing. We went to her. Mira hugged her.

"You need your coat," she said.

Rose was shaking.

"What happened?" I said.

"I told her I'm not going to be her puppy dog just following her around anymore," Rose said. "She acts all sweet and then is, like, 'don't hold my hand,' or whatever, and I'm sick of it."

"What did she say?" Mira said.

"She just left," Rose said.

She threw her cigarette on the ground.

"I'm going after her," she said.

"No, Rose," I said.

Rose started down the driveway.

"Rose, your coat!" Mira called, but she was already in her car, turning on the engine.

"Well, that can only end well," Mira said.

"Should we try to stop her?" I asked.

"I don't think we can."

We watched Rose drive off down the street.

"Let's go in," Mira said. "I'm freezing."

In the kitchen most of the jugs of alcohol had been emptied. Only the gin and the Bailey's remained.

"Where the hell is Sebby?" Mira asked, getting us two fresh cups.

"With Nick," I said. "Always with Nick. Awesome Nick."

"Nick is not awesome. Nick is bad."

"Yeah?" I was laughing without knowing what was funny. Everything was funny now. Or else everything was horribly sad. I couldn't remember which.

"He is a bad news bear. Here." She handed me a gin-and-Bailey's cocktail. "What should we call this one?"

"Disgusting," I said. "We're going to call that disgusting."

"Don't be afraid to try new things, Jeremy," she said.

"I am afraid," I said.

"I'll protect you," she said, smiling. "Cheers." We toasted our plastic cups.

I took a sip.

"Yes, it's disgusting," I said, nearly choking.

"I can't even taste anything anymore," Mira said. "When did we get this drunk?"

"I think it happened pretty recently," I said.

She laughed and leaned her head on my shoulder. We were laughing and holding each other, my arm now around her waist. It felt so nice to have her lean on me, to know how comfortable we were with each other, how well she knew me. Nothing else at this stupid party mattered because Mira was here, and Mira wouldn't leave me. And then suddenly we were kissing, the haze of the alcohol having it all make some kind of sense. Here was her body, my body, our mouths.

She pulled away and some of her drink spilled.

"I'm sorry," I said.

"No," she said. "It's . . ."

She took my hand and pulled me into the hallway.

"It's just . . . too many people around," she said.

And then we were leaning up against the wall, kissing again, her hand feeling along my back, pulling me toward her.

A door opened next to us, exposing us to a flash of light reflected off white bathroom tiles before someone flipped the switch off. Nick came out and headed back to the kitchen, not noticing us pressed up against the wall, frozen together. Sebby was behind him, his darting eyes finding us in the darkness.

Mira's hand stayed defiantly in place.

"What were you doing in there?" she said, a drunken bite to her words.

"What are you doing out here?" Sebby said calmly, a visible twitching in his fingers.

"Nothing," she said.

He watched us for a moment, none of us moving, the noise from the other room beckoning us to rejoin what now seemed like an innocent ritual, a simple high school party, sloppy and insignificant.

His fingers stopped twitching.

"Let's go do nothing together then," he said, finally.

We followed him upstairs to an empty bedroom, unquestion-ing, stuck now inside a game with some carefully coded rules that I did not understand. The king-size bed with a conservative autumnal pattern on the bedspread and matching dark wood nightstands indicated that it was Molly's parents' room. Sebby closed the door behind us and I sat down on the bed, my legs feeling unsteady under me. Sebby and Mira stood together in the half-light of a streetlamp leaking in through the blinds. Monet's *Water Lilies* in an ornate gold frame looking down over it all.

I watched as he took Mira's face in his hands and kissed her hard on the mouth, as if reclaiming something that belonged to him.

He let her go. "You guys are really drunk," he said, smiling.

"Shut up," I muttered. But then he was on top of me, pushing me back onto the bed.

"I thought you didn't like kissing girls," he said. His fingers grabbed at my hair, holding me there. Mira lay down next to us.

"I thought you didn't," I said.

"I guess we don't know everything about each other."

He kissed me and I tried to push back, grab at his neck, thinking of all of those chaste nights spent sleeping next to him. I was angry that he had asked me to keep his secrets. I was angry at myself for all of my stupid insecurities. Now I wanted to push through it all, the drunken static erasing hesitations.

He sat up.

"Kiss her again," he said.

"What?"

He got off me.

"I want to see you kiss her."

Mira was watching us, the tiniest hint of a smile at the corners of her mouth. I leaned over and kissed her quickly.

"Like before," Sebby said, pushing me.

She met me halfway. Her lips felt familiar now, parting just enough for mine, fitting each other.

"You guys look cute together," Sebby said. He was on her now, his hands at her waist.

"Sebby, what are you doing?" she said.

"Nothing," he said. "Don't stop, Jeremy."

He slid down to the floor, pushed up her skirt, let his hand travel up her leg.

"Sebby . . ."

He pulled her closer to him, her skirt falling a little and covering his face. I kissed her, not sure what else to do, following instructions. After a minute she turned her head away from me and grabbed at my hair, held my head next to hers. I stayed in the crook of her neck. At a certain point I realized that I had stopped breathing.

She twisted away from us finally, whispering, "Oh my god," pulling her skirt around her.

He got on top of her, looked at me.

"See, Jeremy, girls aren't that hard to please."

"Fuck, Sebby," Mira said, still turned away from him. "I can't believe you just did that."

He kissed her on the cheek. "For old time's sake," he said.

Her arms were up around her face and I couldn't tell if she was happy or sad, wasn't sure if we had followed or broken those unspoken rules. I touched the top of her head.

"Are you okay?" I whispered.

She took her arms away from her face.

"Yes," she said. "I'm sorry, Jeremy."

"Come on," Sebby said, getting up. He grabbed my hand. "We're ditching this party."

I let him pull me up. He grabbed Mira with his other hand. "Come on."

"Give me a minute, Sebby."

He leaned in and kissed her again to coax her up from the bed. She let him pull her up to her feet, smoothing down the skirt of her green plaid dress as she stood, finding her balance in her worn cowboy boots.

Downstairs we stole beers from the fridge and hid them in our coat pockets. In the living room couples were making out on the couch, less bold girls turning the music up louder to help them pretend not to care that they were dancing alone.

Outside the air was still, the noise from the party fading as soon as we turned the corner. Sebby was ahead of us. Mira held my hand as we tried to keep up.

"Where are we going?" I asked.

"Nick went to this other party," Sebby said. "I said we would meet him there."

The other party turned out to be a large gathering of people in the parking lot behind a convenience store in town. It was the afterparty for those who could not be bothered to make it to an actual party. I didn't recognize anyone, people with elaborate haircuts sitting on cars, every hand holding either a cigarette or a beer bottle.

Sebby left us without a word, dissolved into the crowd. I pulled a beer out of my jacket pocket and looked at the bottle top in drunken wonderment.

"I can't open this," I said.

"Here," Mira took it from me and approached the nearest drinker, a guy with a Mohawk and a ratty peacoat. He smiled as he opened it with his keys, leaned in close to say something in her ear.

Without Mira's hand in mine I had the unfortunate realization that she had been helping to hold me up, and now I worried that I was actually teetering in the middle of the parking lot, looking like a lost and dazed child. Which is exactly how I felt.

"Hey." Sebby was back, next to me. "Come on."

"Where are we going?"

"Just come with me."

"What about Mira?"

"She's fine. She's making friends."

I followed him through the open back door of the building into a storeroom, a dark cave of stacked boxes. Nick and Ali were standing over a sink in the corner.

"Hey," Nick said. Two lines of white powder were carefully arranged on the side of the sink. Ali leaned over it for a minute, then straightened up, leaving only one behind.

The room smelled like cleaning fluid and mold, something eternally wet hanging in the air. Nick pulled a box down from a stack, cut it open, and pulled out two packs of cigarettes. He tossed one to Sebby.

"I'll be outside," he said, walking past us.

Sebby nodded.

Ali handed Sebby the rolled-up bill that she had used and followed Nick out, the back door banging shut behind them.

"Where are we?" I asked.

"Nick works here sometimes," Sebby said. He went over to the sink. "You want some?"

I shook my head.

He leaned over and inhaled the drug, then straightened up and closed his eyes for a moment. His empty hand twitched.

He opened his eyes and smiled at me. My eyes were adjusting to the light coming in from the store. Red nighttime safety lights. Exit signs.

"I think I'm really drunk," I said.

He walked toward me, took my hand.

"It's okay," he said. "You'll be okay."

"Are you mad at me?" I asked.

"Why would I be mad at you?"

"About Dave? What Dave said? Or about Mira?"

He shook his head.

"Everything's great," he said. "Doesn't everything feel great?"

"I don't know. I don't know how everything feels right now."

He kissed me, pressed up against a stack of boxes.

"How about now?" he asked.

"Better," I said.

He kissed me again and then he was on the floor, fumbling with my fly. I tried to say something, but my throat felt numb. Drunk and mute. All I could do was to try to stay upright, not crumple onto the ground next to him. I wanted to touch him but he was like a ball of electricity, moving at its own pace, consuming because it was afraid to stop.

I leaned my head back, feeling the stacked boxes shifting behind me, something shifting inside me too.

And then there was no more room for thinking. There was only the rush of every desire I had ever had. The total forgetting of self.

I let myself slide down to the floor, next to where he had been. He was already up again.

"I'm going back out," he said. "Come on."

"I can't, Sebby. I just need to sit here for a minute."

"Okay." He leaned down. "Are you okay?"

"I don't know."

"I'll get some more stuff from Nick. You'll feel better if you try it."

He was out the door before I could stand. I got myself to my feet and followed him out, but he had moved away, already out of sight. The parking lot suddenly felt like a dangerous place, all faces seeming to be intentionally turned away from me, as if I had done something unforgiveable. And then Mira grabbed my hand.

"Where did you go?" she asked.

"Inside."

"You okay?"

I shook my head. We sat down on the edge of the curb. She huddled up against me. One a.m. on a Sunday morning in a parking lot. None of this made any sense.

"Everything feels out of control," I said.

She looked out over the parking lot.

"I'm really sorry, Jeremy."

"Why?"

"What just happened," she said, "at Molly's house . . ." She looked at me, then looked away. "We used to do that. Me and Sebby. In the hospital. When we felt like we couldn't stand being there anymore."

"I thought maybe he was mad at me," I said, "for kissing you. Like he was trying to prove something to me."

She shook her head. "I don't know. But it was wrong. To get you all mixed up in that."

"I already was," I said. "I want to be mixed up in it." I felt like I was going to cry.

"But you didn't know, maybe, how crazy we are."

"You're not crazy," I said.

"Well, that's generous of you."

She handed me the open beer.

"What are we going to do?" I said.

"I guess we're going to sit here and wait for this night to end. Every night has to end eventually."

**

It was another hour before we saw Sebby again. Nick found the two of us, still huddled together, sharing the last of the stolen beer from the party, trying to stave off the inevitable pain of sobriety.

"Sebby's pretty messed up," he said, and walked away.

We found him along the side of the building, sitting up against a wall, his head in his hands.

"Hey." Mira leaned down and touched his head.

He looked up, his eyes glassy, his hair sweaty and matted.

"What's up?" he said. His voice too small.

"Let's go home," she said.

"I'm not going there. That's not my home."

"My home. Let's go to my home," she said.

We stumbled back to her street, me and Mira on either side of him, holding him up. The porch light was on at Mira's house, her parents asleep inside. She unlocked the front door and we tried to make our way up the stairs to her room as quietly as we could, stumbling as she held Sebby up from the side and I walked behind. Mira put him down on her bed and he leaned back into the pillows.

"What are you doing?" he said.

"You need to go to sleep," she said.

"You're drunk," he insisted.

"I know," she said.

I stood in the doorway of her room, not sure what to do, not knowing if something terrifying was happening to us or if everything was normal, everything would be okay.

"Lie down with him, Jeremy," she instructed, and left the room.

I did as I was told, lying down next to him in her bed. He looked at me, surprised to see me there.

"Jeremy?"

"Yeah," I said.

"Oh, shit, I'm sorry about before."

"What?"

"I just left you. I shouldn't have just left you there."

"No, I know. It's been a weird night."

"Was it . . . okay?"

He was this boy again now. The one from that first night alone in my bedroom. Vulnerable and shy. He looked scared.

"Yes, of course," I said.

"You wanted me to, right?"

I nodded. "Yes," I said.

We fell asleep like that together. A familiar feeling of holding him while he twitched through sweaty nightmares. This was how we knew each other. Unconscious mates.

I woke up a few hours later and saw Mira lying on the floor next to the bed, covered by a quilt. I checked Sebby's breathing, shallow but steady, and fell back asleep.

The next morning we were sick. I had never been hungover before and my brain felt like it wanted to leave my body, go in search of a less hostile environment. I woke up alone in Mira's bed, made my way downstairs to the kitchen to find the two of them huddled over pancakes.

"Hey," she said. "You hungry?"

"I can't tell yet."

She made a plate and handed it to me.

"This will help," she said.

We ate slowly. The house was empty except for us. Her dad had gone into the office for a few hours and her mom was at a Pilates class. We matched the quiet of the house, the noise in our brains still settling. When we finished eating, Mira hid the evidence of her use of forbidden gluten and sugar, sending me and Sebby back up to her room to watch TV.

She met us up there, Sebby drifting off to sleep with his head in my lap, me half watching a show about catching extreme fish or extreme fish catching or something.

I checked my phone to make sure that I hadn't just imagined texting my dad to ask if it was okay for me to stay at Mira's house, imagined getting a yes in response.

The hungover haze of my brain was starting to clear, and images from the night before were coming back to me. The three of us in Molly's parents' bed. Me and Sebby in the dark of the storeroom. I touched his head as he lay in my lap. He was still in his sleep for the first time in a long time. I tried to match him in stillness, wanting him to stay there with me, stay in place.

I was worried that we had gone too far. That things would not be the same now. I felt like I was holding something fragile in my hands that was daring me to break it.

Mira sat down on the other side of me.

"How are you feeling?" she said.

"Pretty terrible," I said. "Probably the same as you."

"No, I mean, about everything."

I shook my head. "Everything's okay," I said, hoping it was true.

SEBBY

You were stopped at a gas station on the side of the highway. Nick went inside to get some candy and you stayed by the car watching the pump, the numbers rolling mercilessly higher. Thirty dollars. Thirty-five. Forty.

You had been up for a day and a half, and the protests from your brain made you feel exhilarated in your own ability to hurt yourself.

"This is nothing," you wanted to tell it. "I'm capable of so much more. You should know that by now."

Your phone was dead in your pocket. There was no reception out here anyway, even if you wanted to take stock of who missed you when you went away. Dead cell phone and a backpack filled with drugs in the trunk. That was how this moment in your life could be summed up.

The past two nights you stayed at a cabin in the mountains that belonged to some of Nick's friends, that served as a place for him to meet up with his supplier. Or else it belonged to no one. A bunch of drugged-out weirdoes happened to stumble upon it during a misguided trek through the Poconos and just never left.

You took mushrooms for the first time and ended up outside lying in the last of the melting mountain snow, looking up at the stars. The air was so clear there that it felt like it was humming at you, a tune at first of wind and water and earth and then speaking words, saying that it had the most important thing to tell you.

You closed your eyes and your entire body listened. The words whispered into you, the secret of the beauty in all of your messy vulnerability. Happiness was always only temporary for you. And so you had started pushing too far, welcoming the inevitable pain that followed.

You lay there in the slowly thawing earth and you understood suddenly that as long as you were here, this is what would be asked of you. To feel such things, such strong, such difficult things, and to know that this is what brings you closest to the divine. This is when you are divine.

On the second night you fooled around with a short guy with dark rings around his eyes. His mouth on your body felt like some kind of witchcraft there in the woods, calling wolves and night creatures to circle the cabin. You imagined that he might devour you when he was finished with you. He was too rough, but you liked it. You wanted to carry around outward signs of destruction like a badge of honor.

"Is this divine too?" you asked the air. "To feel this too?"

Now Nick drove with the window open, speeding down the highway, one hand dangling out with a perpetually lit cigarette. He stopped periodically to do a line to stay alert enough to drive. He offered you some but you were enjoying the way your brain and body felt. Frayed around the edges. Giving in to destruction.

Nick had the radio turned up too loud and you listened hard to try not to fall asleep. Falling asleep would mean giving up. You tried to follow along with the words of a silly pop song. You thought they might contain a secret that could explain how to ignore the past, present, and future all at the same time. This song might know something about escape. But then it was over and there was a loud commercial and you lost your train of thought.

Maybe that was the secret. To try not to think. Try as hard as you could not to think at all.

JEREMY

Mira and I didn't start to panic until the third day that we didn't hear from Sebby. It was normal at this point for him to only sporadically respond to my texts, but Mira had left him a message that if he didn't call her back she was going to start freaking out and there had been no response.

"He's definitely with Nick somewhere," Mira said.

We were sitting at our regular table in the cafeteria. We were alone, since Rose and Ali's fight on Saturday had ended in Rose finally convincing Ali to try to get back together again. Now Rose was spending every free minute sneaking phone calls to her in the bathroom.

"Did you ask Rose if Ali's seen Nick?' I said.

Mira shook her head. "She hasn't heard from him."

Full trays of untouched food sat on the table in front of us.

"Maybe he's just ignoring us," I said.

The cafeteria was emptying out as it got closer to the end of the period. Food eaten too quickly, conversations had too loudly, and now a slow leak of noise until it was just the two of us there in the middle of an empty room. The two of us left behind.

"I can't believe he won't answer his phone," she said. "Why is he doing this?"

This wasn't how it was supposed to go. If Sebby was going to hurt someone it was supposed to be me, the person who let him come and go as he pleased, the one who demanded nothing more than whatever he could get. He wasn't supposed to leave her behind too.

I picked up a french fry for something to do with my hands, put it down again.

"I can't tell my parents," she said. "We can't call his house. Talking to Tilly would be a disaster. I'm sure he told her some lie that he was staying with one of us. We need someone to tell us what to do."

"It's my fault," I said. "I screwed everything up."

"It's not your fault, Jeremy."

We were quiet for another minute.

"We could talk to Peter," I said finally.

She looked at me.

"Do you think that's a good idea?"

"He'll know what to do," I said.

"If there's something really wrong, and we don't do

anything . . ." She was trying to talk herself into it.

I stood up.

"So," I said. "Come on."

Peter was in his office when we got there, eating lunch at his desk.

"Hey, guys," he said, when we came in. "Excited about the gallery opening on Friday? I think we're all set for it."

Mira closed the door behind us.

"Everything okay?" Peter said.

"We have to talk to you," I said.

"Okay," he said. He put down his sandwich.

"We don't know where Sebby is," Mira said.

"He's not answering his phone, and . . ." I looked at Mira, wondering how much to tell. "He might be with this guy. This kid who does a lot of drugs. Who sells drugs." I sounded like a such a loser. *Who cares? Who cares about anything besides making sure he's okay?*

"You have no idea where he is?" Peter asked.

Mira shook her head. "We don't know what to do. His foster mom won't know. I'm sure he told her some lie."

Peter thought for a minute, looked at his desk. "Come sit down," he said. We did.

"Well, the best thing we can do is call the police and report a missing person," he said.

I looked at Mira. She looked like she was going to cry.

"He'll get in trouble, though," she said. "If he's with this guy. He might get in a lot of trouble."

"The most important thing is to make sure that he's safe," Peter said. "If you really think that something's wrong, then that has to be the priority."

Mira covered her face with her hands.

"Okay," she said through her fingers.

"Okay," I said.

SEBBY

Nick dropped you off at Tilly's in the early evening. You figured you could probably eat dinner at Jeremy's house, but something told you that you should put in an appearance for Tilly. Although keeping her expectations low seemed to be working out well. There had been no requests to watch the kids, to take them to church group, to even take out the garbage, for a while now. Tilly seemed to be catching on that the less the two of you had to do with each other, the better.

They were all in the kitchen when you came in, the kids eating their regular five-p.m. dinner.

"Sebastian?"

You stood in the doorway, looking into the kitchen.

"Hi," you said.

Tilly handed the jar of baby food that she was holding to Stephanie.

"Why do I have to do it?" Stephanie moaned.

Tilly took off her apron and came into the living room.

"Where have you been?" she asked. She looked tired, dark circles under her eyes, her bright red hair unwashed in a messy ponytail.

"I left you a message," you said. "I was staying with Mira."

The two of you were standing facing each other in the middle of the living room.

"The police called," Tilly said. "They said that you were missing."

"The police?"

You could feel yourself starting to sweat. Stephanie stuck her head out from the kitchen to try to hear.

"It must have been a misunderstanding," you said.

"This is the second time this has happened," Tilly said.

You tried to smile, like someone reassuring a wild animal that it wasn't a threat. Or was it the smile that indicated a threat? "It was a misunderstanding," you said again.

"I can't have this, Sebastian. I told you that if you're getting into trouble I can't risk having you around the children."

"You're not risking anything," you said, a little too loudly. You took a deep breath to try to relax your speeding pulse. Tilly responded best to calm and agreeable.

"Jonathan convinced me to give you a second chance the last time," Tilly said. "I can see now that that was a mistake."

"Tilly, come on, it wasn't a mistake."

"I told you that you needed to go to school," she said. "And you didn't listen. You don't listen to me. And you obviously have problems that I am not equipped to deal with."

"What problems?" you said, knowing she wouldn't say it. The thing that had kept her from looking you in the eye for almost a month after you got back from the hospital.

"You can't live here anymore." She let that hang in the air, settle down around you, land at your feet. There it was. The truth. You felt a rush of what could only be described as relief, the calm of the inevitable. You had been dreading this moment for so long and now that it was here, you were finally free from its grip.

"You don't do anything to help this household," she said. "You don't go to church with us. You're a bad influence on these children."

"I'm a faggot, too, Tilly," you said. "You can just say that. You don't have to come up with all of those other reasons."

She stood there in silence. Her hands on her hips. You saw Stephanie's head disappear.

"I didn't say that," she said. "Don't say that word."

"Why?"

She sighed deeply and you felt the air around you stir, as if even the oxygen in this room belonged solely to her. There was no place for you here. There never had been.

"I'm calling tonight," she said. "They'll come get you tomorrow."

"Great," you said.

She shook her head.

"I did everything I could for you, Sebastian," she said.

"Yeah, I know you did," you said, going to your room. "It just wasn't very much, was it?"

JEREMY

Mira was having dinner at my house when he finally showed up. She and I were having trouble being apart, as if we were being picked off one by one, and we had to make sure to keep each other in sight at all times.

I hadn't told Dad and Dave what was going on. Part of me thought that I should, that they would know what to do. But then I remembered how angry Sebby had been about Dave talking to him. It seemed like it would be a betrayal.

Mira was helping to clear the dishes when my phone beeped in my pocket. I took it out.

"No phones at the dinner table," Dad said.

"We're done with dinner," I said.

"Then leave the table. No phones at the table."

"Yes. Fine."

I got up.

I'm outside, the text read.

I looked back at my dad. He was clearing away the rest of the dishes. I put my coat on and went out the front door. Sebby was standing on the sidewalk with a garbage bag at his feet.

"Where have you been?" I said, going to him. "We were freaking out."

"Mira's here?" he said. He could see in the front window to the dining room.

"Yeah, she came over for dinner. Are you okay?"

I tried to take his hand. He stepped away from me.

"Did you call the police?" he said.

I looked back at the house for Mira.

"Peter did," I said. "We didn't know what to do. We told him we couldn't find you. We thought something had happened."

"I got kicked out of my house," he said. "Tilly kicked me out. Just now."

"What? Why?"

"Because she doesn't want to deal with me anymore. Because the police called her. Because I'm a fuck-up faggot. Pick one."

I heard the door open behind me.

"Sebby?" Mira said.

"You can stay here," I said. "We'll figure it out."

"What's going on?" Mira said.

"Tilly kicked him out," I said. "The police called her."

She went to him and he stepped back again, away from both of us.

"We thought you might have hurt yourself," Mira said.

"I was fine," he said. "I just wasn't with you guys. I'm allowed to be with other people."

"With Nick?" Mira said.

"It's none of your business," he said.

We stood there for a minute in silence. He kicked at the trash bag.

"This is everything that I own," he said.

"Here," I said, "bring it inside. Let's go inside."

I picked up the bag.

He shook his head.

"You guys seem like you're doing okay without me."

"What's that supposed to mean?" Mira said.

"It means the two of you make a great pair."

"Are you kidding me?" Mira said. She looked at me. "We've done nothing but worry about you for the past four days."

"Well, I'm fine, so you can stop worrying."

"You're not fine," she said. "What's going on with you?"

"Right now? I don't have a place to live. That's what's going on."

"We'll figure it out, Sebby," I said. "You'll stay here."

"No, I won't," he said. "I won't stay here in your perfect house with your perfect dads who are totally overinvolved in your perfect life and give you everything that you need and love you unconditionally. People like me don't get that, okay? I don't get that life."

"Sebby," Mira said, "come on, you're just upset."

"It didn't even occur to the two of you how much it could fuck things up to have the police looking for me, did it? And you told Peter, what, that I ran away?"

"Peter cares about us," I said.

"Peter doesn't have a fucking clue," he said. "And neither do the two of you."

He started walking away.

"Sebby!" Mira called after him.

"Leave me alone," he yelled back.

He kept walking. And we stood there watching him until he disappeared.

MIRA

She tried his house first, but the lights were off and the front door was locked. It was only as she made her way back down the street that she remembered that there was a college fair at school that night.

All the windows were still lit up at St. F, cars emptying out of the parking lot. The air was heavy with the threat of rain.

She went inside and went directly to his office. He was gathering up things from his desk, putting them into his bag, illuminated by the blue glow of his computer screen.

"Peter?"

He turned around and saw her standing in the doorway.

"Hey, Mira. Were you at the college fair? I didn't see you."

She shook her head. Her eyes were red from crying.

"What's wrong?" he said, putting down his things.

She was having trouble forming the words.

"Sebby got kicked out of his house."

"What?"

"Everything's going wrong," she said.

"Come, sit down," Peter said.

"I can't," she said. "We shouldn't have listened to you."

She walked away from his door, made her way through the hall, back out to the parking lot.

"Mira!"

He followed her outside. It had started raining.

"I can't do this," she said. The rain streamed down her face and she stopped to feel it. She was having trouble breathing. She wanted to drown in that rain. She wanted to not have to breathe anymore.

"Come on," Peter said. "It's pouring."

He grabbed her hand and led her over to his car. He unlocked the door and opened the passenger side for her. She got in. He got in the driver's side.

"Tell me what's happening. Sebby got kicked out of his house?"

"It's our fault."

"Whatever it is, it's not your fault."

She shook her head. Her breath was coming in short bursts between sobs.

"Mira, breathe. It's okay, you don't have to talk if you don't want to."

Rain streamed down the windshield.

"It's our fault," she said. "It's my fault."

"Come on. It's going to be okay."

She couldn't stop crying. Couldn't catch her breath. He put his arm around her and held her to his chest.

"I promise," he said. "We can figure this out."

The night that Mira tried to kill herself, she had been crying for so long that she didn't even know why anymore. One year, six months, and eight days before this night in Peter's car, the days that she had counted because she almost didn't get to have them. At that point she was keeping the crying hidden. When it first started, she let people see it because she didn't know what else to do. She thought if they could witness her in the middle of this thing, then they might be able to understand. But they couldn't. It was exhausting for others to watch. For herself to experience. So she stopped showing them.

It hurt so much that she wanted to hurt herself to stop it. At least when she saw her own blood, she could say, "There it is. There's the proof." That she still existed.

But that night it didn't help. So she went further. Too far. And finally realizing that it was too much, that she didn't want that, she wrapped her wrist in toilet paper and woke her mother up in the middle of the night like a little girl with a nightmare. Bleeding onto her bedroom carpet.

She had already been in the hospital for a week when Sebby arrived in the ward. She had been spending the afternoon the way she spent all of her afternoons there, sitting at the window, her eyes drifting out to the courtyard, studying the patch of green through the chain metal on the window. Too green. Back inside to the linoleum floor. She was living in the spaces in between.

She heard footsteps on the linoleum, the squeak of the plastic covering on the chair across from her as he sat down.

"Hi," he said.

He looked pale and medicated. But that came with the territory.

"Hi," she said.

"How's the world looking?" he asked.

"Unappealing."

"Hm." He examined the scene down in the courtyard, pretended to be disgusted by it. "Oh my god. You're right. That is terrible."

She smiled. It felt new.

"You been here awhile?" he asked.

"In this chair? A few hours. In this place? Seven days. You?"

"They just brought me up yesterday," he said.

A group of pigeons gathered around a trash can on the patch of grass, making desperate circles in search of crumbs. Someone had brought an old man in a wheelchair outside and left him near the scavenging pigeons. Sebby stood up, close to the glass, and started yelling.

"Sir! Those are flesh-eating birds! Dear god! Run for your life!"

A nurse stopped in the hallway.

"Sebastian Tate, we keep our voices down in here," she said.

"So sorry, Nurse Ratched," he said, and winked at her.

"Your name's Sebastian?" Mira said.

"Sebby," he said. "And you are?"

"Miranda. Mira."

"Well," he said, "nice to meet you, Mira."

One year, six months, and eight days after she tried to kill herself, Peter drove Mira home from St. Francis and she couldn't stop crying again. A familiar feeling of gasping for air, choking on words that she couldn't even say, "I don't think I can do this."

Her mother drove her to the hospital again on this night, the intake room so familiar it was as if those five hundred and forty-one days had melted into nothing. She was back where she had started. Without him.

There was a rage inside her despair this time. This was about promises broken. If she couldn't breathe, it was because he was supposed to be there to breathe with her. If she couldn't survive, it was because he was taking away the one thing that had saved her.

At least this time they would help her stop it before it went too far. Before the blood dripping onto her mother's carpet. This time she knew what to do.

Try harder to breathe. In and out. Don't think about what it feels like inside. Like a path of shattered glass, bare feet leaving bloody tracks in their wake. At the end of it you can see your half of a heart, still beating somehow, poor heart, trying so hard even though it knows that it is not enough

JEREMY

I called Mira's phone three times that night, Sebby's four times. Neither of them answered. I woke up the next morning to his things still in the garbage bag in the corner of my room.

Mira left right after Sebby did the night before, obviously fighting off tears but refusing to listen to my requests for her to stay. I was left alone with the concerned faces of my dads and no choice but to tell them at least most of what was going on. The three of us sat at the dinner table and drank cups of tea until I finally excused myself and went to bed early. I slept with my phone set on vibrate in my hand, hoping someone would call back, that Sebby would show up in the middle of the night and text me to let him in. But there was nothing.

The next day was Friday and I had no good reason not to go to school besides the fact that I felt like everything was terrible and I had no idea how to fix it. So I showered, put on my uniform, ate breakfast, and walked to St. F.

Maybe everything's okay, I kept thinking as I walked. *Maybe somehow everything's actually okay.*

I had algebra first period, elaborate word problems with Mr. Hepworth. He was still writing the first one out on the board when the dean's secretary came into the classroom and whispered something in his ear.

"If it's absolutely necessary," he said.

The secretary turned to me.

"Jeremy, could you come with me please?"

"Me?" I said.

She nodded. An interested murmur went up around the room as I stood up.

"You'd better bring your things with you," she said.

"Okay," I mumbled, picking up my books.

I followed her, feeling the room watch us go.

"What's this about?" I asked as we made our way down the hallway. She was a nervous bird of a lady, all indirect eye contact and frizzy hair.

"Dean Pike needs to speak to you in his office," she said.

We had our doddering figurehead of a headmaster, and then there was Dean Pike, who really ran the school, a silver-haired man in his fifties who always had a smile and a jovial "Keep that shirt tucked in!" for every student.

The secretary led me to Pike's door and opened it.

"Jeremy Worth is here," she said.

I went in and she closed the door behind me. Dean Pike was sitting at his desk.

"Jeremy," Pike said. "Thank you for coming. Please have a seat."

"Is everything okay?" I asked, sitting down.

"Well . . ." He paused and thought for a minute about how to answer. "We have a little bit of a situation on our hands. You're very close friends with Miranda Powers, aren't you?"

I nodded.

"Have you spoken to her today?"

"No," I said. "I saw her yesterday."

"What time?" he asked.

"I don't know. Around six thirty, maybe. She was at my house for dinner. Is she okay?"

"She's absent today. But we are trying to get in touch with her family."

"What happened?"

Pike cleared his throat before continuing.

"We had a report from a student this morning that Miranda was seen on campus last night," he said. "After the college fair, around seven o'clock. In Peter Sprenger's car."

"Maybe she came back to school after I saw her."

"This student reported that she saw inappropriate behavior going on between Miranda and Mr. Sprenger."

Pike tapped his pen on his desk in a nervous rhythm.

"Inappropriate?" I said.

"Normally I would not take a report without any other eyewitnesses so seriously. I am not interested in an unfounded witch hunt. But Mr. Sprenger has a history of walking a fine line with students when it comes to inviting them into his personal life. And if there is any possibility that he is conducting himself in an inappropriate way with a student, then we are dealing with a very serious situation."

"I'm sure it's a misunderstanding," I said.

"I need to ask you something, Jeremy, and I need you to be honest with me."

I could feel myself starting to sweat.

"Sure," I said.

"Have you ever been to Peter Sprenger's home?"

I didn't say anything. Pike tapped his pen impatiently.

"I need you to tell me the truth."

"No," I said.

"No, you have not spent time at Mr. Sprenger's home?"

"No, never," I said.

Pike sighed and put down his pen.

"I am really disappointed that you answered that way, Jeremy."

"I'm telling the truth."

"You're not telling the truth. Mr. Sprenger himself informed us that you spent a significant amount of time with him at his home last spring after the incident with your locker. Isn't that true?"

Now I was sweating.

"Yes," I said.

"So why did you just answer my question untruthfully?"

I didn't know what to say.

He shook his head.

"This is very disappointing," he said.

"So . . . that was a trap, or something? You just . . . what? Wanted to test me?"

"I wanted to see if the students who are closest to Peter Sprenger feel that they have something to hide about their relationship with him. And I feel confident now that I have my answer."

Just then the door opened and Mira's mother burst in.

"Can I help you?" Pike said.

"I'm Miranda Powers's mother," she said. She was out of breath. "What is the meaning of these phone messages I've been getting all morning?"

"I'm in a meeting with a student," Pike said.

Mira's mom looked at me. She was pale and disheveled, her hair loose around her face.

"Jeremy," she said.

"Is Mira okay?" I asked.

"Why don't you go wait outside, honey? I'll be out in a minute."

I left them alone in the room and sat on a bench in the hallway. I could hear Mira's mother yelling. Pike's secretary was watching the door, looking like she might intervene.

When Mira's mom finally came out of the office I stood up. Pike was with her.

"I think you should go home for the rest of the day, Jeremy," he said. "We'll be in touch with your father."

"I didn't do anything wrong," I said.

"Come on, Jeremy," Mira's mom said. "I'll drive you home."

My head was spinning as I got in the car.

"Where is Mira?" I asked as her mom pulled out of the parking lot.

"She's in the hospital, honey," she said. "She had a little bit of a relapse. But she's going to be okay."

"The hospital?"

Her mom nodded.

"She ate dinner at your house last night, right?" she asked.

"Yes," I said. "She left after dinner. She was upset about Sebby. I didn't know where she went."

"Mira doesn't always handle being upset very well."

"Oh," I said.

"She's going to be okay," she said. "And I know that this stuff with Peter is nonsense."

"I think I said the wrong thing," I said. "To Dean Pike."

"We're going to straighten it all out," she said.

She stopped at a red light.

"Can I see Mira?" I said.

She turned to me. She was crying.

"Oh, not yet, honey," she said, touching my arm. "But soon, okay?"

"Okay," I said.

SEBBY

Couch-hopping your way through Nick's connections was better than any of the possible alternatives. Better than risking staying at Nick's place, a tiny house that his sickly mother never left, stacks of newspapers slowly filling up rooms. Even Nick hardly ever stayed there. He needed to lie low right now too, worried that they had also given his name when they had called the cops. So it was a tour of couches and floors for both of you. Being on the run was less glamorous than it sounded.

When there was nothing around to help you fall asleep, no money for alcohol, no leftover pot to smoke, you lay awake on that night's floor thinking about what you could have said to them to make them understand. What it felt like to know that the two people who cared for you the most couldn't ever really know what your life was like.

Nights spent in Jeremy's bed you had been playing pretend. That his home was your home. That you could go out and screw up but that it would be okay because there was a place to return to. People who would not let you fall. You thought about the beautiful privilege of having normal problems. Not like the ones you had now, trying to decide whether or not lying on yet another floor was better than being inside the system, the bunk beds and behavior control and the madness of others that was promised if you went back.

For now the goal was staying invisible. And helping Nick make enough money for the two of you to be able to eat. Telling them where you were wasn't an option. They believed too deeply in the world's ability to take care of its own. They couldn't understand how easily someone could fall through the cracks.

What made them beautiful was that none of this could touch them. You couldn't blame them for that. It's what you loved about them. But you had always been walking along the edge of it, and now that it was here you weren't surprised. You always knew that this was coming.

Only in this life could freedom mean so much trouble, so much that you were not free to keep. You had been in training for how to give things up for sixteen years now. This was the place where you could take care of yourself. You knew how. But you couldn't take care of them too.

JEREMY

I finally got a text back from Sebby three days later.

I'm okay. Can you bring me my stuff?

We agreed to meet at the diner that night. I called Rose and she picked me up in her car. I was waiting outside my house with the garbage bag when she got there. She popped the trunk and I threw the bag in, got in the passenger seat.

"How are you doing?" she asked when I closed the door.

"Not great," I said.

She had called me as soon as she heard about everything with Peter, asked me if there was anything that she could do. This ride was the first thing I could think of.

"Where do you think he's been?" Rose asked as she pulled out of the driveway.

"With Nick," I said.

At the diner we sat by the window so I would see Nick's car when he drove in. Ali brought us coffees. None of us said much.

I was wearing my ratty blue cardigan, the one that Sebby had picked out for me that day at Arc's almost nine months ago. I wanted it to serve as a symbol, a way of jogging his memory. Couldn't it be that easy? To say, "Remember how happy we were? Remember the wishes that we made? The things we wanted to stop being afraid of?"

I was afraid now. Of losing them both. Of having to go back to the way that things were before them.

It wasn't until a little after ten that I saw the car pull in and Nick and Sebby get out. I left the table and went outside. Rose followed behind me.

Nick pushed past us to go into the diner.

"Gotta piss," he said.

"Great, thanks for the information, Nick," Rose said.

Sebby was leaning on Nick's car smoking a cigarette. Rose lingered behind me.

"Hi," I said.

"Hi," he said.

I paused, unsure for a moment. Then I went to him.

"Are you okay?" I asked.

He nodded.

"Yeah," he said.

"Where have you been?"

"I can't tell you, Jeremy."

"Why not?"

"You would tell your dads. And Mira."

"Would that be so terrible?"

He didn't say anything.

I took his hand. He let me.

"Come with me," I said.

"Where?"

"We'll go to Provincetown. We'll get Mira and we'll just go. Tonight. And everything can be like we said it would."

Nick came out of the diner and got back in the car. He turned on the radio. The music vibrated from the inside.

"It's not that simple," Sebby said, glancing at the car.

"I know that you're mad at us," I said. "For telling Peter that you were gone. For what happened at the party . . . everything just got out of control."

Sebby shook his head. "It's not about that."

"Whatever we did wrong, I can fix it."

"This is just the way that it is," he said.

"It doesn't have to be."

"It does, actually."

I let his hand go, looked at Nick lighting a cigarette in the driver's seat. "Are you with him now?" I asked.

"No," he said.

I could hear Rose behind me, opening the trunk of her car, getting out the bag of his things.

"Hey, Rose," Sebby said.

"Hey," she said, setting the bag down next to him. He nodded his thanks and she went back into the diner, leaving us there alone, Nick's music still blaring.

"What should I tell Mira?" I asked.

"I don't know," he said.

"She's in the hospital again. She's really upset, Sebby."

He looked down at the cigarette in his hand, burning into ash.

"Would you just talk to her?" I said. "Please."

"It's not possible right now." He threw the cigarette on the ground. "I need you to take this one, okay?"

"I don't know if I can."

He picked up the bag of his stuff, opened the back door of Nick's car, and threw it inside, then slammed the door. He turned back to me. He looked far away already. Like he was already gone.

"I know you think that we saved you or something, Jeremy," he said. "That we were stronger than you. But we're not. We weren't. We're all just trying to survive however we can. And the way that I have to survive right now is not going to be something that I expect you to understand."

"I need to fight for this," I said. "For you."

"Fight for her," he said. "That's one you can win."

I grabbed his hand again and he came to me, took my face in his hands, and kissed me, a long kiss that felt like a plea to not make this more difficult.

He let me go. I was crying.

"Please don't hurt yourself," I said.

He smiled. Sad smile.

"How about just a little?" he said.

I shook my head.

He walked away from me and my fingers left the fabric of his jacket, the inches of air sneaking in quickly between us, adding up until they multiplied into an unfathomable distance. Until a part of myself had driven off into the night, leaving me standing there alone.

MIRA

She only had to stay in the hospital for a few days this time, since she hadn't tried to hurt herself, hadn't gotten that far. She was released with new prescriptions and instructions to see a real psychiatrist once a week. Kelly the nutritionist would no longer be considered enough.

Her mom picked her up in the afternoon and drove her home. They didn't talk much in the car. Mira was still sleepy from the sedatives that they had her on for anxiety. But it was better than the alternative. Sleepy meant no thinking.

Her mom handed Mira her phone when she got in the car. She turned it on. Fifteen text messages. Eleven from Jeremy, four from Rose. She scrolled through them quickly, then put the phone in her pocket.

When they got to the house, there was another car in the driveway.

"Julie's here?"

Her mom smiled and they went inside. Julie was standing in the front hall with a bunch of balloons.

"I didn't know what you're supposed to get someone in a situation like this," she said, "but I figured you can't go wrong with balloons."

Mira let her sister hug her. Then their dad was there too, and Mira let them both hold her and wondered how long it had been since she had hugged them like this.

They sat in the living room, Mira, Julie, and their dad all on the couch together, the two of them taking up posts on either side of her. Their mom went into the kitchen to make hot chocolate. Even though it was seventy degrees outside, hot chocolate somehow seemed like the right thing.

"Aren't you missing class?" Mira asked Julie.

"Yeah, it's okay, though. It's just a lecture. I can get the notes from someone else."

They sat and talked about normal things, about nothing. Mira listened to their voices and thought, through the haze of the sedatives, that she was grateful for those voices, for familiar sounds to return to.

After a while she said she was tired and went up to her room to lie down. Her mom had attempted to straighten up while she was away. Her scarves were folded in a pile in the corner, her makeup lined up in neat rows on her vanity.

Mira lay down on her bed and looked up at the wings. Then she couldn't look at them anymore.

There was a soft knock on the open door. It was her dad.

"Is it okay if I come in?" he asked.

"Yeah," she said. "It's okay."

He came and sat down next to her on the bed. He smiled in a way that seemed unsure about smiling.

"How are you feeling?" he asked.

"Better," she said, knowing that it was what he needed to hear.

"We were so worried about you," he said.

"I guess I'm always making you worry about me."

"We just want to know that you're going to be okay."

Mira pulled her legs up, wrapped her arms around her knees.

"I can't make any guarantees," she said. Now she tried to smile. It wasn't sure either. "I want to be okay," she said.

"You'll tell us," he said, "if there's something we can do."

She nodded.

"Okay," he said. He stood up to go.

"You know it's not your fault, right?" she said. "That I'm like this. I think it might just be a part of who I am."

He opened his mouth to say something, then closed it again. He nodded. "I'm just glad you're home," he said.

"Me too," she said.

"I'll let you rest," he said. "You want your hot chocolate up here?"

"No, thanks."

"Okay, honey," he said.

"Dad?"

"Yes?"

"I love you."

"I love you too."

He went out and closed the door behind him, and Mira closed her eyes and let herself sleep.

JEREMY

For the second year in a row, I was missing the end of the school year. It had been almost two weeks since the day that I was called into the dean's office, and I had no plans to go back. Peter would not be there. Mira would not be there. And Sebby was gone.

Mira still wasn't responding to my texts and calls, and I had resorted to calling her house phone to find out how she was doing. Her mother had answered a few days before and said that she was back from the hospital but wasn't ready to talk to anyone.

Rose and Talia finished installing the Art Club exhibit for me, and Rose texted me that I should stop by and make sure it was okay. Our "opening" wasn't happening anymore, and our adviser was banned from the school, but somehow I still cared about it, even after everything that had happened. I told her I would come in after school so I wouldn't have to see anyone.

But on the afternoon that I headed over there, I got to the St. F building and kept walking. There was something else that I needed to take care of first. I made my way down the block to Peter's house. The trees in his front yard were blooming with big white flowers. Summer was so close. We had almost made it.

I rang the doorbell. After a minute he opened the door.

"Jeremy," he said. "You really shouldn't be here."

"I need to talk to you," I said.

He shook his head.

"Please," I said.

We stood there for a minute. Then he stepped aside and let me in.

The living room looked conspicuously neat, some cardboard boxes stacked in the corner.

"Are you leaving?" I asked.

"Yes," he said. "I need to move out of here at least."

"Are they firing you?"

"Probably," he said. "And they don't want me in their housing while they think about it."

"Where will you go?"

"My mother's house. For now. She lives about an hour away."

I sat down on the couch.

"Have you talked to Mira?" I asked.

"I haven't talked to anyone since this all happened, Jeremy. This all looks very bad for me."

"I made a mistake," I said. "When I was talking to Dean Pike. I said the wrong thing."

Peter sat down.

"Okay," he said.

"He was saying that a student had seen you and Mira in your car, that it was inappropriate . . ."

"I know."

"Who would say something like that?"

He shook his head.

"I don't know."

"It wasn't, though, right?" I regretted asking as soon as I said it.

"I don't know what someone thought they saw," Peter said. "Mira was very upset. I was trying to calm her down. We were in my car because it was raining." He looked at me. "What did you say to Pike?"

"He wanted to know if I had ever been to your house. And I thought I should say no. That it would look bad if I had, if they thought you were getting too close to your students or something."

"So you said no."

"I said no."

"But Pike knew that you had been here," he said.

"Yes," I said.

Peter took a deep breath. "He knew because I told him that you were here last spring. After the locker incident."

"I didn't know," I said.

"I wanted them to know because they were very concerned about your situation. Your father was understandably upset and had threatened to sue. And then when the bomb threat happened, you were one of the students who were under suspicion. So I wanted them to know that we were working together on what had happened."

"Oh," I said.

"I didn't want you to know that they suspected you," Peter said. "You were already upset enough. Rightfully so. I'm sorry that I attempted to shield you. I don't know." He put his head in his hands. "To tell you the absolute truth, I'm not really sure how I could have handled all of this differently."

I sat there watching him, sitting among the boxes of his packed-up life. It wasn't fair. That he could help us so much and that this was what he got for it.

I opened my mouth to tell him everything—that he was wrong to have defended me. That I wasn't the person he thought I was. But all that came out was "I'm sorry."

"It's okay," he said. "It's not your fault."

I nodded, realizing that it would be kinder to spare him from this last injustice. What I had done was my own problem, not Peter's.

"Will you be able to find another job?" I asked.

"Getting fired from your last teaching job doesn't exactly make you a desirable candidate," he said. He sat up a little. "But I'll figure it out. Look, I don't want you worrying about me."

"I wish I could do something," I said.

He shook his head.

"Me too," he said. He stood up. "You should go."

I followed him to the door. He opened it, and we stood there for a moment.

"You helped me so much," I said. "Everything you did for me. I just need for you to know."

He smiled. "Thanks, Jeremy."

I walked out and he closed the door behind me.

"Good-bye," I said to myself. "Good-bye, Sebby. Good-bye, Peter. Fucking good-bye, fucking everyone."

I walked down the street, thinking I would just keep going past St. F back home. There was no reason to go there. I didn't care about the exhibit. I didn't care about anything at that place anymore.

As I came up to the school, my phone beeped in my pocket and I took it out. It was a text from Rose.

Are you coming to see it? Talia and I will be in the library.

I put my phone back and looked up at the main building. I had a sudden surge of anger. I couldn't stand it anymore, being asked to accept that I had no control over who left me, over our lives. There had to be something that I could do.

I made my way up the driveway to the front door, past groups of kids headed to their buses. A few noticed me and stopped to look and whisper. I kept walking, in the front door, down the hall to the library.

Rose and Talia were standing there, waiting for me.

"Hey," Rose said when she saw me.

"Hey," I said.

The exhibit looked good. There were a few trippy sculptures and paintings by the emo kids, hands oozing flowers and a man's head growing antlers. Rose's Jenga tower was next to Talia's landscape drawings of trees and mountains. Mira's dress was on the dress form in the corner, hundreds of tiny pockets sewn together with jeweled clasps. And at the end of the hall was my painting. A three-by-five-foot canvas. A cloud of colors, blending from the outside in, forming a cave of paint around three figures. A boy with wings and angel-blue eyes and a boy and a girl on either side of him, each holding a burning stick of incense. In pencil along the bottom I had written the words "fans of the impossible life."

"Does it look okay?" Rose asked.

Talia was straightening one of the sculptures on its pedestal.

"Yeah," I said. "It looks good."

"Have you heard anything else?" Rose asked. "About what's going on?"

"I just came from Peter's," I said. "It's not good."

Talia turned around.

"You saw Peter?" she said.

There was something about the look on her face. Something in her voice. And I just knew.

"It was you, wasn't it?" I said.

Talia said nothing.

"You saw Peter with Mira," I said. "Of course you would be at the college fair. You saw them in his car."

Rose looked at Talia.

"Wait, what?" Rose said.

"And you were, what?" I said. "Jealous? Did you really think something was going on? Or you were that mad at Mira for saying something stupid at Molly's party?"

"Talia? Is that true?" Rose said.

Talia didn't answer.

"Fuck this," I said. "Fuck this fucking place."

I went over to my painting and took it down off the wall.

"What are you doing?" Rose asked.

"I'm taking my shit," I said. I looked at Mira's dress. "I'm taking my shit and Mira's shit." I grabbed the dress form and tried to drag it down the hallway while carrying my huge canvas under my arm. I looked ridiculous. Like the worst art thief ever.

"Jeremy," Rose said. "You can't just do that!"

"Yes, I can," I said.

"You can't even carry it," she said.

"I'll figure it out!"

She came up next to me and took Mira's dress.

"If you're going to be dramatic at least let me help you."

Rose helped me load the painting into the trunk of her car and squeeze the dress form with the dress on it into the backseat, and we drove to Mira's house.

In the car I ranted over Talia, yelled out the window at the injustice of it all. How could she be so blind? She loved Peter enough that she was willing to destroy his life? Well, we were all destroying things left and right. Why shouldn't she have her turn?

Rose pulled up in front of Mira's house. We got out and she helped me unload the stuff from her car. We looked like a deranged garage sale, standing on the front lawn, staring up at Mira's bedroom window.

"What are you going to do?" Rose asked.

I thought about my phone full of unanswered text messages.

"I'm going to sit here and wait."

"Until what?"

"I don't know," I said.

Rose looked up at the house.

"Well, at least you have a plan."

I picked up the painting and propped it against a tree. Rose brought the dress over.

"I can't believe all the work she did on this," she said. She opened one of the little pockets on it, pulled out a tiny folded piece of paper. She unfolded it, looked at it. She opened another pocket and unfolded another piece of paper.

"Look at this," she said.

She handed me the little squares of paper. One said, "Sebby." The other said, "Jeremy."

"Did you see what she called it?" Rose asked. "The wall tag that she made for it?"

"No."

"It's her *What I Love* dress."

Rose sat with me under the tree for a while, not quite understanding why I wouldn't just go ring the doorbell. After about an hour she said she had promised to meet Ali, but that she would check on me later. She drove off and I was left alone with all I had left to show for the past eight months of my life.

After a while longer a car pulled into the driveway and a girl who looked like Mira stepped out. She was taller and leaner than Mira, but they were undeniably related. The same unruly curls. The same eyes and mouth. It was as if, in the strange two weeks that had passed, Mira had transformed into a slightly different person.

"Who are you?" the girl said, standing with her hands on her hips, staring at me.

"I'm Jeremy," I said. "I'm Mira's friend."

She came over and looked at the painting propped up against the tree, looked at me again, then turned around and went inside.

I kept waiting.

It was another ten minutes before I saw the curtain open in the window to Mira's room. The late-afternoon sun glared off the glass and I could only barely see an outline of her. Then she opened the window and leaned out.

"Jeremy?"

"Hey," I said.

She looked at me, looked at the garage sale art show set up behind me.

"What are you doing out here?" she asked.

"Waiting for you," I said.

JEREMY

I was sitting on the same dock that I sat on every summer. So little changed in this town. A fence might get painted. A new ice-cream store opened on Commercial Street. But always the same air. The same light. The same summertime crowds and energy and sense of possibility. This dock was always the same.

There was one post that I liked to sit next to, balance my sketchbook and an iced coffee on. It was good for helping to measure the passing years. I dangled my legs off the side and noticed how far down they went, like reverse marks of height on a wall. I wondered if I still had more inches to grow.

"The man in the pink Speedo is out," I said to no one. He was sunning himself on his bright-green towel on the beach. He had been out for longer than his usual half hour today, rotating himself as the sun moved across the sky.

It was almost lunchtime. Dave would have sandwiches

ready on the table back at the house. Fresh lemonade with sugar and mint.

Now I took another sip of my iced coffee and looked out over the water. I had stopped drawing the bay and the shells and the boats, stopped trying to reproduce what was right in front of me. I still stared off into the water, watching the sun sparkle on the gentle bay waves, but I was looking for something else now. I wanted to draw the places inside myself that felt twisted up like old scars. The parts of myself that needed care. I was taking an inventory of them, one by one. I was figuring out how to put myself back together.

She came down the dock like a mirage, the sun too bright in my eyes. I could see more clearly as she got closer. She had tied her hair up in a scarf this morning, paired with a yellow sundress and pink sunglasses. She saw me and waved. I waved back.

"Did you find your fudge?" I asked when she got closer.

She sat down next to me on the dock, offered up a small box. I opened it.

"Chocolate peanut butter," Mira said. "They've been running out of it all week, but he put some aside for me today."

She pulled off a piece and handed it to me. I put it in my mouth. It melted on my tongue.

"There's no point in eating fudge that doesn't have both chocolate and peanut butter in it," she said.

"Goes without saying," I said.

She smiled.

"Don't spoil your appetite," she said. "It's almost lunchtime."

She stood up and pulled me up with her. I grabbed my iced coffee and sketchbook.

"Pink Speedo's out," she said, looking across the water to the beach.

He was sitting up on his towel, his legs stretched out in front of him. Mira and I were standing side by side, looking at him together, and then she waved. After a moment he waved back. And Mira laughed and took my hand and we walked through the town, through the families and the tourists and the drag queens to the little house where my dads were waiting for us with sandwiches and lemonade.

SEBBY

You have been here before.

The highway winding north through dark New England forests.

You can come back.

Love remembers the places where it touched down.

You can follow it back to them.

ACKNOWLEDGMENTS

Thank you to these readers, feedback givers, advisers, dear friends, loved ones, kind souls: Amanda Villalobos, Laura von Holt, Freddie Scelsa, Vin Scelsa, Khaliah Williams, Mike Iveson Jr., Vin Knight, Lindsay Hockaday, Aaron Mattocks, Lance Werth, Alan Wise, Kaneza Schaal, Linda Kay Klein, Michael David Franklin, Annie McNamara, Susie Sokol, Scott Shepherd, Greig Sargeant, Sarah McCarry, Cristina Moracho, Jessica Olien, Bennett Madison, Julie Murphy, Nina LaCour, Margery Galluzzi, Jon and Elga Goodman, Wayne Kabak, Marsha Berkowitz, Jim Glossman, Rachel Murphy, Chloe Apple Seldman, Greg Zuccolo, Darcy Mentovai, Sabrina Esbitt, Lois Walker Martin, Aram Jibilian, Titus Ulrich, and Sherri Brown.

At Writers House, my superstar agent Brianne "The Shark" Johnson, Cecilia de la Campa, James Munro, and forever to the Fan Grrrls—Bakara Wintner and Andrea Morrison.

At Balzer + Bray, my genius editor Alessandra Balzer, Kelsey Murphy, Jenny Sheridan, Kathy Faber, Nellie Kurtzman, Caroline Sun, Alison Donalty, Jenna Stempel, Mia Nolting for her beautiful illustration, and everyone who worked on the book.

And to my Grandma Rita Bauman, who made many things possible.

JOIN THE

Epic Reads

COMMUNITY

THE ULTIMATE YA DESTINATION

◀ **DISCOVER** ▶
your next favorite read

◀ **MEET** ▶
new authors to love

◀ **WIN** ▶
free books

◀ **SHARE** ▶
infographics, playlists, quizzes, and more

◀ **WATCH** ▶
the latest videos